Reyanna's Prophecy

**Book 1 of the
Forge Born Duology**

By Whit McClendon

Copyrights

Reyanna's Prophecy

Copyright © 2018 by Whit McClendon

ISBN-13: 978-1-7326300-0-0
ISBN-10: 1-7326300-0-3

Cover Art by: Shinji
Copyediting by: Michelle McClish
Published by: Rolling Scroll Publishing, Katy, TX

Website: www.jidaan.com

To join my mailing list to be notified when a new novel is published, go to
http://www.jidaan.com/contact

You can also Like my Facebook page!
http://www.facebook.com/fireofthejidaan/

Acknowledgements

I have an amazing circle of friends and family. They support me in my writing, encourage me when I'm stumbling, and generally keep me moving forward. My wife, Christina, has always been loving and super supportive about my work, and I have to thank her for that. I used to talk to my son, Connor, about the story on our way to his high school, and he helped me work out plot points more than he even suspects. Many of the students at Jade Mountain Martial Arts ask about my writing projects and tell me that they're dying for the next one to come out; that means a lot. Brian Briscoe and Larry Escher have been instrumental in many ways as my writing career has advanced, and their support has always kept me driving forward. Thanks to Michelle McClish for her tireless proofreading and editing of my books, they are always better after she's bled on them. And also thanks to Kathryn Scott, who asked me a simple question about a scene I was having trouble with, and helped jog my brain loose to rewrite the scene much better than before.

For all of you, my loving friends and family, I am profoundly grateful. Thank you.

~Whit McClendon

Dedication

A dear friend let me know that her daughter absolutely adores my books. Ranks it up there with Harry Potter, if you can believe that. Just knowing that someone out there feels that way about your own work is at once thrilling, encouraging, and humbling. I'm so grateful that folks can enjoy my stories that much, and I'm determined to keep writing as much as possible. This book is dedicated to Mary T. Thanks so much for your support and inspiration, Mary.

Also, I want to speak to the dreamers out there who have worlds untold in their imagination, just waiting to be shared with the world. To the folks who are dying to tell a tale, but don't know where to start. To all of you who want desperately to write a book but don't because you're scared it won't work out.

This one is for all of you.

After you read mine, go get busy. Write your own story. The world needs more like that.

Chapter 1

A huge, beefy fist slammed down onto the table, making the mugs of ale jump.

"I want more! You never said there would be Skitters to deal with! Creepy little bastards nearly got me and Tyrel both! We want to be paid for it!"

"Yeah, hazard pay!" Tyrel leaned over his burly friend's shoulder and backed him up. He was none too bright, but knew an opportunity for extra gold when it was laid in his lap. He had not given any thought to it on the trail; he had just done his job protecting the caravan from the spider-like creatures in the forest and did it well. Between he and the protesting Borel, who had decided that their pay had not been nearly enough, they had easily killed over two dozen of the dog-sized, venomous creatures. But Borel got it in his head that they should both get hazard pay. Borel was nothing if not stubborn, and he had talked of it all the way back. So here they were, bargaining for a few extra coins that they would likely drink away in the very same inn and tavern in which they stood.

On the other side of the table, a slight, middle-aged man adjusted his spectacles and looked down at his ledgers with the faintest of sighs. The young tough was new to their outfit, but Oswald was well accustomed to outbursts like Borel's. Oswald had been dealing with mercenaries for a long time, and was quite familiar with their ways. They were not always noble, logical, or intelligent, and seldom were they all three. Oswald ran a hand through his thinning hair, then traced a steady finger down the list of figures in the ledger until he found what he needed.

In a calm, almost bored tone, Oswald replied without looking up from his books. "Borel, you and Tyrel agreed to 10 gold coins apiece when you took the job. That's exactly what you'll receive, and it's generous for that short a route. The risks were explained, as always."

"That's not enough, I said! Those prickly little beasts could have killed us!" Borel spat.

"And I've had nightmares!" Tyrel interjected, attempting to bolster their case.

Borel's huge fist thumped down harder on the table, and Oswald deftly reached out and caught his mug of ale before it tipped over onto his paperwork. He knew he would have to bring his wife in on the situation, and that meant trouble. He had been through this before and he already knew how it would end. He sighed again, silently grateful that he had ordered replacements for all the inn's tables and chairs and had them stored in a nearby barn for the next time someone acted up. Although such confrontations stressed him mightily, he had to admit that he actually loved to see his wife at work. Even though he hated having to clean the blood out of the floorboards, watching his wife deal with troublemakers secretly thrilled him. Oswald looked up into Borel's angry, gnarled face and decided it was probably time to go get her.

With one hand, Oswald slowly and deliberately closed his ledger book. From a chest on the floor next to his chair, he brought out two small pouches and set them on the table before the two men. "Kind sirs, we are happy to pay you the agreed upon amount. If you insist on taking issue with the terms, you'll have to speak to the boss."

Borel looked startled for a moment before regaining his composure. He had only dealt with Oswald up to now, and had not known that there was another in charge.

"Right then! Send him out so I can deal with him!" He rested one hand on his sword hilt and rattled the blade in its scabbard for emphasis. Beside him, Tyrel did the same in imitation.

Oswald carefully packed his ledger, quill pens, and papers back into the chest at his feet, then picked it up as he moved away from the table, leaving the two pouches of gold for the men to take if they came to their senses. "Yes, yes, gentlemen, I'll get her. Please wait a moment."

Oswald opened a much larger chest against the wall behind him and settled the smaller chest inside it before locking it with a large padlock. Once he had pocketed the key he turned and walked to another door, pushed it open a crack, and leaned his head inside. "Kiran, love, could you come out here for a moment? There's a dispute regarding payment."

Through the dim fog that usually wafted around in Borel's brain, he finally caught a hold of the fact that the boss was not a 'he,' but was instead a 'she.' "What, the boss is a wench? Ye gods, that's rich! Send her out here so I can give her a good spanking before she pays us what we're worth!"

Tyrel chimed in helpfully, "Oi, maybe she'll spend some time with us upstairs and we can call it even!" The ruffians laughed at their own jokes, failing to see Oswald's face go pale as the door was jerked open from the other side.

Framed in the doorway was a woman of medium height, drying her hands roughly with a towel. Her pale jade eyes were ablaze with anger, deepening the dainty crow's feet that had appeared at their edges. She was striking rather than pretty, and a few scars only accentuated her fierce glare. Her brownish hair was lightly streaked with grey, bound in a long braid that draped over one shoulder. She wore a man's shirt and pants that could not hide the curves that she lamented over these days. Long gone was her youthful, lean and wiry figure. Although she had put on quite a few pounds since her youthful travels had ended, it was widely commented (though not within her earshot) that they looked fetching on her. Certainly, Oswald thought so. He was not thinking of her curves at that moment, but instead, about the strong cords of muscle in her bulging forearms and the throbbing vein at her temple. He knew that she had heard the ruffians' jokes and had not been amused. At all.

"Now, love, don't kill them!" Oswald pleaded as he looked down at his wife. "They don't know who you are, and they're just being stupid. And we'll have to do all that paperwork for the constable again. You know what a bother that is!"

Kiran tucked the towel into her belt and mumbled in return, "I know, I know. Damned oafs of mercenaries. They're idiots, the lot of them." Her jaw clenched in anger, she strode straight over to the two men, who were still laughing. "Hey!" her voice was loud and sharp enough that

3

it startled them to silence. She glared up into Borel's puggish face. "Your pay is 10 golds apiece. Take it or get out of my inn. I've got more important things to do today than to deal with the likes of you."

Surprised, Borel took a step backwards and looked down at the angry woman before him. She meant business, but Borel towered over her and outweighed her by at least a hundred pounds. Even so, she did not seem the least bit afraid of him. Unfortunately, he was too dim to realize there might be a reason for that. He decided to press on with his demands.

"Look, princess," he saw her nostrils flare and her jaw clench even harder. "We deserve an extra 10 gold for the job we just did. And we're not leaving until we get it!"

"Yeah!" Tyrel added from over his shoulder.

"You just amble over to the chest and pull out some extra coins, or you can bet, there will be some trouble," Borel went to poke her in the chest with his index finger for emphasis. He recalled later that had been a mistake.

Moving with almost supernatural speed and grace, Kiran reached out and grasped his outstretched finger with one hand, twisted, and then held it far over her head, instantly standing Borel up on his tiptoes in agony as he desperately tried to keep his finger from breaking. He squeaked in pain, and Tyrel stared at him with wide eyes while he tried to make sense of what he was seeing.

"I said," Kiran emphasized her words with a slight press that intensified Borel's pain and he squeaked again. "You two agreed to 10..." another press, another squeak. "Gold pieces..." Squeak. "Each. Now I'm sure that you want to uphold your sterling reputations for integrity, don't you?" Borel grunted as tears began to trickle down his face, but he nodded. "Good. Then you can take the 10 pieces of gold you earned and leave quietly so that I don't have to get rough with you. I can just as easily break this finger off and then shove it so far up your arse you can pick your nose from the inside. Gonna be a good boy?" Another nod from Borel. "Ok, then."

Kiran released her hold on his finger and he staggered back a few steps next to Tyrel, groaning and clutching his aching hand. She turned and scooped up the

4

two pouches of gold from the table and held them on her upturned palms, offering them to the pair as their beady eyes glared at her. Right now they were scared and uncertain, and she could feel their emotions as easily as though they were her own. They would either take the gold and make a quick escape, or they would let their pride and anger get the best of them, and there would be trouble. She tried not to grin at the thought. It had been a while since she'd dealt with trouble and she had missed it. She more than half-hoped they would make the mistake of attacking her. Oswald would not like that, though. And he worked so hard to keep the peace. She reminded herself to play it cool and not to start anything...but finishing it would be perfectly fine with her. Kiran jiggled the pouches slightly so they could hear the gold clinking inside, a tantalizing sound. She asked quietly, "What'll it be, boys? I'll even throw in a nice little escort job for you, 3 golds each for guarding a wagon from here to Green Meadows and back, take you less than a day."

Tyrel and Borel glared fiercely at her until she mentioned the job. The road to Green Meadows was known to be safe, and it was a short, easy ride. It was a plum job. Tyrel tugged on Borel's sleeve, and the two exchanged glances. Kiran actually felt their greed get the better of them as they decided to take the gold and the job. Her spirits fell somewhat, but she knew that it was for the best. She jiggled the coin pouches again with a sigh. The two men relaxed and moved forward to pluck the two pouches from her palms. Glancing over their shoulders, they surreptitiously counted the coins until they were satisfied that they had not been cheated, and then they tucked them away with smug grins.

"All right, that's more like it," Borel stood to his full height, towering over Kiran with a lopsided grin. He kept flexing his sore hand, but tried to ignore the pain. He adopted a pompous tone that Kiran instantly disliked. "We'll take it. Where do we need to go?"

Kiran took a deep breath to keep from punching him in the throat. When she had calmed enough, she gave the two louts the details of the job. Oswald had slipped behind the nearby desk and pulled out his ledger again, making

5

notes of the transaction, obviously relieved that there would be no trouble.

"Gentlemen, if you'll just come up and make your mark here, you can be on your way." He turned the ledger book around and offered a quill to Borel, who scribbled the same illegible mark as he had last time, and then Tyrel stepped forward to make his customary 'X'. "Good, then, it's all settled!" Oswald replaced everything in the large chest. "I bid you two good day."

"It'd have been a better day if she'd gone upstairs with us," came Borel's snide reply as he elbowed Tyrel in the ribs. "At least for her, that is! She's got a nice bosom, but she's a little old for me. From the looks of her, she'd have had to pay us extra!" A burst of rude laughter from the two men obscured Oswald's gasp of horror. He immediately stepped through the nearest door and shut it behind him with a slam. It eased open the merest crack as Oswald peeked out.

"Just don't kill them! I mean it!" came his muffled voice from the other side of the door.

Her eyes narrowed in anger, Kiran murmured, "Oh, I won't. Much."

The two men were still laughing when she smashed the table over their heads.

*   *   *   *   *   *

Oswald watched the crew as they brought in a new table and set up chairs to replace the ones Kiran had destroyed in her fight with Borel and Tyrel. Fortunately, it took less than a half hour to get the room set back to rights this time, and Oswald made a note to buy more chairs and a new table to store away. She had not killed Borel and Tyrel, and there was very little blood. The fact that they could both still walk after regaining consciousness had been a good sign that Kiran had kept her temper better than usual. Oswald sighed as he handed over the small pouch of coins he had set aside for the cleaning crew and looked over at his wife of a dozen years.

Kiran sat on a stool nearby grumbling quietly to herself, sipping from a mug of ale. Her knuckles were skinned and a lock of her hair had come loose from its braid, causing her to repeatedly blow it out of the way in absent frustration. Anyone else would have thought she was furious after such a ruckus, but Oswald knew better. Her eyes shone not from anger anymore, but exhilaration. She needed a good tussle now and then to get her blood flowing. He knew she was as happy right now as ever. He walked over to her and placed a gentle hand on her shoulder.

"Are you all right, love?"

For a change, instead of shrugging off his question, she quietly put her hand on his and looked up into his concerned eyes. She smiled.

"Yes, Oswald, I'm just fine. I've fought far worse than those two buffoons. I barely consider them exercise." She looked away and sighed as she continued, "I may look old and fat, but I'm still much more than the likes of those two can handle."

Oswald reached up and stroked her hair the way he knew she liked, and she closed her eyes as she leaned into the caress. His heart nearly burst with love for her.

He had never understood what such an amazing, powerful woman had ever seen in him. He was what he had always been, a man who reveled in numbers and tally sheets and invoices. He was certainly no fighter. She was the strong one. He was no braver than a kitchen mouse, and he shied away from conflict wherever he could. When she had come into the inn where he had been working on accounts, though, he had fallen for her in a heartbeat. In retrospect, he was glad he had not known that she was one of the famous Guardians, even though she carried her Jidaan on her back for all to see. The long-bladed spear with its diamond-shaped pommel rode in its scabbard, the cobalt blue sapphire sparkled over her shoulder as she moved. That should have given away her identity, but he had been far too captivated by her harsh beauty to notice.

Against all better judgement, he had gathered his courage and asked if he could buy her a drink. He had thought she'd laugh in his bespectacled face, but she had not. No, he had seen something blossom in her eyes as soon as she had looked into his own. And he had never been happier. The years since had been like a dream to him.

"Goddess, I love you Kiran," he whispered.

She opened her eyes again and smiled up at him, making his heart jump. Then she stood and pulled him into her rough embrace. For all her strength and toughness, her kiss was tender and sweet. She ended the kiss and held him closer, pulled him down a bit so she could whisper in his ear. "I love you too, my dear Oswald. So very much..." Then, as if she became aware of herself again, she gently disentangled herself from her husband and began to straighten her hair and clothes. "I'm sorry, Honey, I tried not to get angry at them, but...you heard them! I can't let them get away with talking about me like that. I mean, I'm the boss of Guardian Defense Services...they've got to show some respect!"

Oswald adjusted his glasses and nodded. "Yes, love, as much as I hate to admit it, I agree. Without respect, louts like that are apt to make us look bad. We do have a reputation to uphold. I'm sorry it had to come to blows, but it is what it is. I think they'll know better next time."

"Right. They're lucky to work for us. I mean, I even let them keep the job, didn't I? It's not like I wasn't being understanding!" Kiran scoffed at the very idea. "Idiots! Well, since that's all over with, we'd better get back to work. I've got some things to do..."

Kiran's voice trailed off and a pained look crossed her face. A low grunt escaped her and she reached out for Oswald's arm as her legs buckled underneath her.

"Love? Kiran? What's happening? What's the matter?" Oswald helped her down to her knees and went down with her. He had never seen her so stricken. She had never been sick a day in their lives together, and even back in her fighting days, she had been able to take a ferocious beating and recover faster than one could imagine possible. This was something new. His heart raced as he saw the love of his life down on her knees grimacing in pain.

"I'm all right, I'm all right...ow, that hurts, though. Just let me catch my breath," Kiran maneuvered herself into a seated position and pressed her palms into her temples as she steadied herself. "Gaaah...I could have done without that," she mumbled to herself. She took a few lungfuls of air and calmed herself as the pain slowly dissipated.

Oswald was terrified, but managed to keep his composure. "What is it, love? Do we need to fetch a healer? What can I do?" He grasped her arms firmly, reassured by the solid muscle beneath the fabric of her shirt, yet alarmed at the trembling he felt there. He just wanted Kiran to be all right. He needed her.

Kiran finally turned back to her husband, and seeing the concern in his eyes nearly broke her heart. She had always thought he deserved better than her. She was a rough, raggedy mercenary at heart, a Guardian by happenstance. And now, she was the head of the largest mercenary contracting outfit in the northern Realm, for what that was worth. Through all the trials, the fights with rival outfits, the tussles with rebellious mercenaries who refused to work for a woman until she beat them down, Oswald had been there, her rock. When she had wanted to bash everyone's face in, he had been there to calm her. When she angrily wanted to chuck the whole endeavor, he had been the one to point out all the progress they had made and how far they had come. He was always the strong one. She needed him.

Using Oswald's arm to steady herself, she pulled herself back to her feet, a look of confusion on her face. It took her a few moments to gather her thoughts, then she let Oswald walk her to a chair so she could sit down. He called over his shoulder for one of the serving boys to bring her some water, which was brought to their table within a few moments. Kiran sipped it as she tried to put into words what had happened. Shock was evident in her face, but her usual determined expression was not far beneath.

Placing her hand on her husband's arm to reassure him, she spoke quietly. "Oswald, honey, I'm afraid I'll have to go away for a while."

His confusion was obvious. "What? Now? Why? Where are you going?" His brows wrinkled with worry behind his spectacles.

Kiran took a long drink of water before replying. "I have to go back to the Hall of Jidaana, to the Guardians Keep. One of the Guardians is in trouble, and I'm needed

9

there." She frowned. "That's all I know. What hit me was a burst of images and sounds in my mind. It was confusing, but..." she looked into his eyes. "I have to go."

Oswald was silent for a moment, then he looked away. He took his glasses off and began to clean them on his shirt, a sure sign that he was agitated. She hated to see him do that, knowing that it took a lot to get him that upset. She leaned forward and took his face in her hands, interrupting his movement. It took a bit for him to meet her eyes, and when he did, Kiran could see that they were wet. She stared deeply into them, her pale green gaze mingling with his of watery blue. His chest hitched as he struggled to keep his emotions in check. Her voice was firm, yet loving. "I'll come home to you, Honey. I promise."

Oswald sniffed once, then again as he steeled himself. He nodded briskly at her and carefully placed his glasses on the table before taking both her hands in his. Gently, he kissed both sets of her skinned knuckles. When he spoke again, the thin cord of steel Kiran had come to count on was back in his voice and he was all business. "Yes. All right, then. There are some arrangements we need to make, but they won't take long. And I'll need to see you in our office for a time."

Kiran smiled, but began to protest. "Oswald, I need to hurry..." but he firmly stopped her with a finger to her lips. He was having none of it.

"An hour will make no difference there, but it will make a big difference here. Our office. In ten minutes." He raised an eyebrow at her and she could not stifle a giggle. Their 'office' was what he called their bedroom.

She watched him put on his glasses and then head towards the big chest and its ledgers, moving with purpose and vigor. Oh, how she loved him. He was right; it would take weeks for her to ride to the Keep in the Heartstrong Mountains and an hour would make little difference.

Then a cloud fell over her heart as the images and sounds that had assailed her drifted across her mind again. There was trouble coming, and it had already found one of the few Guardians who had survived the war with Mordak two decades past. Kiran looked on the north wall of their inn, where a plaque had been affixed far above the reach of the drunken patrons and mercenaries who frequented the place. The Jidaan of Warding had been mounted there for years, gathering dust, no longer needed. With a flex of magick, Kiran reached out and lifted it out of its brackets and brought it floating easily through the air to her waiting hand. The sapphire in its pommel sparkled as her fingers closed around the shaft, as if recognizing its Guardian.

"It looks like you and I aren't done. We've got work to do." She heard Oswald clearing his throat pointedly as he held open the door that led to their office. "Well...soon enough, anyway."

Chapter 2

Layton sat at his desk and stared off into space as he absently pulled at his short beard. In truth, he was not terribly troubled, but he had found himself drifting more often lately, remembering his younger days. Back then, he had been on the road most of the time, fighting for his life on multiple occasions; a warrior. His weapons were always close at hand rather than left in a dusty chest or mounted on the wall. He sighed and turned his attention back to the papers on his desk. Lesson plans for newer students, supply requisitions, and duty rosters were only some of what he would be fighting that day, rather than the Gholans and Morcats he used to battle. "Some days, I'd much rather a Morcat bust in here to liven things up," he said aloud, though no one was there to answer. Shaking his head at himself, he focused on the sheaf of papers before him and immersed himself in the task. Time passed, and Layton doggedly worked his way towards the bottom of the stack. He was near the end when he heard someone knock on his office door.

"Yes? Come in, please," he called, grateful for the interruption. He had already seen more than enough of the quartermaster's reports for one day.

The door swung open and one of his assistant instructors stepped into the room. The man was dressed for the training hall, and the sweat from the afternoon's exercises was shining on his brow. Layton envied him. The younger man quickly knelt and slammed a fist against his heart in salute. Layton stood and returned it, then reseated himself. "Yes, Daxian? What is it?"

"Headmaster," he began. Layton had only recently become accustomed to being called such, and then only reluctantly. Then again, he had founded the school himself, and trained hundreds of worthy warriors personally over the last decade before ending up behind an administrator's desk. He guessed that counted for something. Layton leaned forward to hear the lad better. "We have a question about one of the ancient two-handed sword techniques. I was sent to respectfully ask if you would come and demonstrate."

There were at least three instructors on duty that morning that Layton knew of who had mastered those techniques. Technically, Daxian should have asked one of them, but Layton fairly burst out from behind his desk, eager to get out into the sun again. His schedule demanded that he train alone in the quiet, predawn hours, and this would be a welcome change from the monotony of paperwork. "Lead on, young sir. Which technique?"

Daxian stepped aside to allow Layton to precede him through the door and explained that two of the instructors had differing opinions on a particular sequence of movements, and it suddenly made much more sense as to why Layton had been sought. The routines, each a series of movements simulating attack and defense versus one or more opponents, were often quite long and intricate, and discussions occasionally arose regarding the choreography. Only Layton knew them all completely by heart, and as the founder of the Green Valley Academy, and creator of its curriculum, he was the unquestioned authority on such things. Daxian explained the portion of the routine that was in question and Layton immediately recognized it. His step quickened in excitement as they neared the huge double doors that led to one of the outside training areas.

Situated just north of Rualtha, only a few leagues from the ocean, the Academy had grown into a sprawling complex since its founding over a decade past. Layton's first graduating class had ended up in some of the most prestigious positions in the Realm due to their high level of skills in combat and strategy. The rigorous mental training they endured and strict adherence to the Academy's moral codes made them impossible to corrupt, and they were highly sought after by the Realm's nobility as advisors and army officers. Grateful nobles had donated massive sums to the Academy until Layton had finally built the organization of his dreams. Those who made it all the way through to graduation were strong and shining examples of strength and good character, while those that took longer in the training often adopted other jobs in the Academy while they continued to study. A few of his best students chose to remain as instructors at the Academy, and those he trusted with not only his life, but with the lives of every single trainee. As they emerged into the sunlight, the sounds of laughter and grunts of exertion washed over Layton in a welcome rush. He had missed that atmosphere mightily. Even though the training areas were only a few yards from his office, he seldom had the opportunity to drill with the students anymore.

They turned off of the covered walkway and into one of the wide training areas left open to the elements, and everywhere Layton looked, there were pairs of men and women in various states of exercise and instruction. Some were naked to the waist, their muscled bodies gleaming in the morning sun, while others wore various uniforms specific to the art they were currently practicing. The ground was hard-packed earth, tramped flat by years of pounding feet. The noises of shuffling footsteps, an occasional impact of a thrown body, and smacks of muscle on muscle were music to Layton's ears. His eyes twinkled with excitement as he strode through them, pleased as always at what he saw. This was home, not his musty office.

As the trainees became aware of his presence, they stopped what they were doing, turned, and saluted. He could feel their eyes on him, and an air of hushed excitement began to grow. Some of the young fighters had never seen him, though his reputation was well-known. In the years following the Mordak War, word of the exploits of the Guardians had spread, particularly his own part in the conflict, and had been embellished in the telling almost beyond belief. To the youngest students, the man now walking among them was a legend. The thought of it made Layton shake his head. He still put his pants on one leg at a time, just like everyone else. Still, his celebrity had its uses, and had helped him establish Green Valley.

Finally, they caught sight of a large group of trainees holding long wooden straight swords, and made directly for them. Porien and Carius, the two instructors who were debating the movements in the two-hand sword routine, were in their midst, loud as ever. Layton knew them both well, and was glad to see them. He was not surprised to see

14

them arguing heatedly, each one holding a steel two-handed straight sword and gesturing with it occasionally. Carius, the taller and more slender of the two, was bald and clean shaven, his pate shining in the sun. Porien was as hairy as Carius was not, sporting a ferocious beard and braided black ponytail that was rumored to hide more than one set of darts and knives, and he was burly as a small bear. Seeing Porien always reminded Layton of the jovial Bjarke, and a brief pang of sorrow struck his heart as he thought of his long-dead comrade.

"No, no, no, it's block, stab, twist, duck, and stab!" Carius insisted.

"I'm telling you, it's block, stab, twist, upward slash left and right, THEN stab!" Porien responded with an exasperated sigh.

"Well just because you're short enough that you don't need to duck, doesn't mean it's not in the form!" Carius retorted.

"Look you beanpole, it's a looping double upward slash, and that's the end of it!"

The two men bickered for a few moments more before they realized that a hush had fallen over the crowd of students. They turned to see their Headmaster standing nearby with an amused grin on his face. They immediately dropped to a knee and saluted.

"Having trouble, gentlemen?" Layton kept the laughter out of his voice, but only barely so. He knew the two men were best of friends and enjoyed bickering as though it was a sport unto itself.

Porien replied, "Headmaster, we seem to have a difference of opinion regarding the sword form. He thinks there's a duck in there and I think it's two slashes." At his side, Carius nodded vigorously.

"It's because there is a duck in there, you sot," Carius murmured.

"Is not, you stork," Porien muttered under his breath.

Layton could not help himself, and he laughed out loud and clapped a hand on each man's shoulder. "In a way, you're both right. Show me." He then motioned for the students to step back to allow the instructors room to demonstrate.

The two men stood and straightened their training tunics, glaring at each other as they prepared to move. The taller Carius went first, sweeping his sword through an intricate series of slashes, blocks, twists and turns. Layton was pleased to see that he had improved since the last time he had seen him perform, no mean feat for one as skilled as Carius. The bald man finished the sequence of moves flawlessly, and as he had mentioned, he had smoothly ducked an imaginary slash at one point, even managing to throw a side-eye at Porien as he did it. He reached the ending position and saluted, receiving applause from the students for his performance.

"Wonderful, Carius. You've improved." The tall man was mightily pleased at Layton's praise. "Porien, you next, if you don't mind."

With a snort at Carius, Porien stepped forward and brought his shining blade to the ready position. He burst into action. Where Carius had been long, graceful, and willowy, Porien was brutal. The movements were the same, but quicker, choppy and powerful. As he swept through the part of the sequence where Carius had ducked, Porien did not, but emphasized the power of the upward slashes. Moments later, he finished, and another round of applause erupted in the training yard. Porien threw a hearty "Hmph!" over his shoulder at Carius, and both men turned expectant eyes toward Layton, each hoping they would claim victory.

Layton's face broke into a grin. "Excellent, gentlemen. You both did that form perfectly."

Confusion crawled over both their faces and a quiet murmuring arose from the crowd of trainees.

"Sir? How could we both do it correctly? He ducked!" Porien insisted.

"Right! And he didn't!" Carius added.

"You had it right when you were talking earlier. Carius, you're much taller than Porien, yes?" Layton saw them both nod and continued, "That point in the routine is meant to represent a defense against a hard horizontal attack. That particular defense for one of your height, Carius, is to duck, then retaliate with two upward slashes.

16

Someone much shorter, like say, Porien, might only need to flex his knees slightly to avoid that kind of attack, which I saw him do. We learn these movements as close to 'perfectly' as we can, and once they are ingrained, we make adjustments to maximize our strengths and minimize our weaknesses. If you please?" Layton held out a hand and Porien offered his sword and stepped back.

The sword felt good in Layton's hand. His own solo training had been single and double axes of late, and it seemed as though it had been months since he had held a shining blade like this one. It was well-made, long and straight and double-edged in the Eastern style with almost no crossguard to speak of. He twirled it once, then again, getting the feel of it as he walked to the open space the trainees had left for him. He stood with his feet together in the ceremonial starting position he had adopted for all of his weapons routines, and all fell silent around him. He took a deep breath, let it out, and the old half-smile appeared on his face as if by magick.

He moved almost silently, save for the swish of his boots in the dirt and the singing of the blade as it cut through the air. His breath moved easily in unison with his movements, flowing with each slash, twirl, and block. He leaped in the air, landed and swept the ground with one leg, and jumped again seemingly without effort as the sword darted out, wickedly sharp in the shining sun. The entire yard was silent as all eyes watched him work, a kind of poetry that they had never seen, but now desperately wanted to understand. This was why he was the Headmaster.

All too soon, the routine concluded, and he found himself standing in the ending position. He sighed and saluted the gathering, and the applause was loud and long. Layton quickly handed the sword back to Porien, who gave him a knowing wink. He and Carius knew Layton well, and they knew that he was embarrassed by the praise. Layton waved off the applause as gently as he could.

"Now, if you were watching, you'd have seen that I, too, ducked at that point in the form. However, I'm taller than Porien, but not nearly as tall as Carius. I ducked as much as I needed to for an imagined slash at that particular height. Once you've mastered this routine and learned the applications of the movements, that's where your individuality starts to assert itself. Make it your own. But first," he smiled and cast his eyes at the young men and women that surrounded him, hanging on his words. "Learn the pattern. And learn it well. Carry on."

As one, the trainees saluted, fists over heart, and then turned back to their work, slowly going over the last movements they had learned. Layton smiled, then sighed as he turned to walk back to his office to finish looking over the quartermaster's reports. *Oh, joy,* he thought.

"I could take ye," a low voice growled from nearby, followed by gasps of surprise and horror at the disrespectful tone.

Layton stopped in midstride and turned to find one of the newest trainees glaring at him from a few feet away. By his accent, he sounded like he was from somewhere in the Iron Hills. He was taller than Layton by a head, and more powerfully built. His hair was close-cropped in the manner of all of the trainees. Layton could see old scars on the skin of his scalp, one of which came down through one eye and continued down the young man's cheek, giving him a fearsome appearance. He spoke again. "Ye move well, there's nae doubt aboot 'at. But ye be small. And weak. I could take ye." At his words, his classmates stepped back in horror, leaving the burly young man standing alone, holding his wooden training sword in gnarled, muscular hands. He was staring at Layton as though the Headmaster had insulted his family and tried to make off with his sister.

"Porien!" Layton called.

The bearded instructor immediately appeared, and when he saw the young man standing nearby, he swore under his breath. "Yes Headmaster?"

Layton tilted his head towards the speaker. "One of yours?"

Porien sighed. "Yes, Headmaster. He's been nothing but trouble since he's arrived, but he passed the initial tests for admittance. He's tough, sir, from the Iron Hills."

Layton nodded. "Ah, I thought I heard that in your voice, Trainee." Layton paused for a moment, then reached out with his senses. It had been long since he had used his magick, but he had never forgotten that it was there. He gently touched the angry looking man and instantly received a shock of rage and resentment. His had been a hard life, and he had survived by being a bully and a thief. It was a wonder that he had passed the exams for entry at Green Meadows. Layton probed deeper, beyond the surface turmoil of his mind, and found what he expected: fear and doubt. There was also a surprising desire to be something more. Wrapped around that core was a strong frustration that he had no idea how to be other than he was, no concept of how to change even if he wanted to. No one liked him, and he liked no one. He had no family, no friends. He had nothing. Deep down, though, he wanted someone to care about him. Layton retracted his awareness and addressed the man. "Your name, Trainee?"

"Bale...sir." Bale had waited long enough that the 'sir' was almost an insult instead of an honorific.

"All right then...Bale. Nice to meet you." To Porien, he said, "Would you loan him your sword, please, Porien? I think he wants to spar with me."

Gasps arose from the crowd. First because they could not believe that anyone would be so blatantly rude to the Headmaster, but also because they knew they might see something interesting. They were fighting men and women, each and every one, and they all knew that this kind of challenge could not go unanswered. They watched Porien grudgingly hand over his sword to Bale, who dropped his wooden weapon carelessly to the ground to accept the true blade. A hint of a smile pulled at one corner of Bale's scarred mouth.

Carius jogged up, presenting his own blade to Layton. "Please, take mine sir." To his surprise, Layton gently pushed it away.

"No, but thank you, Carius. I don't want your weapon to be unnecessarily damaged." Carius raised an eyebrow, but stepped away nevertheless. Layton scanned the training yard for a moment before finding what he wanted. "Water boy! Come here, lad!"

A startled-looking boy of about ten years trotted over carrying a bucket with a ladle inside. He looked up at the Headmaster in awe and shyly asked, "Yes sir? Water, sir?"

"Yes, that's exactly what I need, thank you." Layton took the ladle from the bucket and drank deeply from it. He hefted the large dipper in his hand, testing its balance. Once he had its measure, he looked back at the boy. "If you don't mind, lad, I need to borrow this for a few minutes. I'll get it back to you right away." The boy's eyes went wide and he backed away with the bucket. Layton turned back to Bale with a smile, holding the ladle loosely in one hand.

"Well? If you think you can take me, *boy*, come on, then." Layton's body relaxed as he fell into a state that was as natural to him as breathing. A dreamy half-smile turned up his mouth and made the new lines at the corners of his eyes deepen.

Bale's left eye twitched once, then he bellowed in rage and attacked. He charged and brought the sword up, then down in a brutal slash that would have gutted Layton from shoulder to crotch had he remained where he was. Using skills he had honed for years, augmented by Brunar's training and his own magick, Layton watched the sword's blade arcing downwards at him as if it were moving in slow motion. Without a care in the world, he sidestepped a few inches to his left, allowing the blade to pass harmlessly by. With blinding speed, he whipped the ladle out and struck Bale on the forehead with a loud *thwack!* that brought winces of shared pain from the onlookers. Rather than press the attack, Layton merely stepped out of Bale's reach and watched as the man staggered back, nearly blinded by the pain. Bale managed to keep one hand on the sword, but only barely, and his other hand clutched his forehead as tears of pain rolled down his craggy face.

Layton did not speak, nor did his expression change at all. The happy, absent-minded smile stayed in place, making him look for all the world like he was daydreaming of something comfortable and pleasant. In truth, his mind was both empty and hyper-aware. He had found his inner stillness, that place from which he was capable of using his body to the fullest extent, and although he was approaching middle-age, he was still a Guardian.

Bale squinted through the pain and appeared to find his focus again. He gripped the sword firmly with both hands and pointed it at Layton. He lunged, jabbing it at him once, then again, probing for a reaction. He got none. Layton moved not at all. Bale moved closer and began to circle to Layton's left, away from his live side. Layton simply shifted the ladle into his left hand so that it was closer to Bale's weapon. When Bale was nearly behind Layton, he made his move, stabbing for the Headmaster's neck, but then using the move as a feint, from which he whipped the sword around towards the backs of Layton's legs instead.

Clang! Layton deftly checked the razor-sharp steel with the ladle as his legs pinwheeled over the whistling blade. He landed standing upright next to Bale and instantly slapped him across the face with his open hand so hard that the impact knocked the younger man flat on his back in the dirt. Although stunned, Bale managed to recover quickly, scuttling backwards until he was out of Layton's range, dragging Porien's sword with him. Shaking his head to clear it, Bale got to his feet, a stark purple handprint blossoming on one side of his face to add to the goose-egg that had rapidly risen on his forehead.

Layton continued to smile. Bale was furious beyond measure. His fear and anger combined until his rage burned out everything but his desire to kill the man standing before him, the man with the thinning sandy hair and the dreamy smile. Nothing else mattered. Bale bellowed a clan battle cry and flung himself at Layton, prepared to kill or be killed.

Again, his blade was checked in mid-swing by the ladle, and then both of his hands were struck before he could blink. The sword began to fall from his nerveless fingers, and then the world tilted crazily on its axis as Layton swept his legs out from under him. Bale slammed into the earth again, this time hard enough to knock the wind out of his lungs. Stunned, he could neither move, nor breathe, nor speak.

Suddenly, an immovable weight settled on his chest. Bale looked up to see Layton looking down at him, the Headmaster holding his body immobile with a strategically placed knee. Bale vaguely recalled learning that position last week in one of the training sessions, but no one had made it feel like this. Layton felt like he weighed a thousand pounds. Still too stunned to speak, Bale silently looked up into his Headmaster's face. Layton eased the pressure a bit, and Bale finally managed to catch a hitching breath.

"Yield, son. It's over," Layton whispered just loud enough for Bale to hear.

Something in Bale broke, then. Tears of frustration finally rolled down his face and Bale squeezed his eyes shut in shame. He knew he was done for. This had been his last hope, but they would never let the likes of him stay here now, not after he attacked the Headmaster. He never should have tried to come here. He knew that he was good for nothing. He wished he were dead. Bale sagged in defeat and waited.

"You know," Layton's voice was quiet and amused, "I like you, lad. You're strong. And you've got guts. Not very bright, though. You've got a lot to learn." He sighed. "Even so, I think we can make something of you."

Bale was astonished. Whatever he had expected from the Headmaster, it was not this. He croaked, "Yes...Headmaster,"

Layton leaned over, still smiling, and gently tapped Bale's head with the ladle. "One part of our Warrior Creed deals with humility. I know you can't spell it, but you need to find some. I'm pretty sure that you can find some humility in the kitchen if you look hard enough. Are you willing to do that? I might consider keeping you on here. You've got potential."

Bale could not believe what he was hearing. He struggled to get the words out again. "Yes, Headmaster," he managed to add. "Humility. In the kitchen. I'll find it."

Layton looked up to see Porien standing nearby with a perplexed look on his face. "Porien, would you see to it that this man's conditioning regimen is doubled for the next two months? And that he is also reassigned to kitchen duty during that time? Send him to me after that. I'd like to see what he discovers."

Porien saluted him smartly. "Sir, I'll have it done the moment he leaves the infirmary."

Layton chuckled as he looked down at Bale's battered face. "Yes, give him a day or two to recover, that's fine." He leaned closer so that only Bale could hear. "I'm taking a chance on you, boy. Don't make me regret it. Instead, make me proud. You hear?"

"I hear, Headmaster." Something like hope blossomed in Bale's heart. It had been so long since he had felt anything like it, it was difficult to identify. All he knew was that whatever the Headmaster asked, he would now break his back to see it done. "Sir?"

"Yes, Bale?"

"I'm…" Bale forced himself to say the words. "I'm sorry."

Layton's smile widened. "That's encouraging, son. You might make a warrior yet."

Layton stood and handed the now dented ladle back to the water boy, who looked at it in awe before carrying it off to the kitchen to wash. Leaving Bale in the care of Porien and Carius, Layton bellowed, "Carry on, you lot! Work that sword routine until you don't look like school children with sticks!" Instantly, the trainees shuffled away to begin their drills again, and Layton smiled to see them so eager to train. He knew that Bale would be fine, and he would either stay on after his time in the kitchen or he would leave. He hoped the lad would stay. With a sigh, he walked towards the doors where Daxian awaited him.

"Well, sir, that was…educational," Daxian mused aloud as Layton approached. "You didn't even break a sweat, did you?"

Layton smiled and clapped Daxian on the back as they reentered the huge structure at the doors nearest his office. "Well, I've still got a little bit of fight in me, Daxian. I'm not over the hill just yet."

Daxian laughed, the sound of it reverberating in the hallways of the Academy. "It's got to be a pretty big hill, I'm thinking. You're older than my father, sir, and you handled Bale like he was a naughty child. He's been roughing up the other trainees in his unit ever since he arrived. I'm glad you taught him a lesson."

Layton thought about what he had felt through his magick, what he had learned from the brief connection with Bale. "Well, let's just hope he learns that lesson so that he can be something more than just a thug. That's not who we are..." Layton's words trailed off and he grunted in agony.

Daxian began to reply, but the words froze in his mouth as he saw Layton falter. He reached out and grabbed his arm as he slumped to the floor, obviously stricken. "Headmaster! Sir!" Layton went down to his hands and knees, still unable to speak from whatever was happening to him. Daxian turned and yelled over his shoulder. "Someone fetch the healer! Medic! Medic!"

"No," Layton rasped. He coughed twice, then continued, his voice stronger. "No, I'm...I'm all right. Just let me rest a moment." He struggled to a sitting position, slowly folding his legs beneath him and taking a series of slow, deep breaths to recover his composure. A thin trickle of blood oozed down over Layton's lip, unheeded as he looked within himself to regain his strength.

Daxian knelt beside his Headmaster, silently waiting. It took a small eternity, but finally, Layton's eyes opened, and he wiped a sleeve across his face to clear it of blood.

"Headmaster! What happened?"

Layton paused before speaking, still trying to process the psychic event he had just endured. It had been incredibly painful, feeling like his brain was going to split apart. He had been assaulted by images and sounds, shards of a powerful vision that had overwhelmed him. The last time he had been so immersed in such an intense experience was when he had been Chosen by his Jidaan. But that had been wondrous. This had been agony. It had been fragmented, but at least part of the message was clear.

"Daxian, I have just been called away on urgent business. You know the distribution of duties during my absence. Please make all the arrangements. I'll return as soon as I can, though I don't know how long I will be gone."

Daxian rocked back on his heels. He had not expected this, but he did, indeed, know exactly what to do in the event the Headmaster was away. "Yes, sir. I'll take care of everything right away. Is there anything I can do for you in the meantime?"

Layton slowly got to his feet. "I need my horse saddled, supplies for a long ride, and a pack horse. And fetch my Jidaan and my sai from the museum armory. I'll be needing them, I think."

Chapter 3

Through a red haze of agony, Reyanna saw a man. He was of middling height, lean and strong, not old but not young, wearing a battered old brown hat and a long traveling coat. Wind played with the folds of his coat, whipping it about. He had something long strapped to his back, its wooden handle jutting over his right shoulder, a small leather bag tied on the end as though to cover it.

Odd, she thought absently. The pain in her head kept her from examining what she saw more thoroughly.

The stranger was standing on a grassy rise that overlooked a rocky valley. In the distance, Reyanna could see the stark bluffs and steep crags of an ancient mountain range. The man's face was hidden in the shadows of the hat's brim, but when he turned to look past her, his eyes caught the light, and they blazed a sapphire blue. She had seen those eyes before. *But where?* Through the pain in her head, she could not focus, could not think. She dimly realized that she was on her hands and knees in the grass, but that seemed far less substantial than the vision in which she was immersed.

She heard the terrifying howl of an animal, and then she saw a massive beast top the rise to stand next to the man in her vision. It was a mastiff, but bigger than any she had ever seen. Its muscular body was covered with scars, its face pulled into a permanent snarl that only widened as the dog barked at something that approached. Reyanna felt a rumbling deep in her bones, and saw the two figures stumble as they fought to keep their balance. The dog barked louder as the man's eyes were drawn upward. An enormous shadow crawled over them as an object passed in front of the sun. Something was coming closer. Something big. The intensifying wind ripped off the man's hat, leaving it to dangle behind him by a thin leather thong that encircled his throat, and Reyanna saw his shock of bright blond hair buffeted by the wind. The vicious scar tissue that covered the right side of his face was clearly visible, and the shock of recognition hit her again, followed by confusion. She knew him, but did not.

In her mind's eye, the vision continued, and the man's face took on a ferocious, determined glare. Whatever was coming, he feared it not; he would fight. In one smooth motion, he reached over his shoulder and pulled the unknown weapon from his back, revealing a long-bladed spear that gleamed in spite of the looming shadows. Reyanna felt the man's power rise as he brought the weapon into his hands and fell naturally into a fighting stance. The leather bag that covered the pommel suddenly disintegrated as the emerald beneath it blazed brightly to life, its power burning the covering away. He bellowed in defiance as the huge dog beside him howled its own fury into the wind at the oncoming threat.

And just as suddenly as it had come upon her, the vision ended, leaving her slumped face-first in the grass, her lungs heaving in relief. She lay there for a time, letting the trembling of her limbs subside, then she carefully pushed herself back up to her hands and knees. Spots of blood dotted the grass beneath her and she wiped her nose with her hands, thankful the flow had stopped. She wiped her hands on the grass as best she could, and looked around to take stock of her situation.

Reyanna found herself in one of her favorite places, a tiny meadow surrounded by the majestic trees of the Silver Woods. She was not far from her home, the Weya village of Allinshae, where she had grown up with her adoptive parents, Rask and Shrya. She let the sounds of the forest soothe her as they always did, and tried to get her bearings. *What was that?* she thought with a growing sense of alarm. She had never experienced anything like it. Although her dreams tended to be very vivid and detailed, she had certainly not been sleeping - indeed, far from it. She had only just arrived at the tiny glade, her preferred place of meditation, after a brisk run through the forest. No, she had been awake and exhilarated when the pain had erupted in her head. *What did it mean?* Reyanna turned the vision over in her mind, recalling the details as best she could. However, the pain that yet lingered in her head made that task difficult. She turned and dug through her pack for her waterskin and drank gratefully from it before pouring a small measure over her head. The coolness of the water helped refresh her and she sighed as the pain finally started to dissipate. She unbound her long, raven-dark hair and shook it loose, then quickly rebraided it into a tight plait.

Although she had just arrived at the glade, she knew she needed answers. Carefully pushing to her feet, she shouldered her pack and bow, then set off at a loping run back towards Allinshae. The exercise helped to dispel what ache remained, though it did little to answer her questions.

Who was that man? What was about to attack him? And why did I even see that? I'm no LorMage...I'm just a Ranger. Although the forest spoke to her in a thousand birdsongs and leaves that rustled in the breeze, it gave her no answers. She increased her speed, picking her way through the forest as one born to it, leaving no trace of her passing. Reyanna felt the energy flowing through her as she always did when she ran, as though a current flowed through her, empowering her. It exhilarated her, and she increased her pace. At full speed, Reyanna had been known to keep pace with the fastest of the Weya, if only for a short time. As a human, she knew she could never best them for long at such contests, but that never stopped her from trying. And occasionally succeeding.

As she ran, she reflected on her childhood, spent among the kindly Weya people of Allinshae. She had always been something of a curiosity, a young human girl, her ears lacking the elegant points the Weya possessed, and although her eyes were a striking sapphire blue, they were much rounder than the softly-tilted, jewel-hued eyes of the others. She had always been made to feel welcome, and the Weya children had never been given to teasing, but she still felt a sense of distance from them. She was the outsider. The burn scars along her right arm, jawline, and back had been mostly healed when she had been but a toddler, but she had still been very aware of them. The others did not carry such scars, and again, she felt they identified her as an outsider. The Weya children had never seemed to care, though, and the elders accepted her into Ranger training right alongside their own children. There, she had excelled. Archery, woodcraft, acrobatics, swordplay, and unarmed combat, she had taken to them all as if born to them. She had wanted to make Rask and Shrya proud, and if they

28

were to be believed, she had succeeded mightily. She never quite understood that they would have loved her regardless, but they knew it meant the world to her, so they supported her wholeheartedly.

When she thought of her parents, her spirits lifted. *They'll know what this means, I'm sure of it. They'll know what to do.* With that thought, she accelerated through the forest, dodging branches, shrubs, fallen trees, and anything else that got in her way, more surefooted than any mountain goat.

It took her less than an hour to reach Allinshae, and there she was greeted by everyone who saw her. The Weya were a kindly race, and close-knit. Reyanna waved back as each waved at her, but ran on until she found the small dwelling she had shared with her parents. She slowed to a walk, caught her breath so she would not seem so disheveled, and calmly opened the door.

"Mammai? Patai?" She called out for her parents, but froze just inside the entryway at the sight of a small group of Weya standing in their family room. In one corner, her father, Rask, was in deep conversation with two others, one of whom Reyanna had never seen. Her mother, Shrya, pushed her way through the others to embrace her, a worried frown upon her ageless face.

"Babi," Shrya began, taking Reyanna's hands in her own and looking up into her eyes. Reyanna's concern grew. It had been years since her mother had called her 'baby'.

"What's wrong, Mammai? Who are all these people?" She allowed Shrya to lead her to a carved wooden chair and Reyanna eased into it.

"These are the Elders. You know most of them, I should think." She began pointing them out. "Avigail," she indicated a lovely Weya woman that stood to one side, her hair long and dark. Her robe was simple, but the marks of her office were plain on the sleeves. "Amarin," a male Weya that had once taught a much younger Reyanna how to track a bear nodded his greetings. "Alannia," another female, slightly older than Avigail held her head high, looking slightly imperious, but managed a smile, nevertheless. Shrya gestured at the one remaining Weya that had been

29

quietly debating with her father, "and I don't think you know Calliana."

Calliana turned and bowed low to Reyanna, and the young girl stifled a gasp as she realized that the Weya woman was a LorMage. Calliana's robe was the purest black, inset with blue gemstones. She wore a simple circlet of gold to keep her white hair out of her face, and her eyes were a brilliant, sparkling amber, the likes of which Reyanna had never seen before in a Weya. There was an aura of wisdom and power about the small woman, and Reyanna was thrilled.

"Calliana, my lady!" Reyanna started to rise from her seat, but the Weya gestured for her to sit back down.

"Yes, child, it is good to meet you too. Please, sit. We must talk." With a gesture, she signaled to the others to also take seats, and soon everyone was settled. Calliana remained standing. Reyanna watched her closely and was surprised to see that the LorMage looked tired and worn, in spite of the aura of power she wore.

"My lady, I don't know why you are all here, but there is something I need to tell you..."

The LorMage gently interrupted her. "The vision, you mean?" She saw Reyanna's eyes widen in recognition. "Yes, I see that I am correct. I, too, was touched by it, likely at the same time you were. It appears to have been a Sending, though on purpose or by accident, I know not for certain. I do feel, as do we all, that it is a grave omen, and that is why we are here."

Reyanna's eyes narrowed. "An omen? I don't understand."

Calliana laid a reassuring hand on Reyanna's forearm. "We are not sure that we do either. I was the only one of the Elders here to experience it. I am more connected with this world's magick than the others, though all of the Weya felt its passing, if only as a strange sensation that had no name. However, I do know the man within. He is Gart, who was once a Guardian, a Chosen of the Jidaan. Now, he is a powerful Mage, though he refuses to name himself as such." She chuckled to herself as she continued. "He is somewhat...prickly. But he is a good and decent man. He has kept to himself over the years, but reluctantly took up where Brunar left off as the custodian of the Jidaan."

Reyanna's brows wrinkled at the mention of the Jidaan, the fabled magickal spears that had long ago been created as tools of peace and justice on Talwynn. She had heard of them, of course, as had any child of the Realm. Wielded by the brave Guardians in defense of all that was good in the world, each had a special power, though she had forgotten what some of them might have been. She only vaguely remembered the stories of the devastating conflict that had left the entire Realm with wounds that took years to heal. Her own village had been razed by the evil sorcerer's minions, her human family murdered. She still carried the scars from that horrible night, remembered only in her worst nightmares.

Reyanna searched her memory and found the valiant Mage, Brunar, and the Jidaan-wielding Guardians who had gone to battle against the madman Mordak and his vile army of creatures. Thousands had died, including some of the Guardians themselves. It had happened over two decades past, and the legends of the Guardians had faded for her along with the other hearthtales of youth. She suddenly recognized the weapon in her vision for what it must have been; a Jidaan. If she remembered correctly, the Jidaan of Storms.

"I gathered from the vision that Gart faced a dire threat, though what that threat might have been, I have no idea," Calliana continued. "I know not if this was something that happened even as we witnessed it in the vision, or something that will happen sometime in the future. At first, I thought it could even be a memory from Gart's past, for he has had many adventures since the war."

Reyanna was still confused. "In any event, past, present, or future, what has it to do with me? I have never met the man, nor any of the Guardians. And why did I experience this vision in the first place? I'm just a Ranger, not a Mage."

Calliana smiled and nodded. "Indeed not, little one. Even so, you are involved somehow. Tell me…where were you standing in the vision? Gart was on a hill, yes?"

Reyanna fell silent for a moment, remembering. "Yes, my lady, he was. I was seeing him from behind. Then the wind picked up and he turned around to face me, but..." she turned the memory over in her mind. "He really wasn't looking at me. It was something behind me or above me, something really big. He drew his weapon from his back, and the dog started barking and howling at it too."

Calliana nodded again. "Yes, that is what I saw as well. But I saw it differently. My vantage point was far to what would have been your right. I saw Gart and Beauty, yes. And you."

Reyanna gasped in surprise. "Me? You saw me there?"

"Indeed, I did. Just now you confirmed what I saw. And since you have never seen him before this, I can assume that the vision is not a memory from the past. Since you are here now, it is not of the present. That only leaves the future. A portent like this cannot be ignored." The LorMage gave Reyanna's arm a reassuring squeeze, then she stood and turned away. "I have already discussed this with the Elders and your parents, but of course, you are free to do as you wish, for it is your life and yours alone. We cannot compel you to seek out Gart to find answers."

Reyanna looked at her adoptive parents. Their faces displayed nothing but calm acceptance, though their eyes betrayed the fierce love for the daughter they had raised. "*Mammai*? *Patai*? I would know your thoughts on this." Reyanna stood, knowing it would put her a few inches taller than everyone in the room.

Shrya rushed over and pulled Reyanna into her arms, Rask following only a few steps behind to wrap his arms around them both. No tears were shed, but Reyanna could feel their emotions keenly, just as she always had. There was immense love there, and pride. Fear was there too, yes, but also a sense of resignation.

"My love, we know you well. You would not be able to leave this alone. You would pursue it to the ends of the world whether we agreed or not." Shrya's voice was quiet and loving.

Rask chuckled, "Indeed. You're somewhat pigheaded, if the truth be known. Stubborn."

32

Reyanna was about to protest, but instead leaned into their embrace harder. Rask continued. "It's been time for you to leave us for a while; we were just hoping you would not. You are a grown woman, a Weya Ranger. This may turn out to be something bigger than just us. Go with our blessings and our love. We will be here when you return."

The tears finally came, blinding Reyanna, and it was long before she cleared her throat to speak. "You're right, of course. I'm terrified to leave, but this…I must look into this. I have to know what is going on, why this vision came to me." She lingered in the arms of her parents for a few moments longer before she disentangled herself and wiped the tears from her eyes. She turned back to the LorMage and the Elders of Allinshae and stood to her full height. "All right, then. What do I do now?"

A sigh of relief ran through the Elders. They would never have compelled Reyanna to go, but had been dreadfully concerned at the portents of Calliana's vision. Some of them had survived both wars with Mordak and other conflicts besides, and they knew that such things could not be taken lightly. Calliana gestured to Amarin, who produced two scrolls, one large and loose, the other much smaller, tied with a ribbon and sealed with red wax. Calliana took them both and presented them to the young Ranger. "This is a map of the Realm. I did not recognize the terrain in the vision, so we think the best thing to do is for you to make your way to the Guardians Keep in the Heartstrong Mountains. It is far, but seems the best place to start. The last I knew, Gart and at least one of the remaining Guardians was there, but that was months ago. If you glean new information on the way, then do what you think is best." Calliana sighed, and she sounded sad when next she spoke. "I wish that I could go with you, but I have duties here that I must fulfill." She held up the smaller, sealed scroll. "This is a letter to one of our people who will help you along the way. He makes his home in Shadowy Glen, and he will escort you as long as you require him." A knowing grin crept onto her lips. "If I know Ginn, he will see you all the way to the Keep's very doorstep and consider that just the beginning. You'll likely have a hard time getting rid of him. He has ridden with the Guardians before. He is a canny warrior, and a good friend."

Reyanna accepted the documents and moved to the table to unroll the map. It was beautifully drawn, the towns, cities, and landmarks all made clear with concise Weya markings. Most humans would not be able to read it at all, other than the obvious features they might recognize. She traced her fingers along the paper. Following an easterly course along the Corris River towards Laro, she could eventually angle northward overland to reach the Blackthorne River and buy passage on a boat heading north. Once she got to Green Meadows, she could just follow the mountain range to the west until she eventually came upon the home of the Guardians, high in the western Heartstrong Mountains. Glancing back towards her own village, she saw that Shadowy Glen was not far from Allinshae, and it was on her way. Stopping off to find Ginn would likely not take long.

Looking up from the map, Reyanna glanced around the room, meeting every pair of jewel-hued eyes. "Thank you. Thank you all. I'm still shocked by all this, but I know that what I saw is important somehow. I'm thankful for your guidance." Leaving the map on the table, she faced the gathered Elders and bowed at the waist, showing respect for their wisdom.

They bowed in return. Avigail spoke in a quiet voice that reminded Reyanna of birdsong. "Ranger, the village stands ready to assist you in any way that you need. We will begin to gather supplies for your journey. When will you depart?"

With a quick look at her parents, Reyanna calculated. "The sun is already setting, it makes more sense for me to leave just before dawn breaks. I'll make better time rested."

With another bow, Avigail replied, "As you wish, Ranger. A horse will be made ready in the town stable. Leave at your convenience. May Rowann be with you." The blessing was echoed by all of the Elders, and they each began to make their way to the front door. Each Weya embraced her briefly before leaving, and Amarin, though a hair shorter than she, elicited a squeal from her as he picked her up just as he had when she was a little girl.

LorMage Calliana was the last to depart, and she looked deeply into Reyanna's eyes. "Our hearts go with you, young Reyanna. We know that yours is true. I look forward to seeing you again." She bowed slightly, and Reyanna bowed in return. Calliana moved as if to turn away, but then stopped as though remembering something. She looked back into Reyanna's open face, into the deep blue of her eyes as if seeking. Reyanna suddenly felt embarrassed under such close scrutiny, but could not look away. Their gazes met for what seemed an eternity, then Calliana blinked, and the spell was broken.

"What is it, my Lady?" Reyanna asked, curious after the long look.

The LorMage smiled sadly and shook her head. "I'm not sure, Reyanna. For a moment, I thought...ah, well, it's nothing. Safe journey to you."

Without another word, Calliana slipped out of the door and was gone.

Chapter 4

Kiran rode briskly along the path, enjoying the feel of the sun on her shoulders and the wind in her hair. It had been ages since she had been on a horse, and although she knew that she would be sore for a few days until she reacclimated, it was a welcome change from the mundane tasks at the inn.

The last few years had been good to her, she thought, mostly because of Oswald. It had been his idea to start the mercenary outfit, which had blossomed into something far bigger than she had ever thought possible. They had hired good people to work at the inn so that it mostly ran itself. Even so, she liked to be involved in the day-to-day affairs because it kept her busy, but not so much so that she could not spend time with her husband or keep up her fighting skills with semi-regular workouts. Surprisingly, she had never felt caged as she had feared she might. Her former experience as a mercenary and then as a Guardian had left her with a deep understanding of what was required of the mercenaries and guards in her employ, and she paid them well. Those that knew her personally would fight to the death for her. A grimace crossed her face as she thought of the two newcomers she recently had to put in their place. *Some of the others might still need some convincing.* Then she laughed aloud, a bright and cheery sound. She loved roughhousing with them and she knew it, as did Oswald, no matter the fuss he put up.

She thought of him for a while longer, sweet, kindly Oswald, and a pang went through her heart as she realized how much she already missed him. It had barely been a day. A cloud passed across the sun, further dampening her mood, and she sighed. She decided to think about the task at hand. *Better that than rolling around in sappy feelings,* she reasoned. Kiran listened to the clip-clopping of the horse's hooves on the hard-packed earth of the trail and let her gaze wander across the fields and nearby forest, searching absently for signs of trouble while her mind began to turn over the events she had witnessed in the vision.

Although she had long ago been trained in the use of her magick as a Guardian, both by Brunar during the war with Mordak and by Layton afterwards, she had never been able to use it to see things. Most of her skills had been limited to things she could touch or move. Her perception had become intensely keen once her magick had been fully awakened by the Jidaan in the Choosing, but it was still something she felt rather than saw in her mind's eye. She knew that kind of magick was of another level entirely, far beyond the simple manipulation of physical objects and an enhanced sense of others' emotions.

She realized that what she had experienced had to have been sent to her by someone with infinitely more skill in magick than she would ever have. Gart, she knew, already had the makings of a Mage when they had first met. In the few times she had seen him since, he had done nothing but increase his skills and powers until she suspected that he might have been approaching a level of mastery akin to Brunar's. He certainly could have been the one to send the vision, but Kiran could not be sure. Even so, it definitely had been him she had seen, Gart and his enormous dog, Beauty. She had often joked that Beauty's scars obscured the fact that she was actually a pony rather than a dog, and that had always elicited a smile from the usually stoic Gart.

Mage and canine had been in a meadow near some mountains, and some enormous *thing* had been approaching. She had seen them both turn to face the oncoming threat, but could not see what it was. A young woman had been standing not far from Gart, and at first, Kiran had thought she was the threat. However, the raven-haired girl had looked just as bewildered as Kiran had felt, and Gart appeared not to see her, instead staring at something in the distance. Kiran vaguely remembered seeing other figures standing nearby, also watching, but of them, she had no clear memory. Who they were or why they were there was a mystery, as was the vision itself.

Kiran turned the scene over in her mind as she rode, wondering what it all meant. Her first impression was that something was coming for Gart and that it was evil. She had seen Gart practically lay waste to an entire army once, and that was long before he had spent years improving his skills with the Jidaan of Storms and his own powers. If it was strong enough to threaten Gart now, then whatever it was, it was incredibly dangerous.

"Well, at least I'm sure it's not Mordak," she said aloud to her horse, who said nothing in return. The evil sorcerer had twice tried to take over the Realm, leaving nothing but death and destruction in his wake. Two thousand years past, he had been subdued and imprisoned by Brunar and the previous group of Guardians, and peace had reigned for centuries. Then, just over two decades ago, Mordak had somehow broken free of his prison to again ravage the Realm. Weya, humans, and the powerful ape-people from the south, the Augenan, had opposed him, but it had been a devastating war. In the end, his death had come at the cost of many lives, including Brunar's. The noble Mage had bravely sacrificed himself to stop Mordak's dying attempt to rip the continent apart with his magick. Brunar had grappled with the madman as Mordak sent a beam of energy down into the earth, intending to tear the land asunder. Brunar enabled a magickal amulet, meant to absorb the intense energy, but the forces were far too great to contain. The amulet overloaded in an enormous explosion, releasing all of its stored energy in an instant. The blast had been cataclysmic, and Mordak had been incinerated along with his longtime foe, Brunar. Mordak was nothing but ash, so whatever this new threat was, Kiran had no knowledge of it. "Maybe we'll get lucky and I can just kill it with a good slash and stab. That would be nice. No long battles, no cities destroyed, just a dead bad guy. I'll keep my fingers crossed for that." As usual, her horse listened politely but made no response.

Thunder rumbled in the distance, making Kiran frown. She detested riding in the rain. She looked to the south and saw a bank of thunderheads over the vast forest. She knew that many leagues beyond that forest lay the city of Alverton Falls, the site of the final battle with Mordak. A shudder crawled down her back. She'd just as soon not see that place again. Too many bad memories. The thunder rumbled again and Kiran started calculating how long it would take her to reach the next settlement on her way to the Heartstrong Mountains. Haver's Reach was still a good day and a half ride, so if the storm kept heading her way, she'd be camping in the rain.

"Figures," she sighed to herself. She kept an eye on the distant clouds, thick and gray at the top and nearly black near the bottom, so low they seemed to touch the tops of the trees in the faraway forest. Another rumble rolled across the land, and Kiran spied a zigzag of lightning playing within the clouds. Then another. She was glad the storm was so far away, but something about what she had seen bothered her. She urged her horse to move a bit faster as she kept an eye on the brooding storm, searching for whatever had put her on her guard. Closing her eyes, she opened her senses as Brunar had taught her long ago and tried to figure out what was amiss.

A strong feeling of wrongness assailed her. Her eyes snapped open as she gasped in surprise and revulsion at the oily, disgusting sensation. It was not the storm itself, but something within the storm, something that felt alien and loathsome to her. Not only that, she felt its rage, its hatred. Whatever it was, it was coming for her. At the leading edge of the storm, a dark blot detached itself from the rest of the enormous cloudbank. It looked like a mere speck from that distance. Kiran stared intently at the glob of blackness that approached, then glanced ahead at the nearest edge of the forest, gauging as best she could whether she could make it to the safety of the trees before it arrived. It was much too far, even at a gallop, and uphill at that. Cursing, she looked back at the oncoming, amorphous blotch of ill will only to find that it had already increased in size.

"All right then, whatever you are...bring it on. I've been in a mood for a good fight for a while now, and you'll do." A wicked grin crawled across her face as she reached over her shoulder for the Jidaan she had strapped there. Its brilliant sapphire pommelgem flared to life as she touched its handle. With a defiant battle-cry, she drew it from its scabbard, and the blade rang in the spring air as if happy to be used once more. She held it high, its cobalt light blazing, and turned her horse towards the oncoming threat. The beast snorted and danced in place as it sensed its master's mood. Excited, it eagerly awaited her command to charge.

Kiran's jade eyes narrowed as she watched the swatch of darkness approach, drawing closer moment by moment. From within the opaque cloud, something eagerly, hungrily, watched her as well.

Chapter 5

The road was quiet, save for the songs of birds that sang sweetly in the tops of the trees. They had not a care in the world, it seemed. The sky was blue, the breezes gentle, and spring had brought warmth and light to the forest. Other animals went about their business, eating, hunting, resting, always keeping an ear or an eye out for something higher or lower on the food chain, depending on their own place in it.

Without warning, a shimmering, opalescent circle of energy appeared above the road, silent but for the faint hum of its intense power. A horse's head slowly emerged from it, followed by the rest of the animal's body, guided by the warrior that rode in the saddle. Clad in the lightest leather armor, little more than shoulders and elbow guards, the rider urged the horse forward, but there was little need. It was well-accustomed to traveling through Layton's gates, and it moved ahead without complaint. As they cleared the glowing portal, it winked out of existence, and the shining opal in the pommel of Layton's Jidaan dimmed, its power quiescent once more.

Over the years, the Guardian had honed his skills and gradually built his strength until he could travel much greater distances, with more accuracy, than he had ever thought possible when Brunar first taught him how to use the Gift of Gates. He was not certain how he compared to Dani, the Guardian who had wielded his Jidaan two thousand years before him, but he had been nothing if not diligent in his practice. Two decades had brought him a high degree of skill, though he yet strove for more. He had come across the continent in just a few days and still considered himself lazy.

Though he had seen years of combat as well as peace, Layton still retained much of the look of the boy he had been all those years ago. He still fought with a dreamy half-smile on his face, laughed easily, and found joy and wonder in the most trivial of things. But with age also came wisdom, and a certain amount of cynicism that he sadly considered a part of growing into an adult. He battled it daily with laughter where he could. As he saw it, life was a grand adventure, and abounded with opportunities to make the world a better place. He thought of himself much more as a caretaker than a warrior, and he took that responsibility seriously. That's what Guardians were meant to be.

He looked around at the thick forest that encroached upon the road on either side and found the cracked boulder he had used as a landmark for his Gate. Satisfied that he had arrived as planned, he estimated that he should reach the inn that served as Kiran's base of mercenary operations by sundown. He had almost not recognized her when he saw her in the vision that had struck him. Her hair was much longer and she had grown more comfortable since they had last met, but she was unmistakable. The dark-haired girl, the white-tressed Weya, and the others he had seen in the vision, were all unknown to him. Gart and Beauty, of course, he had known on sight. He figured the best course of action was to find Kiran and see what she knew, since she was more or less on the way to Guardians Keep. If she knew nothing, then at least they would be able to work out something together, and he could transport them much faster than she could ride alone.

The trail opened up as it topped the next rise, and Layton found himself looking down into a wide grassland. The forest from which he had emerged fell away, its edges running southeast and northeast from the road on either side, continuing on for many leagues and shrouding the land in a blanket of dark green. Directly ahead of him, the trail stretched as far as the eye could see to the west, a ribbon of dusty brown cutting through a wide, soft field of pale green grass and occasional trees and shrubs. Thunder rumbled in the distance, and Layton looked to the south to see a storm brewing there, still far away. Enormous, black thunderheads seemed to sit on the distant forest like a mountain of forbidding mist. Lightning played amongst the clouds, menacing even at that great distance. Layton reined his horse to a halt to gaze at the wide vista that spread before him, taking it all in. He would be long gone before the storm even came close, and hopefully, Kiran would help him sort out the vision when he found her.

Thunder rumbled in the distance again, deep and unfriendly. Layton raised an eyebrow at the sound. Something was pricking at the edges of his awareness, and it set his teeth on edge. The Guardian opened his senses wide and instantly found that something within the storm was the source of his unease. It was not the storm itself, but rather a being, a force, within the rumbling nimbus clouds. Layton squinted into the distance, using his magick to enhance his vision as best he could, and was rewarded with the sight of a malignant blotch of darkness detaching itself from the mass of clouds.

It moved with purpose, gaining speed moment by moment, but its trajectory did not seem quite right. If it continued in its path, it would miss him entirely, ending up somewhere ahead of him. He turned his eyes forward and finally saw a speck of movement. There was a rider on the road far ahead, and by his calculations, directly in the path of the oncoming threat. He was about to use his Gift to transport himself there when he saw a brilliant burst of blue from the spot, as though the rider had plucked a star from the heavens and held the shining object aloft.

He knew that intense cobalt flare well; it was the sapphire pommelgem of the Jidaan of Warding, wielded by his old friend and fellow Guardian, Kiran. A smile creased his dusty face. Whatever was coming was going to have its hands full...if it even had hands. He reached over his shoulder and loosened his Jidaan in its scabbard, then checked the twin, fork-like weapons he kept sheathed along his thighs. Although he preferred the Jidaan, he never felt right without his sai. Rather than betray his presence by Gating to her position, he merely kicked his horse into a lazy trot. He'd help if needed, but if he knew Kiran, she'd only be irritated by his assistance. His smile widened and he almost laughed out loud as he realized how much he had missed her.

$$*\qquad *\qquad *\qquad *\qquad *\qquad *$$

Kiran's blood sang in her veins as she kicked her horse into a gallop and burst forward. She would meet the cloud-thing out in the open where she could maneuver. Her horse's hooves thundered beneath her as they hurtled into the wide meadow, and Kiran kept her eyes on the oncoming entity.

It resembled a cloud, but it was much darker; the oily, thick mist seemed to churn and seethe as it approached. Suddenly, it broke into five smaller pieces, each coalescing into vaguely human but utterly nightmarish shapes. Batlike wings appeared, along with long, muscular arms and legs, their digits ending in wicked talons. Their heads resembled those of bulls, each having a pair of forward jutting ebony horns that framed glowing red eyes. Their mouths opened to reveal shiny black fangs, and they all uttered an animalistic cry of bloodlust that echoed over the meadow. Five daemons of the air approached, and Kiran rushed to meet them.

Sliding her hand down to the pommel of her Jidaan to extend her reach, Kiran yanked the reins of her horse to the left and slashed upwards at the nearest creature as it came in range. The short-handled, long-bladed spear cleaved a glowing scarlet line across its chest. It emitted a piercing shriek and veered away, its bat wings flapping crazily as it curled around its pain. Kiran lashed out at another of the beasts as it flew close, and it jerked itself out of the way an instant before losing its head. Without slowing, Kiran thrust the savage point of the blade nearly straight upwards and skewered another of the beasts, which howled almost in her face before sliding off of the blade, clutching the fiery wound as it retreated. The other two creatures hung back, watching.

Kiran pulled her horse around in a circle, invigorated. "Is that the best you can do? You're not even worth the effort!" She taunted them, holding her Jidaan overhead. "Come on and get me, then!" She watched the two wounded daemons struggling to stay aloft, counting them down, but not yet out. She had dealt them what looked like mortal wounds, though they had yet to expire.

Just then, the two wounded daemons flew towards each other, screeching all the while. As they moved, their outlines became less distinct, dissolving as they lost their solid forms to again become the dark, oily mist they had been before. The two nebulous shapes merged and the

44

resulting larger cloud convulsed for a few moments before separating again. From those two blots of darkness, two new daemons formed, each whole and completely healed. They turned their glowing crimson eyes on Kiran and shrieked in anger.

"Well, that's going to make this more difficult, then, isn't it? Looks like I might have to do more than wound you, or else you'll just regenerate. Fine. We'll see how well you fly when you're missing your heads!"

Kiran spurred her horse forward, bellowing in challenge as she stood up in the saddle, her Jidaan held out at full length as she attacked. Her first slash lopped off one creature's clawed foot, and she was encouraged to see that the limb simply dissipated in the breeze and did not grow back immediately. "Ha! Take that, you flying scum!" Suddenly, a fiery line of agony erupted across her back. She cried out and jerked the reins sharply to her right even as she slashed reflexively at the daemon that had wounded her. The shadowy thing took an ugly gash in its right wing before managing to get away.

The pain was sharp and galvanizing. Kiran spurred her horse forward to put some space between herself and the air daemons, but they were fast and cunning. They darted in from one side, then the other, attacking with vicious slashes of their ebony talons. Kiran repelled them all with deft strikes and stabs of her shining Jidaan. Even so, she was soon bleeding from several small wounds, and her horse was beginning to tire.

Fortunately, Kiran had started to catch the timing of the creatures' attacks, and her own thrusts and counters were scoring more often and more deeply. One creature darted in on her left, and she split it from collarbone to groin. Without pausing in her swing, she redirected it to whip around horizontally until she carved a wide gash across another daemon's midsection, nearly cleaving it in two. It slammed into the dirt, writhing in pain. Two more stabs and she had suddenly incapacitated all but one of the dark, malevolent beasts.

The one that remained hovered in the air a few yards away, watching her impassively as its companions howled in agony and frustration. Kiran pointed the blade of her Jidaan at it and bellowed a challenge. "Come on! What's the matter, are you scared of me? Come at me, coward!"

The creature growled in response, but did not come any closer. Instead, it gestured to the others of its kind, beckoning them. Two of them, still struggling with their wounds, swooped down and gathered up the feebly squirming daemon Kiran had nearly cut in half. The others winged towards their leader. When they were all within the thing's reach, the beasts dissolved, their shapes dissipating into a thick, cloudy vapor. One by one, the swirling, inky apparitions merged with that of their leader, the central mass growing larger as each daemon added its own presence to the mix. The resulting cloud was enormous. It roiled and swirled upon itself as flickers of scarlet lightning played within.

Kiran grimaced. "Well, that can't be good. Nope. Not at all."

As if the sound of her voice was a signal, the oily cloud coalesced into a single, gigantic daemon, standing nearly twenty feet tall. Its eyes glowed red with evil power, and it peered down from its towering height at the puny human below. It let out a roar of triumph, then brought its massive fists together over its head.

Kiran saw the blow coming and quickly spurred her brave little horse forward, bursting out of the creature's range just as it struck the earth where she had been only an instant before. The impact rocked her, and nearly knocked her horse off its feet. She could feel the little steed's fear washing over her, and Kiran instinctively sent a sense of calm assurance in return, steadying her mount. It snorted loudly and whinnied as it caught its balance and followed Kiran's lead. She whirled it around to face the huge daemon only to yank her horse sideways as another two-fisted attack came down, shaking the earth with its power. A wave of fatigue hit her as her wounds began to take their toll. She grunted in frustration.

I need some time to deal with these cuts, Kiran thought to herself. *Damn thing is all up in my face, though. Hmph!* Suddenly, Kiran spun her horse around and pulled it to a stop. She raised her Jidaan overhead and ignited its power. The blue sapphire embedded in the weapon's pommel burst to life, its magick joining with Kiran's as it prepared to do her bidding. Kiran watched the creature close in on her. *Just a moment more…*she thought. The dark being's face split into a fanged grin that spread wide in anticipation as Kiran suddenly presented a stationary target. Its two fists raised high again, this time for a killing blow.

With a flex of her will, she created a dome-shaped Ward that completely covered both her and her horse. The daemon's fists slammed into it as though it were made of solid stone, the unexpected impact bringing an agonized howl from the immense beast. Both of its fists became momentarily fuzzy and indistinct, before the injured creature could bring them back into focus once more. With a roar of pure fury, the creature shook off the pain and began to hammer and slash at the glowing blue shield of energy.

Safe within the Ward, the air was calm and peaceful but for the hum of the Jidaan's magick. Kiran caught her breath, frowning at how long it took her to do so. *Getting old…bah!* She reached down and patted her horse's neck to calm it as her narrowed eyes angrily surveyed her attacker. She knew it would never be able to break her Ward, at least, not for a while. She might feel rusty, but she had years of practice under her belt. She could hold such a small shield for some time. The beast would have to be patient if it was trying to wear her down. Unfortunately for the creature, Kiran was not patient at all. She wanted it, or them, dead, and five minutes ago. The creature flung itself at the luminescent blue Ward again and again, desperate to get to her, to pulverize her and then rip her to shreds.

Kiran grunted at it, "Yeah, I know the feeling, you big dumb bastard." *At least the thing had the common decency to attack me way out in the middle of nowhere,* she thought. *No innocents to get in the way. But what to do?* She pondered for a moment, careful to keep a close watch on her levels of fatigue. She gathered a bit of her magick and sent it to the injuries she felt, speeding their healing. Alyssa had taught her to do that a very long time ago. Kiran felt a pang in her heart as she thought of her friend, the tiny healer and fellow Guardian, fallen at the hands of Mordak. The thought made her angry, and she turned her

47

attention back to her huge assailant, who had continued to batter her Ward with its immense fists.

"All right then, I'm getting tired of your crap, daemon. Let's see how you like this…" Kiran held up one hand, palm out, towards the creature and focused on the power of her Jidaan. The Ward expanded slightly, pushing the oily cloud-daemon back a step. It roared in anger and pummeled the shimmering blue shield again. Again, she expanded her Ward, and again, the creature had to retreat a step. It roared in fury and frustration, and began to beat even more ferociously against the powerful dome of sapphire energy.

As it initiated another attack, Kiran suddenly clenched her fist and pulled the Ward inwards, shrinking it substantially. The daemon's scarlet eyes widened in surprise, but it could not check itself in time, and it stumbled as its fists struck air where before there had been solidity. It staggered forward, falling onto the much smaller dome that now protected Kiran and her mount.

In the instant the big creature touched the energy field, Kiran expanded the Ward, opened it, and swept its edges up, over, and around the surprised daemon, completely surrounding it. The sheet of energy snapped itself closed before the daemon could even get to its feet, and when it did, it found itself trapped inside a glowing sphere of magick, completely captive within the translucent blue globe. It unleashed an inhuman scream that would have shattered Kiran's eardrums, but she added power to the Ward and it solidified further, deadening the sound.

Tired, but still strong, Kiran regarded the caged daemon. "Yeah, yeah, tell me all about it. Like I give a crap." With a gesture, she began to shrink the huge sphere, crushing it inwards onto the hapless daemon, who struggled in vain against its confines. As the sphere continued to shrink, the daemon yowled and squealed in agony as its limbs began to compress, pop, and break. While it was solid, it could be hurt. And Kiran was enjoying it. She squeezed the sphere tighter, and suddenly, the daemon's form dissolved into the oily mist she had first seen. Within the frantically roiling cloud, she could see a pair of red eyes, then another, then more. All five daemons were in there somewhere. She reduced the sphere again, compressing the air and daemons inside. As it shrank, the pressure increased within the sphere, and Kiran carefully opened a pinhole to let some air out so that she could shrink it further. One of the daemons lunged for the opening, but she closed it instantly, already satisfied that the sphere was easier to shrink with a little less air inside. She kept going until she had compressed the daemons into a sphere the size of her head. With a gesture she brought it floating through the air in front of her so that she could examine it. She gazed at it, seeing only a glowing sphere of blue around a center of the darkest black.

"If you don't mind my asking," an amused voice drifted across the meadow. "What exactly are you going to do with, um, that?"

Kiran turned and looked over her shoulder to see a very familiar boyish grin. It was surrounded by more lines than she remembered, but the half-smile was exactly the same, nestled within a short, brownish beard. She had traveled the length and breadth of the continent with him in years past, and Layton was more brother than friend.

"I don't know yet. Any ideas?"

"You think a jug could hold it? I've got one here, though it's currently full of wine. I brought it as a gift for you."

Kiran's face brightened. "For me? How sweet of you! I hate to waste good wine on such as..." she nodded distastefully at the black and blue sphere hovering before her, "that."

Without a word, Layton leaned over and plucked one of Kiran's waterskins from her saddle. It was nearly empty. He quickly drained it, then pulled a large, sturdy-looking jug from somewhere. Handling it carefully, he uncorked it, then set about filling the skin with the wine. "Now that I'm here, you won't have to carry so much water. I've got plenty, and we'll make much better time with my Gates anyway." When the jug was empty, he handed it to Kiran. "If they stay in that cloud state, they'll be trapped in there, I'm pretty sure."

Kiran took the jug and held it firmly on the saddle in front of her. Manipulating the power of the Jidaan, she carefully moved the glowing sphere over the open mouth of the jug and opened a tiny hole in the Ward. She could feel the anger and hatred of the beings inside as they struggled to find enough space to change into solid form. "Oh, shut up in there. You attacked me, remember? You deserve what you get." She compressed the Ward until all of the oily darkness was completely imprisoned within the thick confines of the jug, then quickly stoppered it with the cork Layton handed her. She released the Ward and yanked her hand away. The jug was still. She stared at it, watching for any signs of mischief. The jug acted like nothing more than a jug, cold and silent. She watched it for a while longer, just to be sure, then ran a leather thong through the jug's fingerhole and attached it to her saddle.

"Well, now that that's handled, let's see about getting you to the next town. I'm sure you've stopped the bleeding like Alyssa taught you, but you need stitches, food, and some rest." Layton's smile was welcome enough that Kiran did not feel like arguing.

"Layton, that sounds like the best idea I've heard in a long time. I take it you saw the vision too? The one with Gart and Beauty?"

"That would be the one, yes. I figured I'd come get you before heading up to the Keep. That's the first place that Gart might be. At least, that's where he was last I knew." He looked off to the south, from whence the air daemons had come. "Though we could also head that way. That's where your beasties came from."

Kiran shook her head. "No, I want to go to the Keep. Even though they came from that direction, we could be chasing all over the Realm and never find anything definite. We can leave the jug at the Keep, and no one will unknowingly set those things free." A confused look crossed her face. "And...I don't know how to say it, but it just feels right to go there anyway. I've felt that ever since the vision hit me."

Layton nodded immediately in understanding. "You don't have to explain, I felt the same way. It wasn't out of my way to come see you first, but I was headed there too."

Kiran grinned and punched him lightly in the arm. "Nowhere is out of the way for you, you lout. Those Gates get you anywhere you want to be a lot faster than a horse alone."

He smiled. "Well, yes, there is that. Shall we go?"

"Lead on, my good man," she replied with a wave of her hand.

Layton opened a shining, opalescent Gate, and Kiran saw its twin appear on the road far ahead, flaring to life atop a rise at the edge of the forest. Layton gently urged his horse through, and she followed immediately after, leaving the meadow silent and calm once more.

Chapter 6

Reyanna urged her horse, Betina, to go faster, and Betina complied. Shaking her dark hair out of her eyes, Reyanna savored the sensation of the wind in her face and the feel of Betina's sturdy heartbeat. The huge animal stretched its legs and raced for no reason other than that Reyanna had asked her to. Betina's hooves thundered into the earth, and Reyanna laughed in excitement as she felt the animal's exhilaration. It was enjoying the romp as they covered the grasslands between Allinshae and the greater expanse of the ancient forest known as the Silver Wood.

Ahead, Reyanna saw the trees become more frequent, first coming in twos and threes, then clusters, before merging into the edge of the great forest. She let Betina gallop for a few heartbeats more, then reluctantly eased back on the reins. She felt Betina's sudden sadness as she obeyed her master's command, but it was short-lived. As she gradually slowed to a walk, Reyanna's sense of Betina's emotions told her that the horse was happy enough. It snorted loudly as it caught its breath, and then began thinking absently about food, water, and rest, but none of those things were urgent yet. She was content to keep moving were she was asked to go.

Reyanna sighed and patted Betina's neck. "You're such a good horse, yes you are," she said absently. In her mind, she heard Betina agree that yes, she was indeed a good horse, though she did not use words as Reyanna did. Betina had not caught the words, but the thoughts and intent, and responded in kind. Reyanna did not think twice about it. She had always heard Betina, just as she had always heard other things that she did not mention. As a human living among the Weya, she had already been seen as somewhat odd. Even though the others had always seemed to love her regardless, Reyanna had never shaken that sense of otherness that she had always known, even as a young child. She could hear and see things that the Weya children could not. And do things. Sometimes, amazing things. But deep down, she feared being more different than she already was, so she kept those things to herself. She felt no need to rock the boat.

Reyanna expertly guided Betina through the trees until she found herself riding in the shadows of a vast, leafy cathedral. Huge branches met overhead in a dense canopy that rustled and moved in the gentle breeze. The Wood was older than the oldest Weya could remember, and spread its arms far and wide across the land. It often seemed to possess a life and spirit of its own, and it spoke to her almost as clearly as Betina did. Reyanna smiled as she felt it welcome her.

The vale in which Ginn made his home was not far out of her way. Having grown up in the embrace of this forest and others, she felt perfectly at home in the Silver Wood. The birds chirped happily above and the rustlings of other animals occasionally reached her ears as she expertly guided Betina towards Ginn's home.

As the day passed into afternoon, Reyanna finally entered the glade where Ginn was said to be. It was a beautiful spot, brightened by the sun in the center of the small valley, and hugged closely by the majestic trees on all sides. A glistening brook ran along one side, eventually disappearing into the trees to the east. As she approached, she saw a doe and her two fawns pick their heads up from the water to regard her for a few moments before bounding away. Reyanna thought she had never seen a more beautiful spot.

She dismounted and led Betina to the stream, where the horse gratefully dipped her head for a drink. Reyanna left her there, knowing she would not go far, and decided to follow the water upstream. She had no idea exactly where Ginn made his home, but knew that it had to be close by.

"Ginn? Ginn! My name is Reyanna, and I've been sent to find you," she called out, her youthful voice echoing in the little valley. She scanned the surrounding area carefully, but saw nothing but the lush grasses and deep green leaves in the trees. *He's got to be here somewhere*, she thought. After peeking over her shoulder and finding that Betina was calmly cropping grass near the stream, Reyanna sought a place to rest. She found a jumble of stones beneath a large oak tree and sat down upon the largest one, grateful for the sturdy trunk as she leaned back against it. The burbling sounds of water playing and splashing its way through the rocks was soothing, as was the wind rustling its way through the trees all around. Reyanna closed her eyes and relaxed.

Her desire to find Ginn was foremost in her mind as she began to drift, her senses opening up even as she dozed. She felt everything around her, surprised by the energy of life that she felt from every living thing. The silent tree trunk at her back gave off a distinct aura of enduring strength and ancient wisdom, while the grasses all around seemed light and fleeting, their energy sparkling but small. The water was constantly moving and changing, and Reyanna felt its potential for almost limitless power as well as its extreme gentleness. Without understanding exactly how, Reyanna sent her energy reaching outward, away from her, as she unconsciously sought Ginn. It took only moments to find him, deep in the woods to the east. His aura was bright and pure, standing out like a shining star in a dark room, the power of his life essence. Reyanna watched in remote fascination as the Weya warrior carefully picked his way through the forest towards her.

Somehow, she knew that he had only just become aware of her presence, and was attempting to sneak up on her, more as a test of his own skills than to scare her. Drowsily, she chuckled to herself. To her inner eye, the Weya's bright aura was clearly visible, and she could see him easily. She watched him approach until he was barely a stone's throw away. Stifling a giggle, she kept her eyes closed and scooped up a rock with one hand and tossed it into the stream several yards away. Ginn heard the splash, and his gaze turned towards the noise. It only took him an instant to realize that the splash was harmless, and he turned back to the tree where Reyanna reclined only to see that she was gone.

The Weya blinked in surprise. His attention had only been diverted for an instant, surely not enough time for her to disappear like that. Ducking farther down into the shelter of the high grass, he edged forward with extreme care, watchful all the while for the human girl. He saw nothing.

Finally, he stood up to his full height and walked quietly towards the tree, mystified. He was a Weya, after all. A former Ranger at that, and his woodcraft was beyond reproach. *Where could she be?* he thought.

An acorn dropped out of the tree and thunked onto the top of his head. He flinched and looked upwards to see Reyanna there, crouching among the thick branches with a huge grin on her face. How she had avoided detection was completely beyond him, but he could not help but smile at her obvious satisfaction. As she appeared to mean no harm, he removed his hand from the slim dagger at his belt and instead bowed low in exaggerated formality.

"My lady, you have me at a disadvantage, it seems. Please allow me to introduce myself properly. I am Ginn, of the Westburrow Weya. I must commend you on your stealth, lady. I have never been taken unawares like this." His voice was low and warm, and Reyanna liked him immediately.

Moving with practiced ease, Reyanna hung down from the limb and dropped lightly to the ground. She brushed her hands on her trousers before offering both of them to Ginn in greeting. "Amarin once said that I'm good at that sort of thing." Ginn raised an eyebrow at the mention of the Weya RangeMaster. The girl must have been trained by him, but a human trained in Weya woodcraft was highly unusual. She continued. "My name is Reyanna of Allinshae. Rask and Shrya are my parents."

Ginn inclined his head politely as he held her hands. "Well met, Reyanna. I must say that you pique my interest. Even the most skilled of humans are hard-pressed to sneak up on us, though if you've been trained by Amarin, that explains that. If I may ask, why have you sought me out? I've received no notice of a visitor, and I know of Rask and Shrya only in passing. How can I help you, my lady?" He cocked his head to one side, his bright blue eyes shining with interest.

Reyanna stared at his handsome face and she felt a flush creep up her neck. Embarrassed, she gently disengaged her hands from Ginn's as she started speaking more rapidly than she had meant to. "Ah, um, yes...I had a vision a few days ago. It was alarming, and seemed very important. Apparently, the LorMage experienced it too, and came to see me. We decided that I should go and see Gart as soon as possible and try to make sense of it. I have a letter here from Calliana that explains it all." She pulled off her backpack and rummaged within for the scroll.

"Gart? The Mage?" Ginn replied. "Yes, I know him. Or rather, I know of him. I was not there at the battle of Alverton Falls, where he battled Mordak and Balroth alongside the Guardians," Ginn paused for a moment, remembering the brave Bjarke and tiny but ferocious Alyssa, two Guardians who had perished during the final battle. They had been friends as well as allies, and their loss still pained Ginn whenever he thought about it. Shaking off the hurt, he continued, "He seems to have taken up where Brunar left off, although he is a bit of an oddity. No Mage has also been a Chosen Guardian, yet Gart still carries his Jidaan. Nevertheless, he has delved deeply into studies of magick just as Brunar did during his long life. From what I hear, he has made surprising progress for one so young. What has he to do with this?"

Reyanna handed Ginn the scroll and explained the vision that had struck her. He read it as she described the slightly different version of the vision the LorMage had experienced. Ginn tucked the scroll away and nodded thoughtfully as she summarized her meeting with the Elders of Allinshae. His elegant fingers rose to absently stroke his chin as he listened.

"They sent me to ask if you would show me the way to the Guardians Keep in the Heartstrong Mountains. I mean, I don't need a babysitter or anything," the slightest hint of defensiveness had crept into her voice, "but they said you had been there before and having a guide saves time." She sighed and her tone lightened. "Plus, it's always nice to have someone to talk to on the trail!"

Ginn smiled as he turned her request over in his mind. If Amarin had trained her, then she was a Ranger, so he had no doubts of her ability to take care of herself. That said, even Weya Rangers could be slain by accident, misfortune, or even a simple bunch of determined bandits. Two on the road was far safer than one person alone, even if that one was a Ranger.

"Reyanna, daughter of Shrya and Rask, I would be honored to escort you to Guardians Keep. I have been away from the Heartstrong Mountains for far too long, and I welcome the chance to see them again." He bowed low again, eliciting a giggle from Reyanna. As he rose, he continued. "And indeed, I am curious as to the cause of this vision. It sounds important, and although I am not terribly knowledgeable about such things, I agree with the LorMage; it should be looked into."

"Wonderful!" Reyanna was glad Ginn had accepted her request. It sounded like he knew much more about Gart and the Guardians than she, and she was eager to hear more of them.

"It is still early, and I would have us moving on soon. I need to stop at my home and gather some supplies, but that will not take long at all, and then we can be on our way. If we move quickly, it will still take nearly a month to arrive there, so it's better that we don't tarry."

Reyanna agreed and walked over to Betina, who had not strayed far. She put one foot in the stirrup and hoisted herself easily into the saddle. When she looked around, Ginn was simply gone. Before she could open her senses to look for him, an acorn bounced off her shoulder, startling her. She squinted into the shadows beneath the tree she had just left, and finally spotted Ginn, though she was hard-pressed to do so. She laughed.

"My home is just beyond that bend in the river to the north. Follow me, I'll show you. Be sure to keep up, now!" With that, Ginn took off at a lope, leaving Reyanna to spur her horse after him.

Chapter 7

Guardians Keep was quiet. Nothing stirred within the stately chambers that had been chiseled from the living stone of the Heartstrong Mountains. Although the stone was dark, the rooms and halls within the hollowed-out mountain were bright and cheery, an effect achieved by skillful placement of windows and polished surfaces. Enchanted, glowing globes of glass that hung in the highest corners of the room, easily fifty feet above the floor, added even more light, chasing away whatever shadows might have tried to take up residence. Eight enormous columns supported the lofty ceiling, spread evenly over the main chamber, the Hall of Jidaana. Eighty yards long and half that wide, the Hall had long been the home of the Guardians and the Mage who led them. A passageway at the eastern end of the room, decorated with ornate stone carvings on either side, led to an enormous pair of wooden doors banded with steel. As usual, they were tightly locked against the chill winds outside. Although it was Springtime, the air was still cold in the mountains.

At the western end of the room, upon a raised platform, the Jidaan resided. The fabled magickal spears were meant to be wielded only in defense of the land by those specifically Chosen to carry them, warriors of pure heart and will. Each weapon was five feet long, with a blade as long as a man's forearm at one end, the other ending in a diamond-shaped pommel that clutched a powerful gemstone within, each an incredible work of magick. In times of peace, they rested in brackets upon the wall, their blades pointed skyward as they awaited their Chosen. Of the six sconces on the wall, only two held blades, their unblemished steel glimmering softly in the warm light.

Two decades ago, Nessar had reverently placed the Jidaan of Power and the Jidaan of Healing back in their brackets as tears of loss flowed down his craggy face. As a former Master of the Guild of Thieves in Rualtha, Nessar had not been used to having friends at all, much less close ones. The two who had last carried those weapons had been comrades-in-arms, yes, but more than that, they were rare friends, dear to Nessar's heart.

The immensely strong Bjarke, wielder of the ruby Jidaan of Power, had been the jolliest bear of a man that Nessar had ever met. He had been as kind as he was strong. As a man who had single-handedly slain a huge reptilian Killith, then an Ogre, and still held his ground alone against an army of Mordak's rabid creatures, that meant he was very kind, indeed. Equally capable of moving mountains or gently carrying a sleeping child, he had been an extraordinary man.

Alyssa had been as small as Bjarke had been huge, as sweet and compassionate a woman as Nessar had ever known. Raised among the nuns of Rowann, she had found her calling as a physician, a natural choice for one destined to wield the diamond Jidaan of Healing. She knew, though, that some cancers had to be cut out, and the tiny, auburn-haired woman was just as dangerous with her Jidaan as any other Guardian. It could heal, or it could kill, and Alyssa took her responsibilities seriously either way.

Bjarke and Alyssa, had been lovers at the end, though fate would not let them enjoy life together for long. They had died within moments of each other, each felled by the foul sorcerer Mordak at Alverton Falls, the site of the final battle over twenty years past. The world was a somewhat dimmer, sadder place without them.

Many others also died that day, but many more had been saved when the wounded sorcerer, Mordak, tried to rip the very world asunder with the last of his power. Brunar had bravely sacrificed himself to destroy Mordak at the last, thus silencing his evil forever. Since then, peace had reigned, or at least as much as it could in a world mostly ruled by fallible humans. The land slowly healed itself, flower and leaf returned to scorched earth, and life resumed its steady heartbeat from the deepest forests and still lakes to the bustling cities and highest mountains.

The eastern entryway to the Keep was an immense affair. The two enormous doors were built to admit an elephant had it been necessary, though they had been barred and bolted for years. In one corner of the rightmost door was a smaller portal, meant for easier coming and going of the residents of Guardians Keep. Though no one stood near it, the small bar across the door floated out of its brackets and settled gently against the nearest wall in its accustomed resting place. Pushed inward from the outside, the door creaked open. It moved slowly at first, then faster as the old oil in its hinges finally did its work.

"Hello?" Kiran's voice echoed throughout the Hall. "Is anyone here?" Silence was the only answer. She stepped warily through the door, Layton just behind her.

Scanning the area, Layton observed, "Well, there's not much going on here. We'd better go in farther." His eyes wandered over the battle scenes, landscapes, and other intricate carvings that covered the entrance tunnel. The first time he had seen them, he had been so excited at being Chosen and becoming a Guardian that he had paid them little attention. Eventually he learned that Brunar, leader of the Guardians, had carved them himself. It had taken him centuries to complete the work, and Layton smiled at the memory of Brunar apologizing for the relative crudity of the earliest carvings, back when he was still learning the craft. Once Layton had finally taken the time to look at them, they had taken his breath away. He absently traced his fingers over them as he moved down the tunnel that led to the huge and apparently empty Hall.

The pair reached the main chamber and looked around. They had lived in the small rooms that lined either side of the wide-open Hall when they were newly Chosen, learning the ways of their own magick and that of the Jidaan they wielded. That had been long ago, and now, the doors were all closed, the rooms silent. The different gemstones above each door glimmered faintly as they always had, each designating a particular Guardian's place. Kiran noted them all: the blue sapphire that stood over her own door, representing the Jidaan of Warding; the ruby of Bjarke's Jidaan of Power, and the sparkling diamond that shone over Alyssa's doorway. An intensely green emerald glared from over another doorway, echoing the stone in the Jidaan of Storms, Gart's weapon.

As if following her thoughts, Layton spoke, "There's my room, with the opal," and he pointed to the multicolored stone that was twin to the one in the weapon he now carried on his back.

Kiran scoffed. "Yes, you knucklehead. I know it's been a while, but I still remember where our rooms were…" her voice trailed off as she saw that the farthest door on the north wall was open. Her heart lurched as she registered the inky black stone embedded above the doorframe. It represented the Jidaan of Stealth, which was carried by the man who had been more father than friend to her over the years. Although the door was open, and the room seemed to be lit from within, all was still.

"Nessar?" she called out, a note of worry in her voice. The last time she had heard from her old friend, he had been in Tamaransett, a small city just a day's ride from the Keep. However, the letters he had sent her led her to believe that he might have left that town to return to their old training grounds, and might yet be somewhere within its walls.

Immediately following the war with Mordak, Nessar had felt the need to return Bjarke and Alyssa's Jidaan to the Keep where they would be safe. Kiran and Layton had accompanied him and stayed in the Keep for a month before heading in different directions. Nessar had stayed for several months, exploring the Keep as he recovered physically and mentally from the trials of the war. When he finally felt the desire to be around people again, he shuttered the Keep and made his way down to Tamaranset, keeping his identity as a Guardian secret and his Jidaan carefully concealed among his things.

Shunning the larger cities in which he had once lived, he had finally found a small homestead in the countryside and settled down there, even managing to make friends with his neighbors. He stayed out of trouble, tended a garden, and kept a few farm animals, all the while feeling like he was getting away with something. When the mood struck him, Nessar would hire a local boy to care for his tiny farm and then head back up to Guardians Keep to check on the Jidaan and enjoy the solitude for months at a time.

On one such occasion, Gart had finally turned up at Guardians Keep, his emerald Jidaan strapped to his back and his enormous canine companion, Beauty, at his side. Gart had spent time with Agatha, Nessar had written, a contemporary of Brunar's. She had tutored him in the use of his magick and that of the Jidaan as Brunar had once meant to, and the young man's skills had grown considerably. His quiet and somewhat surly nature found its twin in Nessar's, and the two got along famously in the Keep. Nessar had written that, although Beauty had made him nervous at first, even they had come to enjoy each other's company.

Upon arriving, Gart had entered Brunar's chambers easily, using nothing more than a wave of his hand to dispel the powerful wards the Mage had left behind. Gart had then begun some kind of research, using Brunar's books and papers and spending hours in the Keep's massive library. Nessar never knew what Gart had been studying. The two had been content to share their time in mostly companionable silence, not getting in each other's way, but somehow comforted at the other's presence.

She had not given it much thought at the time, but Kiran was glad that Nessar had written so much about Gart's visits to the Keep. It was not a lot of information, but it was something. And besides, Kiran had always enjoyed receiving his letters; seeing his distinctive scrawl had never failed to lift her spirits. Now, she hoped he was there. And suddenly, she hoped that he was all right.

"Nessar? Ness? Are you here?" she called again. She strode across the wide space, her boots ringing on the stone. She reached out with her senses and found nothing, but even so, she pulled her Jidaan from its sheath at her back. She knew there should be nothing to fear anywhere in the Keep; it had been a home to all of them. But she always felt better with a weapon in her hands. With Layton trotting alongside her, she quickly approached Nessar's door. With a trembling hand, she pushed it open to peer inside the small chamber and froze at the sight.

Nessar was there, in his bed, with eyes closed and his mouth open slightly. He was fully dressed, boots and all, as though he had fallen into bed and immediately fallen asleep. Before Kiran and Layton could say anything, they heard Nessar's buzzing snore, assuring them that he was alive. Kiran was not sure whether to scream in anger or cry with relief. Layton barely managed to stifle a chuckle. As they watched, Nessar snored again, but more softly.

Kiran could take it no longer. She walked over and kicked Nessar's bed frame lightly, stepping back just as quickly afterwards, for Nessar was not one to take kindly to such awakenings. "All right, old man, thanks for scaring us to death. Now, wake up!" To her surprise, Nessar did not respond. Her brow furrowed. Usually, Ness would have slipped out of bed with a dagger in hand, ready for action. He'd always been that way, especially after his powers had been awakened by the Choosing. She glanced at Layton, only to find him just as concerned. She stepped forward again, more gently.

"Ness? Hey, it's Kiran and Layton. Wake up, man. Ness?" Moving slowly and deliberately, she sat on the edge of his cot and placed her hand on his arm. She was shocked at how bony he had become. Reminding herself that he was well-past eighty now, she gently shook him. He slept on. Kiran's eyes roved over the deep creases and lines of the old man's face as if seeing his years for the first time. He had always been there, ever since she was but a child, and he had seemed eternal. Seeing him still, silent, and aslumber like this disturbed her deeply. It was not right. Her eyes fell on the nearby nightstand, and she saw a cloth, stiff with brown stains, and an overturned mug. She knew old blood when she saw it. A glance confirmed that Nessar's shirt was stained with it as well, though he did not seem to be wounded.

"Something's wrong," Layton observed quietly. "I can't do what Alyssa used to, but let me try and help him. I have a thing my old teachers passed on to me; it might work." He sat on the edge of the bed next to Kiran, placing his own hand on the sleeping man's shoulder.

"A thing?" Kiran scoffed, more out of habit than any real disbelief. "What, they gave you a magic wake-up ring or something?"

Without bothering to answer, Layton gently placed his other hand on Nessar's back and took a calming breath. Long ago, he had learned a technique from his Eastern masters, teachers skilled not only in fighting, but also in other areas of spirit, mindfulness, and even healing. It took

Layton only moments to find that place of silence and stillness within himself. Fleeting memories of his early training, when he struggled for hours to reach his spiritual center and stay there for only a few precious heartbeats, crossed his mind. Now, he could go there easily, and often did when contemplating a knotty problem, or in an effort to rejuvenate his body when tired. From deep within himself, Layton assessed the level of his own energy, noting that it was steady and strong. Satisfied, he began to gather some of it, separating it from the flow that his body needed to function. Once he had the amount he desired, he channeled it down his arms and out through his hands, into the sleeping body of the old thief.

As his own energy merged with Nessar's, Layton was shocked and dismayed to feel how exhausted the old man was. His ki had dwindled nearly to the point of death, though he had not yet crossed that line. Layton stayed focused on the energy that connected them, sending his own through Nessar's body, using it strengthen his friend's bodily functions. Layton had learned much since the war with Mordak, and suddenly was glad of it. Moments passed, and Layton was rewarded with a quickening of Nessar's heart, a subtle warming of his leathery skin. As the old thief finally began to stir, Layton shut off the flow of energy and sighed heavily in relief. He would need to rest, but he felt Nessar returning to them, and was satisfied.

Nessar shifted, snorted, and then began to stretch. He groaned as though he had just enjoyed a solid night's sleep, and finally opened his eyes to focus on the two figures that sat at his bedside. It took a moment to realize what he was seeing.

"Layton? Kiran? Oh, Goddess, it's good to see you both! Your hair's so long, Kiran...and what's wrong with your eyes?" Nessar pushed himself up to a seated position on his cot, and Kiran took the opportunity to hastily wipe her tears on her sleeve.

"Nothing, just a cold, you old sot," she retorted, relieved beyond words that Nessar was not in danger. "How long have you been here? Are you all right? We almost thought you were dead when we found you."

Nessar put his hands to his face and then massaged his head and neck. "Whew. Theonas' balls, that was awful. I feel fine now, though, perfectly all right." He raised an eyebrow at Layton, taking in the younger man's features. His hair was still cut short as it had been when he was a youth, and the half-smile still lent him a boyish aspect. Even so, the years had matured him into a rugged looking man, wider through the shoulders and thicker through the chest than the wiry boy that had danced with death at the walls of Laro. "You did this." It was not a question.

Layton sighed with fatigue. His energy would replenish itself soon enough, but for now, he was tired. "Yes, old friend. You needed a bit of energy to get you going again. I just helped out a little."

Kiran interrupted him. "What happened? I've never seen you like that. I thought you were…" she could not voice the thought.

Nessar could, though. "Dead? Well, baby girl, I was close, I think. That vision just about knocked the life out of me.

"You saw it too?" Layton asked quietly. "That's why we're here."

Nessar rubbed his face again, then shooed his fellow Guardians away so he could swing his legs over the side of his bed and sit up. "Yes, yes, I sure did. That's what laid me up, I think. It hit me so hard, I'm pretty sure I passed out. I came to and managed to get to my bed, here, and my nose was bleeding something fierce. I tried to clean up, but I was just so tired that I laid down and that's the last I remember." His stomach growled loudly, sounding like a caged animal in the small chamber. "Sheesh…seems like I need some food. Come on, let's head to the kitchen while we talk. Feels like I haven't eaten in a week, and I'm famished." Nessar stood on somewhat unsteady legs, but quickly found his balance and led the way out of his chamber. Kiran followed after a sidewise glance at Layton.

Well, at least his appetite is what I remember it being, Kiran sent the thought to Layton, causing him to smile. They followed him out the door and across the open Hall to the corridor that led to the kitchen and dining chambers.

I'd be hungry, too, Layton answered dryly as he hurried to catch up with Nessar. *His body must have slowed down to conserve energy. Anyone else would have starved or died of dehydration days ago.*

"I know you're talking about me back there, so just cut it out. Come up here and join me in some beef and potatoes and we'll talk this thing out," Nessar's voice drifted back to them, echoing from the stone walls. Always one to cut to the chase, Nessar wanted to get to the bottom of the visions just as they did. At the mention of dinner, they both quickened their pace, silently agreeing that they had always done their best thinking on full stomachs.

Chapter 8

The moon had just risen, and she cast her silvery light over the forest. Ordinarily, Reyanna would have made camp hours before, but both she and Ginn had felt the same vague sense of urgency that kept them traveling past sundown. They had long since abandoned the path, and they slowed to carefully wind their way among the trees. Reyanna tried to let the coolness of the wind and the sound of the rustling leaves soothe her, but the feelings of restlessness and unnamed anxiety continued to plague her.

"Something does not feel right," Ginn's low voice confirmed that he, too, was affected.

"Yes, I agree with you. I don't know what it is, but something is amiss here. Is there anything about this part of the forest I should know?" Reyanna had grown up in the deep forests surrounding Allinshae, but had never experienced such a dark feeling of foreboding.

Ginn carefully scanned the trees ahead and on either side as they moved. "Honestly, there should be nothing to set this part of the forest off from the rest. Certainly, there are sections of the wood that have a fell aura about them from evil done long past, but those I know of are far from here. There should be nothing to warrant this disquiet."

A chill ran down Reyanna's spine as the feeling of dread gradually intensified. "I don't like it. Not at all. Maybe we should camp for the night and find a defensible spot."

Ginn was about to agree with her when something caught his attention. He reined his horse to a stop and Reyanna did likewise beside him. "What is it?" she asked, keeping her voice at a whisper.

He peered through the trees and quietly replied, "I thought I smelled a fire, though it was faint. It's stronger now, and I see light over there." He pointed and Reyanna followed his gaze until she, too, could see the faintest hint of a flickering light among the trees up ahead. She breathed in deeply, trying to catch the scent as Ginn had, and she found it, just at the edge of her senses.

"Should we check it out? Or pass it by?" Reyanna's immediate inclination was to angle towards the light and see if it was another set of travelers. There was strength to be had in numbers, and if something dangerous was roaming the woods, joining others might be smart.

Ginn replied quickly. "Let us be on our guard, for the sense of ill remains. We know nothing of whomever is up there. For all we know, they are the cause of our unease." He loosened his sword in its scabbard, then unslung his bow. He pulled a handful of arrows from his quiver and held them and the bow in his left hand, where he could bring them into play in an eyeblink.

Reyanna held her bow likewise, just as she had been taught. As quietly as she could, she urged Betina forward, making her way towards the flickering light with Ginn at her side.

As they approached, she began to smell the smoke of a campfire more clearly. It was not long before another smell reached her, and the hairs on the back of her neck stood up as fear touched her.

Whispering, Ginn confirmed what she already knew. "I smell blood. Stay quiet, and be ready."

Reyanna carefully nocked an arrow to her bow, holding it in place with her left index finger, then focused on guiding Betina forward as quietly as possible. When they had come to the edge of the clearing, Ginn gestured for her to halt. Without a word, he slipped out of the saddle and crept forward to get a better look. As an afterthought, he turned to tell Reyanna something, only to find her noiselessly creeping along right next to him, her bow at the ready. Ginn smiled. She was young, and a human at that, but her stealth skills were on par with his own, and she was not about to be left out of anything. He turned and continued to make his way towards the light. A faint buzzing sound reached them, along with the quiet crackling of the fire, but otherwise, the woods were silent.

When they both reached a sheltered spot where they could see, they wished they had not. Reyanna's lips pressed to a thin line in horror at the sight, but she did not turn away. Ginn's face was stoic, but standing this close to him, she could feel his alarm. When they were certain that no further threat was imminent, they pushed their way through the branches to examine the scene.

68

The campfire had been carefully laid within a small ring of stones, and not long past. There was plenty of wood left to burn, and a small stack of firewood close at hand. Two horses lay dead, still tethered to a nearby tree branch, their bodies viciously ripped open. Flies buzzed around the carcasses, eagerly taking sustenance from the gaping wounds. Splatters of blood covered the clearing, causing Reyanna and Ginn to be watchful of where they stepped.

"There. A body. Or part of one." Ginn pointed, and Reyanna saw what looked like a human arm lying on the ground near a great splash of crimson. The bloody hand still clutched the handle of a huge forester's axe.

"Where's the rest?" she said, making a face as she spoke. "Oh, wait. There." She pointed with the arrow that was currently nocked to string in her bow. Even as she said it, she realized that she was seeing a different body, headless and savaged almost beyond recognition. The clothing was different, and it seemed too big to match the first arm. Ginn saw it too.

"It looks like two different people. This didn't happen long ago; the blood has yet to dry. We should take care." Ginn scanned the forest for any signs of a predator. Even as he did, he knew that none of the creatures of the forest would do this, not even the big cats. They killed for food. Whatever had done this had been certain to kill everything in sight, and then left the bodies where they fell.

Although there was a quaver in Reyanna's voice when she spoke, there was steel there, too. "Whatever did this...we need to find it. If it's a bear that's gone rabid, or a big cat, we need to put it down. It will kill again."

Ginn nodded. "Indeed. We need to track this beast and..." his words suddenly ceased and he froze.

His sudden silence unnerved Reyanna, but she did not speak. Instead, she followed his gaze. His eyes were locked on a spot on the opposite side of the clearing. A thrill of fear coursed through her as she realized that a pair of glaring yellow eyes was staring back at them. She heard a low, rumbling growl as the thing announced itself before pushing through the leafy branches that had hidden it from view.

It was a nightmare. Dagger-like teeth gleamed from a sharp, canine snout, still stained with blood from its last kill. At first she thought it an impossibly large wolf, but then Reyanna saw that it walked on two legs. Even hunched as it was, it towered over them, its hugely muscular torso and unnaturally long arms displaying the enormous strength of its body. It had hands rather than paws, tipped with razor-sharp talons that glistened scarlet in the firelight. It growled again, louder, and then howled its hunger to the silver moon above, the sound of it chilling the two Rangers to their bones. Then, it sprang at them, all fangs and claws, ravenous and deadly.

Reyanna's arrow struck it in mid-leap, right in the center of its forehead, but its skull was far too thick and the arrow glanced off, leaving naught but a trifling cut. She dove out of the way as it landed, rolling and coming up into a run, already nocking another arrow to string. Ginn had already leapt to safety in the other direction, having loosed his own arrow only to see it lodge in the thick muscles of the creature's chest. With a howl of anger and pain, the beast snapped the arrow and flung the broken shaft away before turning back to Ginn.

The Weya Ranger stayed calm, and instantly released another arrow. It sped for the vulnerable eye socket, a sure path to the brain beyond. The creature flung up a beefy, black-furred arm, intercepting the arrow. It went right through the meat of its forearm and lodged there, largely ignored by the beast. With frightening speed, the man-wolf lashed out with one overlong arm and swatted Ginn. There was an audible crack as his bow arm snapped under the creature's impossible strength, and Ginn's body was flung in a heap across the clearing like a rag-doll. He lay there, still and silent.

The enormous man-wolf stalked over to Ginn's unconscious body, its jaws dripping in anticipation of a fresh kill. It loomed over him, black lips skinned back over its deadly sharp teeth.

Thup, thup, thup! Three arrows penetrated the thick muscles of its back, and the monstrous creature unleashed a ferocious howl of pain. Its yellow eyes turned and lighted on Reyanna, who had another arrow already nocked. The

70

beast snarled and began to stalk her, watching her closely as it moved. It knew the danger of a well-placed arrow, but it was confident it could protect itself as before. It took a step closer to Reyanna. And then another. A low, rumbling growl rolled from its throat as it crept towards her, its huge talons clicking. It paused for a beat, then lunged towards her.

Reyanna loosed her arrow, and it struck the beast in one shoulder. It howled in pain, but quickly yanked the offending arrow out. With a snarl, it broke the arrow in one hand before discarding it. It took another cautious step forward, watching her every move.

Too close for another arrow, Reyanna juked right, then flung herself to her left in an attempt to escape, but the creature was far too quick. It snatched her in mid-stride and slammed her down on her back, knocking the wind out of her.

The pain was intense. Reyanna felt her consciousness slipping away, but she grimly clung to it. The beast leaned in towards her, growling in triumph as it opened its jaws wide for the kill. Reflexively, Reyanna reached up and jammed her bow deeply into its mouth, locking its jaws open.

The creature grunted in surprise and tried in vain to close his jaws on the struggling girl, but it could not get through the sturdy, Weya-made bow. Finally, it yanked the bow out of her hands and spat it aside, out of her reach. Triumphant, it leaned over her again, gloating, its deadly smile widening as it prepared to crush her skull.

Looking up into what would surely be certain death, Reyanna felt her magick awaken within her. It was a growing heat that squirmed and writhed like something alive. It felt ready, even eager, to be used. She gathered it up within herself, a swell of heat and pressure, and encouraged it to grow until she felt she would burst. With a furious yell, she released her power and thrust it at the body of the man-wolf.

The beast flew away from her as though it had been yanked by a team of horses, its furry arms and legs pinwheeling in the air as it flew across the clearing to slam into the nearest trees, cracking their trunks with its bulk. It

71

bellowed in rage and pain, and scrambled back to its feet, already on the attack once more.

Still on her back, Reyanna reached one hand towards the campfire, beckoning it, calling to it. The meager fire answered. She felt its heat growing, quickly consuming the wood that fueled it. From embers it suddenly became a roaring blaze. The creature turned to assess this sudden brightness, and without knowing fully how, Reyanna sent the intense flames towards the beast, the fire lunging straight at it as though it had a life of its own.

The flames swarmed over the beast's face and neck, and it unleashed an agonized howl as it writhed and beat at the fire with its deformed hands. Frantically, it whirled and struggled, but there was no escape from the flames.

Reyanna struggled to her knees as she wheezed and tried to catch her breath. She knew she had to act quickly. Gathering her strength, she dove across the clearing, rolling on her shoulder and coming up with the huge forester's axe. Praying to the Goddess Rowann that her aim would be true, she leaped as high as she could towards the thrashing creature and brought the axe down on the back of its neck with all her might. She was rewarded with a sickening *thunk* that cut off the beast's tortured screams. The man-wolf fell face-first to the earth, its huge, clawed hands clenching and unclenching in the dirt. The flames dwindled, and Reyanna wrenched the axe free from the hideous wound only to see the beast weakly try to rise again. Bellowing a cry of anger and desperation, Reyanna raised the axe and brought it down again. And again. And one more time, finally severing the creature's enormous head from its body. It rolled erratically before coming to a stop, its yellow eyes still glaring, its great tongue lolling free of its fanged mouth. Its body spasmed once, then relaxed completely as death came for its shattered soul.

As Reyanna's heart thundered in her ears, the rest of the world settled into a heavy silence. She tried to step backwards, away from the bloody beast she had slain, but she stumbled and fell flat on her backside. Reyanna sat there, dazed, for what seemed like an eternity before she caught her breath and wrapped her mind around what had just happened. It had only taken a few moments, scarcely longer than a minute, but she had fought for her life and won. Barely.

Shaking her head to clear it, she crawled over to where Ginn had fallen. She winced as she saw his forearm, obviously broken by the beast. She knew she would have to set it before she did anything else, and having an immediate task brought a semblance of calm back to her.

"Ginn," she said quietly as she gently probed the break with her fingers. "Ginn, your left arm is broken. I'm going to have to set it." He did not respond, but Reyanna was relieved to find that his pulse was strong and his breathing was deep and even. *If I'm lucky, he'll stay out long enough for me to get this done,* she thought.

She positioned herself next to him and carefully placed her right leg around his fractured arm to hold it firmly in place. Using both hands, she grasped his arm at the wrist and took a deep breath.

In that moment, as she focused on Ginn's arm, she felt a swell of the same warmth and pressure inside her that she had when she flung the beast away. It was much smaller, but more focused, a tight swirling in her abdomen. Instinctively, she allowed it to flood her body, and Ginn's arm suddenly became very clear in her mind, almost as though she could see right through his skin. Instantly, she knew how to manipulate the bones exactly, and she pulled Ginn's wrist until the edges of the breaks were lined up perfectly again. She continued holding Ginn's arm, peering into it, feeling the energy swirling inside her. A thought occurred to her, a wish, a simple desire that Ginn's arm would heal well and strong. The power inside her leaped and rolled, then eagerly pulsed along her arms and out of her hands, directly into Ginn's arm. She gasped at the intensity of the flow, but held on. The energy flowed for only a few heartbeats. Then fatigue washed over her like a wave of ocean surf, and she knew no more.

Chapter 9

The stone wall of the chamber flared an ugly scarlet. Arcane designs chiseled in the stone glowed brightly for a moment, then suddenly writhed towards each other until they connected to form a rectangular shape. The stone within the squarish borders instantly disappeared to reveal a darkened, shadowy corridor. From within its depths, a cloaked and hooded figure stumbled, coughing and using its hands to feel its way along. The instant the figure had exited the passage and stepped into the room, the doorway vanished. The ancient, glowing symbols crawled back to their original positions and then faded, leaving only the rough granite wall behind.

"The girl? And her Weya companion?" A man reclined in a chair in one corner of the shadowy chamber, the dim candlelight reflecting from his smooth pate. His nose was hooked like a falcon's beak, and his eyes glittered with malice within a nest of old wrinkles.

The cloaked figure, still hunched in seeming exhaustion, did not reply immediately but coughed a few moments longer. When it had finally stilled, the figure stood straighter and slowly lowered its hood with delicate hands. The man revealed beneath seemed barely more than a boy, but the others in the room knew differently. Tousled brown hair, a boyish face, and a pair of gold-rimmed, circular spectacles hid a soul as black as pitch, far older than his youthful appearance suggested. Arkhan hated to give his report, but knew he must.

"They live, damn them. I sent a greater Joining to attack them, and they somehow survived."

"The beast failed? I told you to send two, you idiot!" Barovius ran both hands over his hairless scalp as he fumed. He had feared that Arkhan would make a mess of things, no matter how skilled he was at shapeshifting magick.

"Two?" Arkhan's voice was cold. "Do you even know what it takes to create a single Joining of that size? No, you don't, because it would be completely beyond you. Casting that spell and getting back here nearly killed me as it was, you sniveling little toad, and you could have done no better. It's not like your bright idea worked either." Arkhan adjusted his tiny gold spectacles to hide his frustration. His face remained expressionless, though he took consolation in the fact that where he had failed, so, too, had his unlikely companion.

"Why, you swine...the only reason my air daemons didn't get that sow of a Guardian was because of her damned Jidaan! You just had a single Weya and a girl to deal with, and neither of them are Guardians! Incompetent!" Barovius felt his lips curl into a sly smile. He enjoyed the bickering, the chance to lord it over the young-seeming Arkhan. Barovius knew he was the stronger of the two.

"Be silent." The woman's voice was ice and steel in the darkened chamber, and at her command, both of the men snapped their mouths shut and turned wary eyes towards her. Though - in theory - they were all equals in this endeavor, something about her made the two men uneasy. They had heard things about Melidia; dark and terrible things. They were careful around her, and they were not men who scared easily.

Her hair was the color of blood, bound in a single, thick braid that fell down her back nearly to her knees. Eyes of chipped emerald turned on the two men, who struggled not to allow their nervousness to show. Melidia's face was ageless and beautiful, and both men knew that many young women had died so that it could stay that way. While the two men were driven by simple lust for power and wealth, they could both tell that Melidia was driven by something darker. What it was, they could not say. She secretly terrified them, but without her, they could not hope to achieve their goal. She had sought them out, and they followed her lead. For now.

"You have a suggestion, Melidia?" Arkhan was used to being polite, and his tone hid his misgivings well. Barovius, however, scoffed and folded his arms as he leaned back in his chair, always the curmudgeon.

Melidia walked over to the window and opened the shutters, letting the cool night air raise gooseflesh on her exposed skin. She let her gaze travel over the forest below, and the mirrored surface of the still lake that adjoined her estate. She could see the reflection of the moon in it, making the lake look beautiful and sweet, rather than revealing it for the brackish muck that it actually was. The trees that bordered its waters were stunted and angry-looking. It had once been a lush paradise, but over the years, Melidia's spell-casting had leached something vital from the land surrounding her castle, leaving the area twisted and malformed. Somewhere in the distance, she heard an inhuman yowling that was suddenly cut off as a larger creature caught and killed its prey. A cold smile appeared on her lovely face, though it did not reach her eyes.

Without turning, she replied, her voice both cold and sensual. "We need to focus our efforts on the Mage. The Guardians that remain will not be able to stop us from taking him when the time comes, especially since they don't know where he is."

Barovius leaned forward in his chair with his elbows on his knees. "Are you sure about that? They've already started to gather at their blasted Keep! Someone or something is helping them, and if they find him before we do, we'll never be able to get our hands on him! As it is, he's powerful, maybe more powerful than Brunar was. How are we supposed to deal with that?"

Melidia cast a look over her shoulder at the wizened man in the corner and felt Barovius' pulse quicken at the sight of her beauty. "He's powerful, yes. But he's unschooled. He cannot hope to cram a thousand years of knowledge into two decades. For all his strength, he's no Brunar. Together, we can subdue him and then I will have what I need. I have a plan." Her green eyes glittered in the light of the fire, and her smile was both lovely and frightening.

Yes, you idiots, she mused to herself. *And you two are but small parts of it. Do as I bid you, and you might just survive afterwards.*

Melidia's plan had been much longer in the making than even Arkhan and Barovius knew. Her scrying had made her privy to many events long before they occurred, and of all she had seen, Gart's path had been the most clear to her. *If Gart continues on his way, then everything will come together nicely,* Melidia thought. *Everything he strives to accomplish will only serve me in the end, no matter what he thinks!*

Chapter 10

"So you saw the same thing we did?" Kiran sat across from Nessar as he feasted on a huge platter of meat and vegetables, with a hunk of bread close at hand.

The old thief nodded vigorously as he chewed and then he half-drained the mug of water he had poured himself. He belched in satisfaction, then replied. "From what you're saying, yes, I sure did. I was standing far away, but I recognized you two and Gart right off. The others, I didn't know, though the girl who was closest to him seemed familiar somehow. There was a Weya there, too, but she was hazy, almost transparent."

Layton held up a piece of meat on his fork, examining it idly as he spoke. "Do you think it's a vision of the future? It's certainly not a memory, not for any of us." He finally judged the meat up to his standards and put it in his mouth.

Nessar shook his head. "No, it's not a memory, but I don't know if it's truly in the future, either. All I know is that, for a short time, I was *there*. I still don't know what to make of it, but I do know that the experience was strong enough to put me on my arse for nigh unto a week." He leaned back in his chair and rested one hand on his distended belly. He burped again and politely covered his mouth with a fist while doing so. Kiran rolled her eyes at him anyway.

"Where is Gart now?" Kiran asked. "It's obvious he's at the center of all this, even though we don't know what 'this' is. Is he here somewhere?"

Nessar shook his head. "No, he left a couple of weeks back, almost right when I got here. Took that humongous dog with him." A sad look crossed his face at that. "I kind of got used to the beast, to tell you the truth. She may be as big as a pony, and scary to look at because of all those scars, but she is as sweet as can be. We get along just fine." He tore off another piece of bread and toyed with it before putting it in his mouth. "Anyway, Gart spent a lot of time in Brunar's room and in the archives over the years. Sometimes he would be here when I came up from my little farm, and sometimes not. He never really said what he was doing, exactly, just that he was looking into some things." Nessar paused for a few moments as he considered his next words. "He seemed pretty excited when he left, though. Gathered up his things in a hurry and hustled out of here one afternoon, saying he'd be back in a month or two, that he was going to check on something that he'd found."

"No idea what that might have been?" Layton leaned forward, eager to hear more.

Nessar shook his head. "No, none at all. When we would talk, it was always about trivial things. Whenever I did ask him about his work, he would always slide around the question. Said he was just trying to get things organized. I can tell when someone is hiding something, but I have to say, he was smooth about it. Truth be told, it never even occurred to me to dig any further. He seemed perfectly at ease, not shifty or secretive. I never once thought that he was doing anything that might cause trouble, or else I'd have called him on it, right then and there."

"Hmph," Kiran was none too pleased. "I say we go looking through Brunar's chamber to see if we can piece something together. Unless he tidied up everything before he left, he's bound to have left some clues in there." She stood and left the table with her plate to wash it, and the others quickly followed her.

Minutes later, they stood in Brunar's study, a large room off the corner of the Hall of Jidaana. Where Brunar had left the entrance hidden with a spell, Gart had chosen to leave the chamber open and unguarded simply because he lacked the spellcraft to do otherwise. He had dismantled Brunar's ward easily enough, but then destroying something was always easier than creating it. The three moved carefully inside.

A bed resided in one corner of the spacious chamber, and shelves cut into the stone of one wall held various mundane items. An enormous desk sat in the corner opposite the bed, and their attention was immediately drawn to it. A globe of white glass hung in the air over the desk, its magickal light illuminating the workspace. When

Brunar had lived here, the desk had been kept neat and orderly. Gart, however, had a different sense of organization, and now there were untidy stacks of books, parchments, and scrolls in an arrangement that must have made sense only to him.

"It looks like he's been working hard," Kiran quipped. "But on what?" She stepped up to the desk with the others and began to carefully sift through the books and papers. One book still lay open on the desk, and Layton slid it closer to himself so that he could read it. Nessar took note of a stack of blank parchment. He gathered the pages up and turned to walk out of the room.

"Hey, where are you going with those?" Kiran called after him.

"To try something. I'll be right back."

Kiran rolled her eyes, but went back to her work. The books were ancient, and ranged from tomes of ancient history to some on simple spell work. She started to read some of the books on basic spell casting, but the dialect was archaic and hard to follow. "Well, that's no help at all," she muttered, moving to the next book.

"Uh, Kiran?" Layton's voice held a note of alarm.

"What is it?" Kiran turned to see what he had found.

"This book talks about summoning spirits," Layton said, his finger holding a place on one page. "That can't be good...right?"

Kiran moved beside him so that she could see the page he indicated. Sure enough, the ancient book held detailed ritual instructions that appeared to offer a way to recall the souls of those who had died. The wording was difficult to follow, but not impossible. Frowning, she read as much of it as she could before raising her eyebrows and turning to face Layton.

"Are you getting the same thing from this that I am?" She hoped Layton would prove her suspicions wrong.

"If you're thinking that this is a way to bring a spirit back from the dead, then I'd say you're right," Layton confirmed. Kiran felt a knot of dread appear in the pit of her stomach.

"Well that's just peachy. I'm not a Mage, and I only know how to use my own magick in a handful of ways, but

80

even I can tell that's just a bad idea. Something could go wrong. Right? Dealing with dead spirits and such, surely something awful could happen. Does it say anything about that?"

"Let me look, hold on." Layton scanned the book, turned the page and continued. He let out a low whistle, but said nothing further as he kept reading. Kiran's patience started to fray, but she held her tongue. Layton turned another page and read it, followed by another. Finally, he turned what looked like the last page in the chapter, and then all the color drained from his face.

"What?" Kiran asked. "What is it?"

Layton took a deep breath and let it out before he spoke. "OK, yeah. It's bad. The warning's in the back, here." He stepped forward, moved the book to the center of the desk, and moved aside so that Kiran could see better. He pointed to the final paragraph, written in red ink.

"The ritual is supposed to summon a single spirit, presumably so that someone can speak to it, for a couple of minutes at best. It has to be done during an eclipse of the sun, which according to this," Layton picked up a piece of parchment and then laid it back down, "is only a few weeks away. There are a couple of problems that jump out at me. First, it looks like the spell creates a portal, a window similar to my gates, but it opens onto the netherworld and you can talk to the spirit through it, I think. That window has to be strongly warded, because the pull of our world is powerful enough to yank the spirit through to our side otherwise. If that happens, the spirit will become trapped here and lose its sanity, essentially becoming a daemon." As he read, Layton suddenly looked like the weathered warrior he had become, his worried frown stealing the boyishness from his face.

"OK, right, that's pretty bad. What's the other problem?" Kiran felt like she could handle a single daemon. *Hel, I have some air daemons locked away in the Keep's vault right now,* she thought.

Layton raised his eyes to her, and Kiran's breath caught. She had never seen him so serious, not even during the war.

"If he leaves the portal open long enough, or his concentration wavers the slightest bit, other spirits are going to start pouring out of it, pulled from their afterlives and attracted to the light and energy of our world. If they pass through the ward that the summoning spell provides, they, too, will go irrevocably insane the moment they arrive here. With that insanity will come the power to manifest in this world. They can kill anyone they come across. They can even possess living bodies and commit unspeakable acts that their former selves would abhor. They'll be monsters."

Kiran stared at him silently for a moment. "Sooo, you're saying that hundreds of vicious daemons would just appear here in our world and start killing people?"

"No, I'm saying thousands of them will," Layton corrected. "Thousands upon thousands, and thousands again. How many souls have passed on to...wherever? Just the souls of people who die naturally every year would be overwhelming, but ALL of the souls? From every death, from forever?" he slowly shook his head. "I can't count that high, Kiran."

Kiran blinked at him, at a loss for what to say. When she found her voice, she asked, "Surely, he knows the risks? Who could he possibly want to see that badly?"

"That would be his wife, Gennie," Nessar answered as he walked back into the room. In his hands, he held a single page of parchment, its surface smudged and dirty. "He spoke of her a few times over the years. Those were the only times I ever saw anything like emotion come out of him, but according to this, she's the one." He strode over to the desk and tossed the page on top of the book where Kiran and Layton could see it.

"What's that?" Layton said as he leaned over to examine the page. "And why is it so dirty?"

"I rubbed charcoal on it so I could see the indentations of whatever he wrote on the page above it. Fortunately, Gart presses down too hard with his quills, or we'd not be able to see anything." Nessar summed up his discovery. "This is basically a letter to Gennie, but it's written as though he's using it as notes, rather than an actual letter. It's like he's preparing a speech." He paused for a moment, feeling a twinge of guilt for intruding upon the man's privacy, somehow. "He's asking for forgiveness for not being able to protect her."

"Protect her from what?" Kiran asked as she looked over the notes Nessar had uncovered.

"Jor Dayne," Nessar replied, making a face as though the name tasted bad in his mouth.

"Oh, him," both Layton and Kiran responded simultaneously, and with the same tone of distaste. The being that had called himself Jor Dayne had been a hugely muscled warrior, nearly as big as Bjarke. He had been the leader of Mordak's forces, a powerful battle lord that had ridden at the head of the evil sorcerer's army, created by Mordak to be his second-in-command. His demonic origins had been evident in the slitted pupils of his yellow eyes and his sharp fangs.

After waging Mordak's war across the lower half of the continent, he had finally died at Alverton Falls, slain by Alyssa. She had seen that Jor Dayne was a blend of daemon and man, and knew what she had to do. She had attacked him, heedless of her own safety, and brought him down. She had both healed and killed him, banishing the daemon even though that freedom ended the life of the man underneath. Moments later, she had died at the hands of Mordak, himself. Maddened by grief at her death, Bjarke had attacked Mordak single-handedly. The big Guardian had almost killed him, but the sorcerer had managed to turn the tables and it had been Bjarke that had fallen. The memories were thick among the three Guardians as all this flashed through their minds at the mention of Jor Dayne. Kiran was first to break the silence.

"So Jor Dayne killed her? That must have been long before we ever met him. I thought he was married to Ishabel, that Iron Hills woman."

"No, no, they met much later," Nessar explained. "They were dear to each other, yes, and they had some grand adventures after Alverton Falls, according to Gart. He never struck me as one who exaggerates, either." Nessar scratched his stubbly chin as he spoke. "But they drifted apart. She was a clan chieftain, after all. She had duties, and Gart felt drawn here. No, Gennie was his first wife, the mother of his daughter. That big bastard, Jor Dayne, killed them both long before we ever met Gart. That's why he finally came and accepted his Jidaan, though it was months after we left here to head for Laro before he showed up here to claim it." Nessar shook his head as he remembered. "He told me about her once. He said that he's never forgiven himself for not being able to save her and his daughter. Based on that," the old thief jabbed a gnarled finger at the smudged page of notes, "he wants to call her spirit back so that he can ask for her forgiveness."

Kiran blurted, "But that's crazy! Has he lost his mind?" She pulled the book into her lap where she could read it better, and started back at the beginning of the section that contained the summoning spell, looking for answers.

"Oh, no, far from it. He's very rational, very logical, that one. But his emotions run deep. If what we're thinking is correct, then he's convinced himself that talking to her is worth the risk. You know, I could never get a sense of him, connect with his mind the way we all can, you know, feel each other. He was closed off as a King's treasury. Somehow, it doesn't surprise me to discover that he thinks he can pull this off. He's intensely focused, and strong. Honestly, I think he's almost as powerful as Brunar was, he's just not nearly as experienced."

Layton looked up from the page of notes Nessar had laid down. "Why doesn't he do the ritual here? It's quiet and secluded. If he is planning to summon her, then where has he gone?"

Kiran raised a hand to quiet them, then pointed to a passage that had been lightly underlined. "It says here that he's going to need..." she struggled to pronounce the words, "The Heart of Corria, and," she squinted, "the Blood of Nimshi. And just what in the blue Hel are those?" She looked at Nessar, hoping that he would have an answer.

He shrugged his narrow shoulders and raised his hands in resignation. "I haven't a clue. I'm a thief, not a Mage. If you tell me what and where they are, I could probably steal them for you, but I've never heard of them before."

Layton laughed. "Yes, I bet you could, Grampy." Nessar smiled. Layton had not called him that in over

84

twenty years. The younger man continued, "Fortunately, we can travel faster than Gart. We just have to figure out where to go. Any ideas?"

Nessar leaned over and pointed at the smudged parchment on the desk. The bottom of it was the faintest, but a few words were still visible there. "It looks like he's made a connection between the Heart of Corria and the Corris River in the south. Was there ever a city by that name?"

Layton was already looking through the pile of maps that Gart had scattered across one corner of the desk. Kiran closed the huge book of spells and moved it aside so they could work, and Nessar picked up Gart's sheet of notes. Layton skipped over the newest looking maps and began checking the older, more brittle ones. He opened up one large map and cried, "Aha! This might be it!" He spread the map out for them all to see. "Right there. Look, Gart made some notes on this one. How old is this thing?" He looked down at the map's faded legend in the corner and whistled. "Gods, this map was old when Brunar was a boy. It still shows old Caldea." Layton peered closer at the map and saw that Gart had drawn a light charcoal circle around one area. "Well, the area he's circled covers a lot of ground north and east of there. My guess is that's where Corria would be, judging from the river and all. It's possible that someone in New Caldea would know something, but that's a long shot at best."

Nessar nodded. "Well, that's something, at least. We can start there. What about that Blood of Nimshi? Anything on that map about that?"

Layton scanned the map carefully. "No, nothing that I can see. That one has me stumped."

Kiran spoke up, "What about the Weya? Wouldn't they be able to help us? They have their LorMages, and certainly must have some historians who would at least know where Corria was, or what in the Hel the Blood of Nimshi could be."

Nessar nodded his agreement. "Exactly, yes. How to contact one, though? I'm at a loss there. They keep to themselves, and I haven't seen or spoken to one since the war with Mordak. I haven't the slightest idea where the nearest Weya village might be."

Still poring over the map, Layton answered, "I know a few. I've been training with them off and on over the years, and I've been to Valendell, which is close to my school, but that's far from where we're going. They told me of another Weya settlement deep within the Shadowed Forest, not that far from the Rowook Home where Alyssa came from." His face fell at the mention of the brave Guardian, but he turned quickly back to the task at hand. He tapped one finger on the map at the rough location of where he knew the Weya settlement to reside. "It's on the way to New Caldea. We can be there in five days. Less if we hurry."

Kiran nodded. "Thousands upon thousands of spirits, no, *daemons,* pouring into our world to cause trouble if Gart messes up? I'd say let's hurry."

Chapter 11

Reyanna's eyes opened to see fluffy white clouds drifting lazily across the sky above her. The chirping of birds was sweet music, familiar and soothing. She nearly closed her eyes and went back to sleep, but then the memory of a fanged creature looming over her startled her fully awake. She gasped and sat up. She remembered the attack, the enormous wolf-thing, and Ginn's body lying on the ground, lifeless and unmoving.

"Ginn? Ginn! The wolf!"

Suddenly, he was there, kneeling beside her with a calming hand on her shoulder. "It's all right, Reyanna, I'm here. You killed it. Most decisively, I might add." There was a hint of laughter in his voice, and admiration as well.

"What do you mean? Wait...oh, yes. The axe." She rubbed the sleep from her eyes and looked at Ginn, searching for signs of injury. "Are you all right? Your arm? Why is it not in a sling?"

Ginn held out his left arm and flexed it a few times, then wiggled his fingers. "I'm somewhat bewildered about that. I distinctly remember it breaking when the creature hit me. I've broken bones before, and I know the feeling. I hit my head when I landed over there, though, and must have fallen unconscious. When I awoke an hour or so ago, my arm was fine. It aches where I remember the break occurring, but it appears to be relatively unharmed. What did you do?"

Reyanna frowned. "I don't know. I thought for sure it was broken. I tried to reset it, and was glad you had knocked yourself on the head so you didn't have to feel that pain. Did I just imagine that?" she asked, but continued without waiting for an answer. "But after that, I don't know, I..." her voice trailed off as she tried to remember. "I must have passed out from the shock of," she made a face and made a shooing gesture at the clearing where they had fought for their lives, "all of that. What was that thing?"

Ginn flexed his left arm a few times and then decided to leave well enough alone. He shrugged and walked across the small space to where something lay on the ground.

"Well, although the creature was obviously wolf-like, it resembled a Morcat," he began, mentioning the massive, humanoid cat creatures that had sided with Mordak in years past. "But they are an intelligent race, with their own culture and history. They are considered evil by our standards, but even they can be spoken to and reasoned with. This was something else, entirely; some joining of man and wolf by sorcery. I've never seen the like. Come and see." He drew his sword and prodded the object on the ground at his feet.

Reyanna stood and walked over to find a horrible sight. Where before, there had lain the headless body of a single, enormous wolf-thing, now there were *three* headless figures on the ground. A naked man, his back covered in bloody sigils and symbols, was flanked on either side by the bodies of two dead wolves, all severed at the neck. A few feet away, two silent, snarling wolf heads lay nearly on top of a bloody human head, its face contorted in permanent agony. The three disembodied heads lay close together, as though collected and placed there on purpose. She vaguely remembered the wolf-thing's head rolling in that direction after she had lopped it off, and her stomach lurched at the thought.

Unperturbed, Ginn continued. "After you killed it, it must have reverted, changing back into the individual beings that had been used to create the single, huge beast that attacked us." He shook his head. "It takes powerful and evil magick to do something like that. I didn't even know it was possible. I've heard tales, but..." his voice trailed off.

Reyanna stared at the remains for a few moments longer, then sniffed and turned away, angry. "Well, apparently it is. We should probably try to track it, see where it came from. If this creature was made on purpose, I'd just as soon be sure there's not another one out there."

Ginn nodded his agreement and began to walk the clearing, looking for signs he could follow. Reyanna did the same.

It took them only a few minutes to find the wolf-thing's trail at the edge of the clearing from which it had sprung upon the travelers. They followed it through the forest, carefully easing their way through the trees, arrows

88

nocked and ready to loose at the first signs of danger. They were only met with the songs of birds and the rustle of leaves in the wind.

The trees cleared and the pair stepped into a roughly circular open space nearly twenty yards across. Huge, dark stones, each twice as large as a man, circled the edge of the clearing, forming a border around a flatter central stone of the same black substance. A nasty, oily sensation began to crawl around in Reyanna's belly the moment she saw the stones, and her head began to ache. They felt wrong.

"I do not like this," she said as she placed one hand on her roiling stomach in an attempt to calm it.

"There is a fell energy here. It is strong, and malicious." Ginn confirmed. He scanned the area carefully, but saw nothing to indicate that anyone was nearby. "We need to examine the center stone."

"It looks like an altar of some kind," Reyanna ventured, taking a deep breath to steel herself against the ill sensations that assailed her. Gradually, the queasiness subsided, though the sense of wrongness did not. She readied her bow once more, then stalked toward the squat block with Ginn at her side.

The smells that reached them were noxious and stifling, and they easily found the source. The remains of a small fire were visible on one end of the block, which stood about waist-high on Reyanna. Ginn moved towards it and prodded the ashes with a dagger.

"Yes, as I thought. A spell was cast here, a powerful one. Herbs and other things were burned as part of the ritual." Ginn saw what some of the other things were and a shudder crawled up his spine. "Whoever did this had nothing but ill intent."

Reyanna heard him, but did not answer. She had put her bow away and was examining the rest of the huge altar stone. It was inscribed around the edges with markings that seemed to wriggle and writhe when she looked at them, leaving her feeling dirty inside. She moved her gaze to the flat surface of the stone and found evidence that confirmed Ginn's earlier assessment. "There seems to be wolf hair on this stone, Ginn. And blood." She recalled the symbols carved into the skin of the dead man's back. "Yes, this is the place where it happened. Why would anyone do such a thing?" She frowned as she thought it over. "I mean, what purpose would creating a beast like that serve? And way out here, so far from any city? It just doesn't make sense." Just then a thought occurred to her. "Wait, maybe it was sent to kill those two travelers! But again, why? We'll probably never find out." She clenched a fist in frustration.

Ginn walked over to her, carrying something gingerly in one hand. "It was sent to kill someone, yes, but I think the travelers were just in the wrong place at the wrong time. Look at this," he said as he handed her the charred piece of wood.

Reyanna wrinkled her nose as she took the piece from him. It appeared to have been a few inches square and flat, though the bottom half had been burned away. She squinted at it, then gasped as she finally saw what Ginn had seen. Carefully inscribed in deep lines in the wood was an uncanny depiction of her own face. She gaped at it for a moment, then looked back to Ginn, who confirmed her worst fear even as it blossomed in her heart.

"That beast was meant for you, Reyanna. It was sent to kill *you*."

Chapter 12

"Ness, hey, are you in here?" Kiran poked her head through the open doorway of Nessar's chamber, thinking that he would be inside, but the room was empty. She started to pull away, but something caught her eye, and she leaned a little farther into the room to see. In one corner, the desk that had always been empty when they had first lived in the Hall of Jidaana so many years ago was now covered in books and papers.

Kiran raised an eyebrow and, after looking around to see that Nessar was not nearby, decided to venture inside and take a look. Feeling vaguely guilty for snooping, she walked over to the desk and leaned over to see what Nessar had been working on. There was a small stack of newly bound, slim volumes on one corner of the desk, and another stack held older, larger books that looked like they had come from the Hall library. Leather and glue and other binding materials had been pushed off to one side. There was a sheaf of carefully written pages in an unusually neat version of Nessar's scratchy handwriting, a stack of blank papers next to that, and a single page half-filled with writing lay right in the center of the desk, a quill and inkwell close at hand.

Her curiosity rising, she reached for the topmost book in the stack of slender volumes, and eased open the cover so she could read the title page.

"Passion's Heat, by Vanessa Hills," she murmured. She flipped a few pages and saw that, again, the handwriting was Nessar's, though painstakingly neat. Fairly bursting with curiosity by then, she closed the book and picked up the half-written page from the desk and began to read. Her mouth dropped open after only a few sentences.

"Hey, what're you...?" Nessar's voice startled Kiran, and she turned to greet him with a look of disbelief and shock on her face. "Hey, you shouldn't be digging around in my things! Give me that!" A note of alarm and embarrassment ran through Nessar's gravelly voice as he stepped over and reached for the page Kiran still held. Still gaping at him in astonishment, she quickly stepped away from him, holding the page out of his reach. When he saw that she was not going to just give the page over, Nessar sighed and walked over to sit on the bed. With a wave of resignation, he mumbled, "Go on, then, say what you will."

Kiran stared at him for a few seconds longer, then lowered her eyes to the page and began to read. "Her breath came in ragged gasps as the heat from his hands seared her skin. 'I want you. I want you now,' Luke whispered urgently in her ear. 'Yes, yes, my love, I am yours, now and forever.' Luke reached up and ripped Lora's bodice open as though it were naught but paper'..." Kiran fell silent. Her eyes were round and her mouth stayed open as she regarded the man who had been her father for most of her life, a hard-bitten thief who had killed men in the dark, ruled an entire Guild of thieves, fought at her side and faced an army of hideous creatures and the undead.

And he was apparently a romance novelist.

"You wrote this?" Kiran's voice was incredulous.

"Well, of course I did," Nessar snapped. "And it's good, too! People actually enjoy my stories!" He folded his arms defensively. "Look, I started writing years ago, just to amuse myself. When I moved to Tamaransett, I made the mistake of letting a neighbor read one of my little books. Told him an old friend had written it. Wouldn't you know it, soon everyone was clamoring for one. I'm not going to lie to you, I enjoyed that. Moreover, I like writing my stories." A smile finally crept across his face, washing away his embarrassment. "It's...fun for me. Creating the characters, figuring out who they are and how they fit into the story. It makes me happy." Nessar rubbed his chin absently as he spoke. "That's why I come up here...to write. I love working my little farm, but there's always something that needs doing, some chore or other that's screaming for my attention. Weeding, planting, cleaning, even people stopping by just to chat, especially after my books got around. Don't get me wrong, I actually love it all, even tending to the animals. But I just can't write there. Here," he gestured with one hand, indicating the whole of the ancient Keep, "this place has been sitting here for centuries upon centuries. It doesn't really need me. It's quiet. There's no rush, no hurry. I can just sit here and write.

Whenever the mood strikes me, I just pay some neighbor boys to take care of the farm for me. I come up here for a couple or three weeks, check on the Keep, and get some serious writing done. When I'm ready, I head back to town and sell 'em to make a little extra money."

He straightened up then, assuming a stance of unaccustomed dignity. "And I'll not apologize for what I write, either. I enjoy it, and that's enough for me. Others enjoy it, too." He slowly lifted a finger and leaned towards Kiran, pointing at her. When next he spoke, he jabbed her gently in the chest for emphasis. "And there's nothing. Wrong. With that."

Kiran looked at him, then back down at the page in her hands. She knew as well as Nessar did that, as Guardians, they had unlimited access to the vast sums of treasure stored in the Keep's ancient vaults. Nessar could have bought a palace on a whim had he chosen to do so, and not made a dent in the treasury. Money was not the point, and she knew it.

She stood and carefully placed the page back on the desk, then took the topmost book from the stack and brought it with her as she wandered back over and sat down next to Nessar on the bed. She made a production of sliding the little book into the top of one of her boots, next to her hidden dagger. A sly grin crawled across her face, lighting up her eyes as she turned back to face him.

"Nope. Not a thing wrong with that. Nothing at all." She slowly shook her head, still grinning.

"You're never going to let me live this down, are you?" Nessar glared at her.

Kiran could no longer keep her laughter in check, and she surprised Nessar by reaching out and giving him an enormous hug, which he returned. With her face buried in his shoulder, she said, "Not a chance, Vanessa. Not a chance."

I love you, you old fool. Her words echoed silently in his mind.

I love you too, you disrespectful little shit.

93

Chapter 13

"Me?" Reyanna asked in disbelief. "Why would anyone want to kill me?" She looked down at the flat, charred piece of wood held between finger and thumb. Her face stared back at her without giving up any answers.

Ginn shrugged his shoulders. "I'm not sure, Reyanna. I do know that they are using some very dangerous and evil magick in order to do it, though. Look over here." He strode to one of the huge standing stones opposite the altar, drawing his sword and using it to point. "See this? More of those same symbols you see on the altar, but these seem to frame a door or portal of some kind."

Reyanna eyed the marks he indicated. They moved and wriggled under her sight, as had the ones on the altar. She felt a slight vibration from them that had not been present on the altar, and she slowly moved forward to examine them more closely. At the very edge of her senses, she could feel a raspy hum, a faint current of power. It intensified as she came closer to the stone, and she saw the carved symbols begin to glow with a faint reddish hue.

She raised one hand towards the stone to shield herself, but then she felt an answering vibration deep within her body. A swirling energy gradually grew inside her. It grew stronger, and she felt it move throughout her limbs, washing away her hurts and anxiety. She sighed with relief and moved closer, hand still upraised.

"Reyanna, what are you doing?" Ginn moved a step away, uncertain as to what was happening. She did not answer.

Through her raised hand, she felt the oily, dirty energy that emanated from the symbols. It felt almost alive, and it pushed against her, hateful and loathsome. She pushed back with her own power, and she could feel the scarlet energy fleeing before her. In an instant, the symbols turned from bloody crimson to a shining gold. They began to swirl and move, elegantly forming a rectangle of soft, golden light. Within the borders of the shining doorway, the stone disappeared, and an empty corridor stood waiting.

"Oh, look..." Reyanna called to Ginn, her voice filled with wonder. Before he could respond, there was a hideously loud sound, an inhuman shriek that drove them both to their knees as they desperately covered their ears to shut it out. The sigils turned scarlet once more, burning brighter than ever, their bloody glow shining over them both. Moving on instinct, Ginn reached out and grabbed Reyanna's belt, hauling her bodily away from the stone and stumbling with her as fast as he could manage. When they had reached the far side of the great, blocky altar, Ginn helped Reyanna down to the ground and then sheltered her with his own body.

The shrieking had risen in volume and intensity until the entire stone finally exploded in a scarlet burst of evil magick, throwing huge chunks of debris in all directions. Several bounced off the altar, but sheltered as they were against it, Reyanna and Ginn were spared any injury. Gradually, the dust from the shattered monolith settled, and silence returned to the stone circle.

Reyanna carefully sat up, her head still ringing. "What just happened, Ginn? What was that?" She dusted off her shirt and slowly stood up, then leaned heavily on the altar that had sheltered them.

Ginn got to his feet and looked over to where the misshapen pillar of rock had stood moments before. "That was how the summoner of the beast made his escape. There was a doorway there, to where, I know not." He turned his sparkling eyes to Reyanna, whose startling blue gaze met his. "How did you open it? I've heard of such things, but I could not have done that, and I do have some skill."

"I..." Reyanna began. "I don't really know. I just...felt something when I got close to it. It pushed at me, wanted me to go away, but I think I pushed back. I'm not exactly sure how, though. I don't know how I opened it." Reyanna was uncertain. It had been years since she decided to hide that part of herself, the power to do things that no one else could do. She was already an outsider, no need to be more of one.

Ginn smiled, reassuring her. "You have a way of magick about you, that's obvious. Did no one ever teach you how to use it? I would have thought the LorMages would have come to help you."

Reyanna shook her head. "No, I never told anyone."

Ginn nodded, still smiling. "I see. Well, that is definitely interesting. You have a Gift. That's probably why you saw the vision in the first place. I suggest you start figuring out how to use that Gift, for it might come in handy at some point. You know, since there are evil sorcerers trying to fling wolf-creatures at us, and all."

Relieved, frightened, and determined all at the same time, Reyanna simply nodded her agreement. *No sense in hiding it now,* she thought.

Chapter 14

The rider brought his horse to the top of the hill and reined his mount to a halt. A breeze picked up, making his long, brown coat flap lazily. As he had done thousands of times before, he reached up to be sure that his ancient, floppy hat stayed secure on his head. Almost without thinking, he moved his hand from the hat to the haft of the short spear that jutted up over his shoulder. He wore the weapon in a sheath that held it blade-down across his back, and he moved as though it had long since become a part of his body. He sat there on his horse for a few moments, scanning the area and taking in the sights, while an enormous mastiff ambled up to stand beside them. It was nearly the size of a pony, and thickly muscled, though the black and brown fur had gone frosty around her muzzle.

Gart absently patted Bessie's neck as she shifted beneath him. He looked down to see that Beauty was looking up to confirm that they were stopping. He nodded at her, and the huge, scarred mastiff walked in a circle before settling her haunches to the ground. Her mouth, disfigured in dogfights decades before, hung open in a frightening, angry-looking snarl as she panted, though Beauty was actually quite content. Where her Master went, so did she, and as far as she was concerned, all was right with the world when they were together. They had traveled the Realm for years, and although no longer a young pup, she was still remarkably strong. Gart looked down at her and smiled. He had grown very fond of Beauty over the years, and had often used his magick to heal her wounds and keep her healthy far beyond the lifespan of most canines. He had been unable to heal her scars, though they never seemed to bother her. They reminded him of his own, a patchwork that covered the right side of his face. In truth, he had grown quite fond of her, scars and all; he knew the spirit of the dog behind the snarl. Leaning over in the saddle, he scratched her ears the way he knew she liked and was rewarded with a happy groan.

Sitting back in the saddle, Gart took off his weathered hat and ran a callused hand through his blond hair and looked around. "Well, now...let's just see what we can see, eh?" Eyes of icy blue scanned the horizon ahead, trying to see it all at once. The mountains had given way to rolling foothills, and they had come to the top of one hill only to see the beginnings of a forest spreading out for miles in all directions. It had taken him weeks to get this far south, but he planned his mission carefully, and there was still ample time remaining.

Gart pulled a thick leather journal from one of his saddlebags and carefully thumbed it open to a page near the back, covered in sketches and notations. He looked them over for a time, then raised his gaze back to the forest that lay before him, seemingly stretched out to the horizon. He scanned the thick, green carpet of trees carefully, but saw nothing but the canopy of leaves gently moving in the wind's fickle breezes.

With barely a hint of effort, Gart engaged the powerful well of magick within him, and found it instantly ready to answer his call. He reached out with it, exploring the countryside before him, his senses expanding to take in far more than they could without the magick to aid them. He closed his eyes, though he actually saw much clearer without them now than before. Using his power, he rapidly covered miles upon miles of terrain, probing, searching, wandering without moving. Beauty barely flicked an ear at him, having long since grown accustomed to his use of power. It tingled on her skin and buzzed in her ears, but it was just Gart being Gart. He did that sometimes.

Suddenly, far away to the southeast, Gart detected an area of ill, of darkness. Invisible to the eye at that distance, Gart's magick made it feel close by, and a chill went up his spine as he explored the edges of it with his enhanced senses. It festered there, miles away, like the rotting bruise on an otherwise perfect apple, a place that seemed to vibrate with a sense of anger and resentment. Gart saw fleeting visions of trees grown twisted, of animals falling ill and being born with monstrous abnormalities from being too close to the borders of that sickly, evil place. No matter how high the sun, Gart knew that it would always be dark in that part of the forest. Other things brushed against his consciousness. Dangerous things. He had only vague comments in ancient books to tell him what had taken place there in the distant past, but the land felt the impact of those events, even now.

That's it, he thought. *Nimshi. That's where it waits.*

Gart pulled his power back within himself and opened his eyes. He took a cleansing breath and then let it out. Looking back down at Beauty, he saw her looking back at him, her simple love and adoration plain on her battered face.

"Well, Beauty, let's enjoy the sunshine and beautiful forest while we can. I have a feeling we'll be missing them both soon enough."

Beauty did not care one way or the other, and snorted as if to say so. Gart smiled sadly and gently nudged his horse with his heels, urging her forward. As he rode Bessie down and out of the hills with Beauty alongside, Gart wondered again if he was doing the right thing.

Right or not, I'm doing it. I must, Gart reminded himself. He knew what he was going to attempt would be dangerous, and it might even cost him his life. But it would be worth it. He was strong enough now, and his skill with magick had improved beyond anything he had ever dreamed possible. He could do this.

Gart allowed himself to picture his deceased wife's face, her beautiful smile, as it had been over two decades past. She had loved him back then, loved him as no one else had ever loved him. If he were strong enough, and careful enough, he would see her face again.

I'll bring you back, Gennie, he thought. *I'll see you soon.*

Chapter 15

After burning the bodies and leaving the stone circle far behind them, Reyanna and Ginn worked their way through the trees and found themselves on a wide trail that led to the north.

"At last," Reyanna sighed with relief. She was a trained Ranger, thoroughly at home in the forest. However, being attacked by an enormous man-wolf was enough to shake anyone's confidence, and Reyanna had been more than a little jumpy over the last two days.

Ginn agreed. "I, too, am glad that we've reached the road. We should arrive at the next town by midday tomorrow, if my calculations are correct. From there, we should be able to catch a ferry north. We'll be on the river for a couple of weeks, but that will get us closer to Guardians Keep." A laugh crept into his voice. "Now, at least, we only have to keep watch for brigands of the road, snakes, and the occasional wolf, though they would be of the usual variety rather than what we fought back there."

Reyanna laughed. "All those things we can handle. What I want to know is why am I being targeted?"

Ginn stayed silent for a time, thinking. "You received the vision, along with several others who are users of magick. You have some power in that area, though you say you don't know how to use it well."

"I can do some things, like move objects and such. I stopped using my powers when I was a little girl, afraid that I would be made fun of. Or worse, taken away from my new parents." The remembered fear from back then, even though long past, was still strong enough to put a lump in her throat. She loved Rask and Shrya deeply, and the notion that she might have to leave them if anyone found out that she could use magick still terrified her.

Ginn shook his head. "They'd have taken you, all right, but not as a prisoner. Most likely, you'd have simply apprenticed with a LorMage, probably Calliana. She lives in your village, so you'd have spent your days with her and then gone home to your family."

Reyanna scoffed. "Well that's information that might have been handier back then as now."

Ginn laughed, the sound startling birds in the trees above. "Yes, well, it's highly unusual for even a Weya to display such talent; much less, an orphaned human babe. Tell me, do you know anything about your birth parents?"

Reyanna frowned. Memories flitted past in her mind, too fast for her to grasp. A woman's face was foremost, with a beautiful smile and long, dark hair like her own. She guessed that might have been her mother, but the woman's features had become hazy over the years. Of her father, she knew nothing. There was also screaming, monsters, and fire. A shudder took her and she turned her mind away.

"Very little, I'm afraid. Not anything that could help. Mostly just nightmares."

Ginn nodded in sympathy. "I'm sorry to hear that. Had we known your birth parents, we might have been able to find out some things about your power. Maybe one of them had it too. Then again, sometimes individuals are simply born different, more in touch with the magick of the world. You might be such a one. Either way, I wish I had knowledge of the arts so that I could direct you. Unfortunately, the few skills I do have are not helpful here."

They fell silent for a time, Reyanna mulling over her situation. Someone had marked her for death, but why? Did her magick have something to do with it? As far as she knew, the fact that she had any power at all was a secret. Even her adoptive parents had not known the truth, so how could anyone else know? And why would that someone want her dead?

Ginn suddenly spoke up, startling her out of her musing. "You said there were others in the vision, did you not?"

Reyanna blinked a few times, thinking. "Why yes, there were. The LorMage was there, I know that. She saw me in the vision. I remember seeing other figures, too, but they were hazy, and I don't remember much about them." She turned to Ginn, frowning. "You think that someone in my vision is trying to keep me from reaching that man and his dog, that...Gart?"

Ginn shrugged his shoulders. "I don't know anything for certain. But it stands to reason that only the people who shared your vision, who saw you in it, would know that you were involved at all, whether you have power or not. If someone with ill intent saw you, they may have thought that you could be a threat to them and whatever they are plotting."

"But who could that be? And what could they be plotting that would require me to be out of the way?" Reyanna was shocked that such a thing might be possible, but she could feel the truth of it.

"I don't know," Ginn responded. "But it certainly seems to me that if someone is evil enough to send that creature out after you, then they would be your enemy. From what little I know of Gart, he would never do something like that. I don't know what role he plays in all this, and they may be after him as well."

Reyanna thought about that for a moment. "I guess we're on the right path, then. If we can find Gart, then hopefully, he'll shed some light on all this."

"Indeed," Ginn agreed. "Let's just try to keep ourselves alive until we find him."

Chapter 16

The lush forest was alive with birdsong, the buzzing of insects, and the rush of water nearby. The sunlight pushed through the thick leaves overhead to make spotted patterns on the ground below, leaving great swatches of shadows in which various animals made their homes and went about their business.

Suddenly, one of the larger shadows burst into opalescent light as a magickal doorway appeared out of the nothingness that had been there before. Within its border, a swirl of rainbow colors played on a field of crackling white energy, its power holding a way open from elsewhere.

Layton rode through first, his dappled horse navigating the Gate with the ease of long practice. Its hooves thumped in the dirt as it made way for the other two horses as Kiran and Nessar rode through the Gate right behind. The instant they were through, Layton let the portal vanish with a faint pop. He sighed and wiped a sleeve across his sweaty brow. They had come a long way in a short time, and he was feeling it. Repeated use of his Gift left him with a bone-deep fatigue, and although he was still strong enough to travel for many more miles if necessary, he would not turn down a chance to rest. He surveyed the thick foliage that surrounded them.

"We're just going to have to ride through this part. If I can't see where we're going, I can't safely put a Gate up ahead."

"Actually, I think we're nearing the Weya settlement you spoke of," Nessar suggested, poring carefully over a notebook in his hands. He had taken the time to jot down as much information as they could glean from what Gart had left behind, as well as sketches and maps of their destinations, and the little book had already served them well. "What's the name of the place again?"

The feminine voice that answered him was obviously neither Layton's nor Kiran's. It carried a sweet, melodic lilt to it, almost as if the speaker were on the verge of singing or laughing, or possibly both. It echoed among the trees, seemingly coming from everywhere at once.

"You have reached the borders of Elarin Glen, Guardian. We are honored by your presence, though we had no word of your coming."

Nessar and Kiran stifled gasps of surprise, but Layton had spent time with many Weya over the years, and had been expecting just such a welcome. "Hail and well met, milady. We would certainly have sent word had we been able, but we left Guardians Keep and came straightaway."

The voice did laugh then, and the Guardians felt their spirits lift at the sound. "Your method of travel would have easily outpaced any missives you might have sent in any event. I am ValElder Sissia. How can we help you?"

Almost without transition, six figures appeared from the surrounding forest, each shorter by a few inches than Kiran. Their skin was pale ivory in the dappled sunlight, and they were clothed in an elusive blend of grey, green, and brown that made them difficult to see if you did not know where to look. Their ears were sharply pointed, and six pairs of sparkling, jewel-hued eyes regarded the Guardians. The Weyas' hair ranged from golden blonde to raven black, and each Ranger wore a welcoming smile.

Their leader stepped forward, her jet-black hair tied back from her face with a braided leather cord. Aside from her confidence and stunning presence, the only sign of her rank was a sash of darker green that belted her waist. Both Layton and Nessar felt their heartbeats quicken at the sight of her. Layton simply took a deep breath to calm himself, for after spending so much time with the Weya over the years, he was less affected by their intense beauty. Nessar, however, just stared, goggle-eyed, and said not a word.

Kiran, too, had forgotten the almost physical impact that the diminutive Weya had on humans, and she felt her face flush at the sight of the stealthy warriors as they stood watching her, faint smiles on their comely faces. Her coping mechanism was simple stubbornness, however, and she allowed her irritation at being affected in the first place to bring her back into focus.

Layton replied to the ValElder. "Milady, we are on our way to lost Corria. We were hoping you might know something that might help us. A Guardian turned Mage may be attempting something that could bring peril to us all, and we would like to prevent such, if we can."

The tiny Weya raised one arched eyebrow and her expression grew more serious. "Lost Corria, you say? You delve deeply into the past, Guardian. And a particularly dark chapter of it, from what I've been told. You'll want to speak to the LorMage. He will be able to tell you more than I, by far. We will take you to him straightaway, and we would be honored if you would also join us for the evening meal." A look of concern crossed her face then, as though she were deciding whether to speak further. "He is...not well. Please be gentle with him." With that, she signaled her companions, who melted back into the trees as though they had never been there at all. "Follow me, please."

Layton glanced at Kiran and Nessar, surprised at the mention of a Weya being ill, and not only that, but a LorMage. Kiran's voice instantly echoed in Layton's mind.

Did I hear that right? Their LorMage is sick? I thought that Weya never took ill! And LorMages are their best healers!

Layton kept his expression neutral as he thought back to her. *I've never heard of such a thing either, and I've spent time with them. I hope it's nothing serious.*

Nessar said nothing, but worry and sadness had filled him at the first mention of the Weya's illness. All his life, he had known the Weya to be powerful, beautiful, and everlasting. They were wise and kind, as well as formidable warriors. As he had lived his hard, gritty life, the idea of them had always secretly uplifted him. Their immortal existence had been a source of hope, something he could count on. They had always been there, and always would, only dying by accident or combat. No illness he had ever heard of could take hold in a Weya. Somehow, the thought of a Weya taking ill had shaken him to his core in a way that nothing else had.

ValElder Sissia flitted like a ghost through the trees, occasionally stopping to see that her charges were keeping up. Lost in their thoughts, the trio followed, each dealing with their worries as best they could. As they rode, the light slowly faded from the forest.

Chapter 17

The change was sudden. The forest through which Gart and Beauty traveled was beautiful and lush. Birdsong followed them as they moved through the trees and grass, until the air suddenly stilled and they walked into an area that seemed to draw shadows as moths to a flame. The birds fell silent, though Gart could still hear them, their songs falling farther behind them as they walked. Trees became twisted and gnarled, and the grass became brown and brittle. A faint smell of decay and rot made Beauty snort repeatedly as she tried to clear her nose of it before she finally became accustomed to the stench. Gart's piercing blue eyes scanned the woods ahead, and he slowed Bessie to move more carefully. There was danger here. They could feel it.

Gart reached over his shoulder and checked that his Jidaan was still firmly strapped there. The butt-end of the short spear jutted up from the back-scabbard that held the long blade down and out of Gart's way. Although he had long since learned to call upon its Gift of Storms without touching it, he had carried it for so long that the feel of it reassured him. At his side, Beauty growled low in her throat. She did not sense any immediate threat, but the atmosphere weighed heavy on her.

"There, there, girl, I know. This is a foul place. We'll only be here as long as necessary, I promise. I just need to find something and we can be on our way."

Although Bessie was reluctant, she obediently moved forward when Gart gently dug his heels into her flanks. The air was dead and flat, and left Gart feeling listless. Before long, Bessie's hooves clattered on stone, rather than the soft floor of the forest. Gart looked down to see large square flagstones beneath them. Though mostly covered with dirt and brown grass, he could just make out the edges of a narrow road, just wide enough for two riders to travel side-by-side. A thrill went through him. He knew he was close to his first goal. If he could find the Blood of Nimshi, then he'd be halfway there. Eagerly, he searched the sickly forest ahead for more signs.

After several minutes of riding, Gart saw two moss-covered shapes on either side of the road. They were each waist high, and roughly cylindrical, though their true outlines were hidden beneath a thick layer of thorny vines. Gart pulled Bessie to a halt and dismounted. Beauty sat, her mouth wide and panting. Gart moved closer to one of the structures and pulled a black-bladed dagger from his belt. He gently probed the tangle of vines and felt the tip of his blade meet stone. Carefully, he cleared away some of the jagged, sickly vegetation that hid the pylon, and found a worn stone cylinder, carved with sharp symbols all the way around the top end.

Gart pulled out his notebook and checked the symbols against the ones he had meticulously copied. They were a match. He had found Nimshi. Moving more quickly, he tucked the book away and remounted Bessie. With a curt whistle to Beauty, Gart moved forward again, eager to fulfill the first part of his mission.

The road became clearer as they pressed forward, and other structures began to emerge from the malformed, sinister-looking undergrowth. Finally, the stunted trees and gnarled bushes gave way to a wide open space with a low stone wall that stretched away to the east and west. A gray-green, thorny ivy had grown over most of the granite, but its outlines were still plainly visible against the pale, dry grass that clung tenaciously to the foul-smelling earth below. Beyond the wall were stone pillars and archways. A few squat buildings still stood, also covered with the thorny growth. Gart felt a deep sense of sorrow and regret that lingered somehow in the stones. This had once been a beautiful place, a temple of reverent study and worship. Now, its former beauty had been broken, perverted into something foul and revolting. Gart wiped a sleeve across his mouth and nose as a draft of ill-smelling air threatened to gag him. In spite of the unwelcoming atmosphere, he steeled himself and rode a while longer before reining Bessie to a stop. He pulled his notebook from his pack and checked the notes again. Once he was sure that he knew where he was, he dismounted, keeping the journal in one hand.

Gart knelt and ruffled Beauty's fur as she came close and licked his face with her massive tongue. She whined quietly, which she almost never did. Gart grimaced in sympathy. He could feel the oppressive atmosphere just as he knew Beauty could, and she was far more affected by the awful smells of decay and rot than he was. Gart roughly hugged her neck as he spoke.

"I'll be back soon. You stay with Bessie and keep her safe."

Beauty whuffed and whined in response. She did not like that idea one bit, and Gart knew it.

"I know, girl, but if something happens to Bessie, it'll slow us down more than I can afford. Watch after her. I'll hurry."

Beauty's warm brown eyes locked with Gart's bright blue gaze for a moment, then she looked away and lazily panted in spite of the stench in the air. Gart knew that she would do as he asked, even though she hated it almost as much as Gart hated leaving her there. Still, it was the prudent thing to do. He scratched her behind the ears one more time before standing up to regain his bearings. Glancing at his notes again, he started towards the west, walking along the inside of the waist-high wall.

He did not have far to walk, for he soon came upon a slender, round structure, a short tower only three stories tall. It had a conical roof, once beautifully tiled, now mostly open to the elements. The ancient wooden door had half-fallen off its hinges, so it did little to bar his way. Gart put away his notebook and pulled the wicked-looking black dagger from his belt. His Jidaan was less agile in closed places, and the black sword at his belt was similarly too long. Although his magick was always at the ready, he just felt better with steel in his hand. He eased himself into the entryway, avoiding contact with the evil-looking vines that snaked along the doorframe.

The first floor was mostly bare, though piles of wood might have been furniture at one time. Gart stepped carefully over to the stairs that hugged the wall to his right and began to move upwards. The second floor looked much as the first had, but it had fewer plants and less debris. One floor remained, and Gart worked his way up the stone steps to see if his notes were correct.

As his head passed the level of the floor above, he saw what he at first took to be a bundle of sticks covered by a moldering blanket just a few feet away from the stairs. In the center of the room, a stone pedestal arose, a few feet high and carved with ancient symbols that Gart recognized from his research. He reached the top of the steps and startled a handful of birds from their roosts in the rafters overhead. They squawked as they flew awkwardly away, and Gart glimpsed one bird that seemed to have two heads on its malformed body. He stifled a shudder and moved towards the pedestal, sheathing his dagger and laying aside his traveling pack as he did so.

The top of the pedestal was bare, and Gart slid his hand across it. Leaning over, he checked the runes that had been chiseled along the rim of the piece and grunted to himself. The pedestal was clearly marked in an ancient tongue. Its meaning, "Water," was clear enough. But there was supposed to be something else, an artifact of some kind. Gart frowned and examined the pedestal from top to bottom, but found nothing more. He stood, deep in thought. He needed the artifact, nay, needed four of them. Even one out of place would foil his quest before it had even begun. He turned and let his eyes roam the chamber as he considered his options.

When his gaze fell on the bundle of sticks on the floor, it caught his attention. He cocked his head to one side and then slowly approached it. Drawing his sword, he carefully reached out with the tip and prodded the ancient blanket that covered the pile.

The fabric crumbled at a touch, revealing not a pile of jumbled twigs as Gart had first thought, but bones, instead. The skeleton lay curled in a fetal position, wrapped around something it had held close for hundreds of years. Gart moved closer and knelt beside the bones, carefully reaching among them to extract its tightly held treasure. The bones crumbled as he moved them, and in moments, he held a dusty vessel in his hands. He blew the dirt away and wiped his thumb across it to reveal brilliant blue stone. The lapis lazuli had been painstakingly sculpted into a vase of great beauty, inlaid and accented with gold runes around its rim. Gart pulled a cloth from his pack and cleaned the vase before setting it back on its pedestal, aligning the runes on the vessel with the runes on the stone below it. When he felt that all was in place, he rummaged in his pack and brought out a plain bowl and his water skin. He placed the bowl at the base of the pedestal and filled it with water from the skin, and then quickly shouldered his pack and made his way back down the steps and out of the tower, his steps quicker now that he had accomplished the first task.

From the northernmost tower, Gart made his way along the circular wall towards the western tower that he knew would be there. His eyes kept scanning the empty buildings within the temple grounds on his left, keeping alert for any movement, but he saw nothing except the overgrown vines and hollow shells of the ancient temple of Nimshi. His notes said that the temple had once boasted a large library that had been sought after by priests and scholars from all over the Realm, and a small museum that housed remnants of an earlier age. Gart was interested in none of it at the moment, only the Blood of Nimshi, which the temple had been built to protect.

The western tower came into view, and its door was in better shape than the last. As he drew close to the tower, Gart took off his pack and rummaged around in it until he produced an empty jar. Kneeling, he scooped up handfuls of the rank-smelling earth at his feet and deposited them in the jar. Once it was full, he stoppered it tightly and stowed it again in the bottom of his pack before sliding his arms through the straps and settling it into place on his back.

Refocusing on the tower, Gart reached out with his magick and took hold of the door, gently easing it open. Some of the planks fell out of the iron binding as it moved, but it stayed mostly intact, and Gart slipped past it. The tower was similar to the last, and he moved to the stairs as he had before.

Sprawled at the bottom of the stairs was another skeleton, covered by a decaying piece of fabric whose color was lost in the distant past. On a hunch, Gart pulled his sword again and gingerly probed the ancient, desiccated corpse. The fabric disintegrated, and Gart saw another vessel clutched in the body's bony arms. It was dusty and antiquated, just as the other had been, but it was wider, and much shorter, almost like a shallow cooking pot. Gart sheathed his sword and then gently pulled the vessel away from the skeleton's arms. Fishing the rag from his pack again, he began to clean it up. It was a deep, dark brown color underneath the covering of centuries worth of dust and grime. Gold runes encircled the low rim of the vessel, and Gart knew without pulling out his notes that this was the artifact that corresponded to "Earth." Holding his prize carefully in the crook of his left arm, he pulled out his sword again and made his way up the stairs, glancing at the pile of bones as he went.

That fabric looked like priests' robes, he thought. *It looks like they were trying to steal the artifacts. But why?* The ancient books he had found had never fully explained what had gone wrong in Nimshi, only that one priest, bedraggled and raving, had escaped. The terrified man's final words had been a warning to let the forest reclaim the temple, lest its evil be released upon the rest of the world. Those few who set out to discover the truth behind the dying priest's words were never heard from again, and the temple at Nimshi faded into obscurity.

Gart shook his head at the folly of those who had come before him. He cared not for the ancient mysteries. If there had been some kind of treasure here once, he had no interest in it. Even the priceless artifacts he had already found were nothing more than a means to an end. Beyond that, he was content to let Nimshi fade into the forest as the old priest had suggested, as long as he found the Blood first.

As he reached the top of the stairs and his body emerged beyond the level of the stone floor, he heard something. Instinctively, he froze in place as he tried to interpret the sounds. The roof of this tower had lost many more tiles than the last, and the afternoon sun shining through had momentarily blinded him after the relative darkness of the rooms below. Gart closed his eyes against the glare and reached out with his magick, using it to probe the layout of the room. He had only just begun to make sense of what he felt when he found himself fighting for his life.

Something slammed into Gart's backpack, knocking the breath out of him and sending him sprawling onto the top steps and the floor beyond. The ancient urn hit the stone floor with a dull ringing sound before it rolled away, while his sword spun out of reach. He heard a loud hissing as something wrapped itself around his kicking legs and squeezed them together with incredible strength. Gart continued scrabbling with his arms as he attempted to crawl towards his weapon. When that failed, he struggled to turn and see what was attacking him.

A cold, reptilian face floated before him, its black, fathomless eyes staring back. Its huge hood flared out, framing its wedge-shaped head. It was beautiful, and deadly. Gart felt a ferocious jerk from his backpack and then another head joined the first, its three-inch fangs still dripping with venom from the strike that had fortunately struck Gart's pack instead of his body.

The snake was immense, a black and gold monstrosity that gazed at Gart with both sets of eyes, both heads swaying hypnotically in a soothing motion even as its body tightened further on his legs and began to move up his torso.

Gart knew that if he cried out, Beauty would find him in a matter of moments. The snake was faster than she, by far, and he wanted to keep her safe. He grunted softly under the stress, but then found his composure at last. He sent his magick over the surface of his body, covering every inch of his skin from his chest down to his feet, sliding it easily between the serpent's constricting scales and himself. Once he felt completely sheathed in his own power, he expanded it, pushing away from himself until he had created a couple of inches of space. Though slight, it was more than enough to completely relieve the pressure from the snake's ropy, muscular coils. He breathed a relieved sigh as the crushing weight was lifted from him, and then refocused on the more immediate danger.

Gart's hands shot out and gripped a throat in each, just below the fanged jaw of each head. Both heads hissed viciously at him and the end of its tail thrashed violently where it wasn't coiled around Gart's lower body, but Gart was far stronger than anything the snake had yet encountered. Gart had always been wiry and strong, and with his magick singing through his body, his grip was ferociously powerful. The snake struggled mightily to maintain pressure on its prey and escape its clutch at the same time, failing at both.

"Sorry, snake, but you picked the wrong lunch today," Gart grated through clenched teeth. "I'd let you live, but then I'd have to worry about Bessie and Beauty out there. Can't have that, can we?"

With a sharp flex of both muscle and magick, Gart crushed the throats of the two-headed monstrosity and then flung it away from him. It released its hold as the pain hit its reptilian brains, and it squirmed frantically, coiling around itself in a vain attempt to protect its vitals. With a gesture, Gart used his magick to retrieve his ebony-bladed sword, floating it through the air until the grip was settled in his hand once more. He watched the snake's movements intently for a few moments, then swung the blade in a carefully timed arc that neatly beheaded the mutated creature. Scarlet blood sprayed the walls, and although the snake's long body continued to writhe and squirm, the hissing heads fell silent at last.

Gart watched for a few moments, then when he was certain that the snake was no longer a threat, he turned and looked for the urn, suddenly concerned that it had been damaged. He saw it in the shadows across the floor where it had rolled on one edge, seemingly intact. He quickly moved towards it, laid his sword on the floor, and knelt to examine the urn. His fingers roved over the entire surface of the deep brown pot, searching for cracks. He breathed another sigh of relief as he found that there was no real damage on the piece. He wiped its surface again with the rag just to be sure, then carefully placed it atop the central pedestal, taking time to align its runes with those on the stone pillar.

Gart pulled his pack in front of him and noted the two huge holes that the snake's fangs had made in the thick leather. He unbuckled it warily and opened the flap, hoping that nothing was terribly damaged inside. He saw that the small blanket he had rolled up inside his pack had taken the

114

brunt of the snake's attack. Gart carefully pulled it out, noting that it seemed heavier than it should have been. A green, syrupy substance oozed out of the blanket's folds, and Gart tossed the sodden fabric to the floor. A strong, acidic smell assaulted Gart's nostrils, and he was suddenly very relieved that the snake's venom had not gotten into his body.

After reassuring himself that no further damage had been done, Gart pulled out the jar of earth he had gathered from below. He unstoppered the lid and put it aside, then placed the open jar at the base of the pedestal. Satisfied with the arrangement, he buckled the pack shut and hoisted it over his shoulders, adjusting his Jidaan in the process. He picked up his black-bladed sword and headed for the stairs, keeping a decidedly more watchful eye out for possible dangers. He still had two more towers, two more elemental artifacts to put into place, and then his real work could begin. The Blood of Nimshi was as good as his.

Chapter 18

The afternoon sun had already passed out of view behind the trees, but night was still a long way off. Reyanna and Ginn kept to the road, moving along as quickly as they dared without overly tiring the horses. She chafed at their lack of speed, but knew they were actually making good time. In a few more days, they would reach the river and could head north to Green Meadows. From there, the trip west would be much shorter, and then they would reach Guardians Keep. She hoped that Gart would be there and that he would have answers for her.

"Hold a moment," Ginn's soft voice brought her out of her thoughts. She eased Betina to a halt next to Ginn's mount, and turned to see him gazing into the forest to the east. His view was obscured by trees and shrubs, but she knew that he was 'looking' with all of his senses, not just his eyes.

"What is it?" she whispered, scanning the area herself. A flock of birds, startled by something, flew out of the trees farther to the east and over the riders' heads as they tried to find safer places to rest. Somewhere far off in the distance, Reyanna heard what might have been men yelling, though the sounds were indistinct.

Before Reyanna could reach any further with her senses, Ginn stated the obvious. "There is a commotion over there to the east. Shall we investigate? It could be...interesting." One eyebrow raised and the hint of a grin was visible at one corner of his mouth.

Reyanna was torn. She was on a mission. She had been marked for assassination by strangers, and had already faced death once as a result. She desperately wanted to keep moving forward, to reach their destination in the hopes of finding some answers. There was no telling how long such a detour could take, or if it was even worth their time.

Before she could speak, the wind shifted, bringing the distant voices closer. She heard the faint echo of a woman's voice, yelling in anger and protest, followed by more masculine shouts, heavy with malice. She cocked her head, trying to hear more, but the words were indistinguishable. Their tone, however, had been quite clear. A woman was being attacked, and from the sound of it, by more than one assailant.

Reyanna turned her eyes back to Ginn. The humor in his expression had vanished and was replaced with a much harder look. She nodded silently and the pair began readying their weapons as they guided their horses towards the ruckus.

Soon, the voices became clearer; the riders found themselves no more than a stone's throw from the fight. Reyanna and Ginn found a sheltered spot and tethered their horses, knowing they could melt into the forest more easily without them if need be. They held arrows to string and crept through the last bit of cover that separated them from the conflict. As they peeked between the branches, they were both astonished at what they saw.

A group of a dozen hard-looking, dirty men were brandishing weapons and yelling at a woman they had surrounded. She was dressed in the simple robes of a priestess and wielded only a steel-capped staff in her defense, but that was not what had widened Reyanna's eyes; it was the massive spider that the woman rode upon.

Easily taller than a horse, and much broader, its spindly legs skittered with unsettling quickness. It gnashed its two long, ebony fangs at its attackers as the priestess guided it with her knees and a set of reins. She rode it as though it was a warhorse, but the swords and spears of the men appeared to be keeping the creature at bay.

"I've told you louts, I have no gold! Leave us be! We're not hurting anyone!" Sunlight glinted from the steel ends of her short staff, and she held it like a lance, knowing that the men were out of her reach for the moment. Frustration and anger were plain on her face, and fear as well. However, as Reyanna watched, she suddenly understood something.

"She's not afraid for herself, Ginn;" she whispered to her companion, "she's afraid for the spider!" Ginn nodded silently as he watched. Moving slowly, he returned his arrow to its quiver and slung his bow over his shoulder.

He made a short sequence of hand-signals to Reyanna. As a Ranger, she understood him as plainly as if he had spoken aloud. She smiled a grim smile as she moved away to her left, keeping her bow at the ready. Ginn faded into the forest on his right. They would attack together from opposite sides of the clearing and hopefully convince the men that they were surrounded. If they could distract them for even a few moments, the woman could escape.

Just then, one of the braver men darted forward and lopped off the lower part of one of the spider's legs. It did not make a sound, but it shied back, hiding its injured leg close to its furry body. The priestess screamed, "No, you bastards! Don't hurt her!"

The men laughed. The biggest one, a blond-bearded fellow with missing teeth, bellowed in return. "Hey, we can't let a vicious beast like that roam free! Perhaps if you come down from there and give us your gold," and then he glanced at his companions with a sly leer, "and maybe spend a little time with us, we'll let you both go!"

They laughed again as the priestess registered disgust and rage on her pretty face. She knew what they wanted, and they knew she knew.

And she had definitely had enough of their nonsense.

The big man started to speak again. "You know we won't let you go until we get what we want! Come on down, be nice!"

Reyanna, still watching from behind a tree, saw the woman's expression shift and was surprised to see her burst into a wide, and somewhat evil grin.

"You want me to come down, do you?" The man's smile froze on his face as his prey suddenly did not seem at all afraid of him anymore. "Fine! You'll think better of that after I get down there, arseling!"

Before the leader could dig a suitable response from his limited vocabulary, the priestess slid off of the spider's back and launched herself at him, a blur of brown robes and flying black hair. The short staff in her hands separated in the middle and became a pair of steel-shod fighting sticks that sang a vicious song of pain.

She slammed one stick into the leader's head and he dropped like a stone, but she was already on the next thug

118

before the first had settled to earth. The other men shouted in fury and tried to swarm her, but although they had swords and a few spears, she danced through them all, untouched. Weapons dropped to the ground as she broke hands and fingers at every turn with precise strikes of her sticks, and the air was alive with yells of surprise and pain from the men.

The instant the spider was unburdened, the beast spun around to face the two men who had circled behind to hem it in. It reared, its front legs held high and its enormous fangs dripping venom as they clicked loudly together. The men blanched in fear, suddenly terrified that the beast had turned on them. Before they could decide whether to attack or flee, the spider had thrown great, white gouts of sticky silk over them from its spinnerets, covering the men completely. They fell to the ground in terror, thrashing furiously, but the sticky webs held them fast. The spider came closer, and the men froze in horror as its hairy bulk came to rest on their bodies, holding them completely immobile. The tips of its dagger-like fangs gently scraped along the silk that covered one man, terrifying him to stillness, but it held its bite.

The priestess was a whirling tornado among the shouting, fighting men. They swung and stabbed viciously at her, but to no avail. They could not touch her. One by one, each was silenced by a sharp rap of her whipping sticks and sent, unconscious, to the ground. Within moments, she was the only human still upright in the clearing. She adopted a fighter's crouch, her sticks still held ready for any threat. A faint spatter of blood speckled her pretty but stern face, but she paid it no mind. The warrior priestess scanned the trees for a moment, then stood tall and pointed one stick at a spot directly opposite Reyanna's hiding place.

"I know someone is there! Step out where I can see you! If you make me come in there after you, you'll regret it!" Her expression was grim and determined, and clearly displayed that she aimed to make good on her promise if need be.

Ginn's calm voice floated across the clearing in response. "Milady, I daresay we would! I am Ginn, a Weya.

119

I'm a former Ranger. My companion and I heard the commotion and came to aid you," Reyanna could hear Ginn's smile as he continued. "However, it seems that you had things well in hand."

The priestess quickly looked around, but kept her stick pointed at Ginn's position. "Your companion? There are only two of you?"

"Priestess, we are friends," Reyanna spoke up, and the woman instantly turned to point her other stick in her direction. "As Ginn said, we came to help. May we approach?"

The priestess considered her words for a moment, then finally relaxed her stance and lowered her sticks. "Yes, please. I could use some help moving these," she gestured with one stick at a pile of unconscious bandits, "*fools*, if you would be so inclined. You'd think the sight of a giant spider would be enough to send them packing, but apparently, that wasn't the case. Greed and lust can be powerful motivators, it seems." She put the two ends of her sticks together and gave them a firm twist. There was a stout *click*, and the sticks became a single staff once more. She put it aside and moved quickly towards the spider, which still sat on the two men it had ensnared.

Reyanna and Ginn eased their way through the trees with their hands held up and their weapons sheathed. As soon as she caught sight of them both, the woman's face burst into a wide smile. "Well met, you two! Thank you for coming to help me, that was most kind." She turned her attention to the spider, and Reyanna and Ginn saw that there was a small but clever saddle affixed with a leather strap to the juncture of the spider's thorax and abdomen. A backpack was buckled to the rear of it, as well as a couple of extra pouches, which the woman dug through as she searched for something. "I must tend to Drusilla, for these louts hurt her. A moment, please."

She found what she needed and began to make cooing, soothing noises to the spider as she moved towards its injury. "There, there, Drusilla, you'll be just fine. This salve will help the sting, I promise." She gently took its injured leg into her hands, singing softly in a language that Reyanna had never heard before. The spider stayed mostly still, though its legs quivered at her touch and the small pair of pedipalps that flanked her fangs moved incessantly. Over her shoulder, the priestess said, "I am Teryn, of the priestesses of Rowann. Those bastards surrounded us as we were about to leave our campsite, and Drusilla could not make it to the trees through their spears and swords."

Reyanna's eyes were still wide to see a spider of such immense size, much less a priestess that obviously rode one. She cast a glance at Ginn, only to find him gazing just as intently at the pair as she was. As ancient as Ginn was, seeing the enormous arachnid seemed to enchant him as though he were a child. Reyanna addressed the priestess.

"I am Reyanna, milady," she said, moving closer as she spoke. "We were just passing by and heard the commotion."

Teryn opened the small jar she had retrieved from the saddlebag and set about smearing a dollop of its contents on the end of Drusilla's injured leg. The spider did not pull away, and the priestess quickly replaced the jar and began winding a strip of cloth around the stump.

"Yes, well, I certainly appreciate your willingness to help. Usually, we avoid such ruffians with ease, but they surrounded us. They would have hurt Drusilla if she had attacked one of them before I had them occupied." She tied off the bandage and eased the leg to the ground. It was shorter than the others, but the spider seemed to have little trouble putting weight on it. "It could have gone either way, and had I been hurt, your help would have been most welcome."

"It she hurt badly?" Ginn ventured. It had been many years since he had seen one of the giant spiders, children of the Spider Queen Kulcania, last seen in the cliffs somewhere between fallen Laro and Rualtha, and they were a wonder to him.

Teryn's laugh sparkled on the air like music. "Fortunately not. She will regrow the leg by her next molting. She'll need to eat a bit more in the meantime, and it will take her some time before she can bear my weight again, but she'll be just fine." Satisfied that her companion was properly tended, she turned her attention fully to her benefactors. "Drusilla is young, and in my care. I hate that she was injured, but it could have been much worse. Thank you."

Ginn bowed deeply, with the grace that only Weya could manage. "Though we did naught but observe, 'twas our pleasure, milady."

"We should go," Reyanna suggested. "These idiots will rouse eventually, and I'd just as soon we not have to deal with them. Where are you headed? And, if I may ask, how did you come to travel with such a…" she hesitated, staring into the silent spider's many eyes. They had fastened on her as she spoke, and Reyanna had been struck by the way they shifted colors in the sunlight. "Such a beautiful creature?"

Teryn smiled in response. "That is kind of you to say, for although Drusilla cannot speak, she does understand." She gestured with one hand as she continued. "We are headed north for a time, then west. I am returning to my home in the Shadowed Forest so that another may take my place with the Spider Queen Kulcania."

Ginn's face, usually inscrutable, actually betrayed his intense interest. "Fascinating. I would love to hear the full of this tale, but I agree with Reyanna; we should move on. We, too, are headed north. Do you wish to ride with us until Drusilla can carry you again?"

Teryn moved a lock of her dark hair away from her eyes with one hand, relief plain on her face. "That would be most welcome, yes. She can forage on her own and will stay nearby. She'll let me know when she can carry me. It should not be long at all, a day, maybe two at most. They adapt quickly to such things. Here, let us deal with these ruffians, and we can talk further."

Moving quickly, Teryn grabbed the nearest of the unconscious men and dragged him to rest with his back against a nearby tree. Then she grabbed another and repeated the process. With Reyanna and Ginn's help, it took only a few minutes to round up all the men and lay them against the rough bark of the wide tree trunk.

"Drusilla, dear, please come and help me. I need your silk." Teryn waved at the spider, and she immediately raised herself off of the two men upon whom she had been sitting, eliciting muffled cries of relief from underneath their silken cocoons. "Oh, drat, I'd forgotten about those two. Ginn, Reyanna, would you be so kind as to use your daggers to cut those louts free enough to bring them here as well. You might leave their mouths covered, though. No sense in listening to anything they have to say."

Ginn allowed himself a chuckle as he strode to the two prone bodies, Drusilla making way for him and Reyanna. When he had mostly freed the first one, the terrified bandit began to struggle mightily. Ginn clouted him in the jaw in a ruthless, efficient motion, and the man went limp. Ginn raised an eyebrow at the other man, who was being freed by Reyanna, his eyes round as saucers underneath the webbing. "I suggest you do not give Reyanna trouble. She bites."

The ruffian's eyes shifted to Reyanna, who snapped her teeth at him ferociously, and he froze in fear, allowing her to cut him free without any further struggle. The two were dragged over to the tree with their brethren and placed alongside them. Teryn then called for Drusilla once more.

The great spider skittered close to the tree, then turned so that her spinnerets were pointed in its direction. Teryn raised her hands as she murmured a series of archaic words. The hair stood up on Reyanna and Ginn's necks as the priestess's magick came alive. Using her will and magick, Teryn drew a thin sheet of sticky silk from Drusilla's spinnerets. This she carefully, slowly guided through the air to encircle all of the seated, dozing men…and the one still awake, but too terrified to move. The floating sheet of silk surrounded them, a ribbon of white a hand's-breadth wide, coiling around their chests two, three times, then a fourth. The flow of silk ceased, and Drusilla moved away, leaving Reyanna and Ginn watching, fascinated. With a gesture, Teryn jerked the silk tightly around all of the men and sealed it closed, imprisoning them firmly against the tree, but leaving their legs free. The lone, wakeful ruffian finally began to scream beneath his silken gag, thrashing and kicking his legs in a futile attempt to escape. The words of Teryn's chant changed slightly, becoming more melodic. It drifted into a calming lullaby, aided by subtle gestures that

123

focused her intent. The man's struggles slowed, and soon, he was dozing peacefully alongside his fellows. Teryn dropped her hands and her song stopped.

"What did you do to them?" Reyanna asked, curiosity eating her alive.

Teryn ran a hand through her dark locks and let out a deep breath before looking at Reyanna. "Oh, I cast a spell that will put them to sleep for a couple of days. The silk will weaken, and they'll be able to work their way out of it after that. They'll be less trouble in the meantime if they're sleeping, and they won't need any food or drink while they're under the spell. Actually, they'll waken quite refreshed." Teryn frowned at that, and after a moment's thought, stepped forward and kicked the sleeping leader hard in the ribs, and then the man who had wounded Drusilla for good measure. "Well...refreshed and nursing some cracked ribs, anyway." She quickly looked over her shoulder at Reyanna and blushed, embarrassed. "Oh..um...Rowann forgive me!" she said, making a quick gesture of supplication.

Satisfied that her unpriestesslike behavior would likely be pardoned by the Goddess, Teryn moved over to the great spider and unbuckled her backpack from behind the saddle, pulling some items from other pouches and putting them in the pack. The spider swayed gently at her touch, its pedipalps constantly moving as if testing the air. Teryn leaned in and whispered to her for a time, then stepped away. The only thing Reyanna caught were the words, "No, you may not eat them. I know they hurt you, but still, no." When Teryn had finished, she stepped away from Drusilla to give her room to move. In a flash, the enormous creature scampered up into the stately trees above and then vanished into the forest, heading northward.

"Oh, my, gaaaaaah..." Reyanna could not suppress a creepy-crawly sensation that ran up her spine at the sight, and she clenched her fists tightly to her chest until the chill had finally had its way with her. Ginn looked at her sternly, but Teryn burst out laughing.

"They had that effect on me too, at first. Very, very creepy. Imagine an entire colony of them! Gave me the willies, to be sure." Teryn flashed them both a brilliant smile. "But then I got to know them, and lived with them, and now I see them for the amazing and wondrous creatures that they are."

Reyanna blushed. "I'm so sorry, I couldn't help it! She's beautiful, yes, but," she looked up into the trees where the spider had disappeared, "OK, yes, a little creepy."

Ginn spoke up. "Indeed, I agree on all counts. A wondrous creature. And somewhat...startling. Shall we go?"

Chapter 19

Elarin Glen was far different from the elegant but simple Weya settlements that Layton had visited in the past. Their guides led them through the thickest part of the forest by way of a hidden trail. It wound through the rising terrain and was all but invisible unless you knew exactly where it lay. When they emerged into the narrow valley, Layton heard Kiran and Nessar's gasps of surprise at the sight.

A river ran through the center of the glen, flowing over ruddy stones and soil that shone scarlet through the clear water. Its bloody cast might have been frightening, but somehow, the burbling of the water and the sunlight glinting off its surface made it seem welcoming instead. On either side of the river, the craggy stone walls rose almost straight up into the sky, the grey granite covered almost entirely in lush green plant life. Craning their necks, the trio gazed upwards to see a slender ribbon of blue sky above, bordered on either side by the tall cliffs.

Carved directly into the stone of the sheer rock faces before them were doors and windows, walkways and terraces, balconies with railings, and even gardens. Weya could be seen here and there, going about their daily tasks. Some raised hands to wave at the newcomers, obviously friends since they were escorted by the ValElder. The beauty of the tiny, hidden city had taken the Guardians by surprise, and their eyes were wide with delight.

"Welcome to Elarin Glen," ValElder Sissia's voice brought the Guardians' attention back to their guide. "We will leave your horses there," the Weya pointed to a larger opening closer to the level of the river. Over the sounds of the rushing water, they heard whinnies and snorts that indicated a stable. "Then I will take you to see the LorMage." A pained expression appeared on Sissia's face, and she rid herself of it with some effort. Without elaborating, she led the Guardians towards the nearest set of stairs that led into the heart of the cliff city.

Nessar, Kiran, and Layton exchanged looks, but said nothing. They were all very interested in seeing the

LorMage. The Weya LorMages were highly respected among their own people and humans, alike. Most numbered their years in millennia rather than decades, and had spent their time learning the history, arts, and magick of the world, then teaching it wherever it could be most helpful. They were well-known as masters of healing and gentle magick, though at one time, their destructive powers had been almost godlike. Back then, they had not been the wise, benevolent sages into which they had eventually evolved.

Aeons ago, when the world of Talwynn had been new, a quarrel had broken out among two rival groups of Weya. The exact origin of the disagreement had been lost in antiquity, but the results had been catastrophic. The Weya had been rash and arrogant, quick to anger and slow to forgive. A madness had overtaken them, and war ensued. The land became a battlefield, utterly devastated by the LorMages as they strove to impose their will on their opponents. The land was torn asunder. The legends spoke of rivers of fire, exploding mountains, vicious ice storms, and fell, monstrous creatures brought to life and sent into battle. Years passed, the earth bled, and every living thing on Talwynn suffered. Many Weya fled for their lives, and still the LorMages made war on each other, no longer knowing or caring what started the war in the first place, striving only for dominance.

Finally, one Weya LorMage saw the folly of what they had become, and it broke him. He wept to see the misuse of such power, and the hurt that he and his brethren had caused. Inspired by his insight, he climbed the tallest mountain on Talwynn and cast a spell of such magnitude that he shone like a second sun. The brilliant fire was too bright to look upon, even from miles away. He reached out with his power and somehow laid hold of the magick held by the other LorMages. With a ferocious flex of his will, he forcefully ripped their abilities and knowledge from them, leaving them empty and defenseless. All over the world, the warring LorMages stumbled to their knees, and a staggering silence fell.

The lone Weya spoke to them, his voice echoing across vast distances, and they heard. He spoke of life, love, and responsibility. He spoke of pride and forgiveness,

127

and described to them a Weya people united in the creation of a better world. His words shamed the other LorMages, and their hearts were turned. They wept as they realized what they could become if only they worked together, if they chose to change. Chastened and bereft of their power, they took his words to heart. The LorMages rose up and gathered together as brothers and sisters once more to begin again.

Spent and weary, the single Weya who had ended the conflict vanished from Talwynn, taking knowledge of many of the most powerful arts with him. And so began a new age of Weya wisdom, an age that continued to the present.

Layton, Kiran, and Nessar hoped that the ailing LorMage possessed enough of that wisdom to aid them on their quest. They handed off the reins of their horses to young Weya, each hoping to find the answers they sought.

They were escorted along a walkway carved directly into the side of the cliff, which then turned and headed straight into the stone. A long series of halls and chambers had been built into the rock, snaking through it in a sophisticated and beautiful arrangement of living spaces.

"We are close," the ValElder spoke over her shoulder to Kiran, who was nearest her. "Please keep your voices down and your movements measured. We do not wish to startle him overly. He is quite frail." Kiran nodded her agreement and turned to see her companions doing the same. They would be respectful of the LorMage's condition.

A few moments later, they came to a beautifully carved wooden door, a bit larger than most they had passed. ValElder Sissia knocked gently. She was answered almost immediately by a male Weya, who opened the door and smiled at her.

"There are Guardians here who wish to speak with the LorMage," Sissia spoke in a hushed tone to the Weya assigned to look after the ancient one.

"Guardians?" The nurse's eyes widened as he looked up at the trio with admiration. "Why, yes, of course. They are always welcome," he replied, stepping aside and pulling the door wide. "Please enter, friends." They filed inside, their eyes immediately taking in their new surroundings. It was a small chamber, but not cramped, each of the walls completely covered with shelves. Neat stacks of scrolls dominated the shelves on one wall, while others held books of all shapes and sizes. The same kind of small, glowing globes they had seen Brunar use at Guardians Keep were in each corner of the room, throwing a warm glow over all.

From an adjoining room, they heard a tremulous voice call out, "Trian, who comes?" The voice was faint, but aware. "I was not expecting anyone, but it is a welcome…" the voice paused as though gathering strength before continuing, "diversion."

Trian thanked the ValElder for bringing their guests and she departed with a wave. Trian then turned to the Guardians. "LorMage Eldwynn has been resting. He is not well, but as he says, he occasionally welcomes visitors. This way, please." He turned and gestured toward one of the open doorways that led into the dwelling. Layton took the initiative and moved forward, the others following closely.

In the next room, light streamed in through a set of open doors that led to a sunlit patio. The breeze carried hints of the nearby forest, and fresh flowers had been placed in pots around the room, giving it a subtle, sweet smell. A desk sat in one corner, looking as though it had once been used hard, but not recently. A small bed sat in the center of the room, and in it, propped up by a number of pillows, sat a tiny, wizened Weya. His hair was completely white, and braided into a long plait that trailed over his shoulder and under the sheet. The pointed tips of his ears poked through the straight, snowy locks. Deep lines and wrinkles covered the pale, ivory skin of his face, and his eyes appeared to have a grey cast to them. He was alert, peering across the room as he tried to see his visitors.

His voice was reedy and thin, but held a note of authority and mirth that could not be hidden. "Hello, strangers, and welcome. I apologize for not standing to meet you, but I am tired of late." He squinted at the three humans for a time before shaking his head and sighing heavily. "Alas, my eyes are not what they once were. I can see you, but not near as clearly as I used to." The effort of speaking seemed to tire him and he paused for a few moments before continuing. "What brings you to see me, children?"

Nessar snorted loudly, and Kiran smacked him in the arm, glaring at him for being rude. Instantly, the ancient figure in bed loosed a gentle laugh. "My apologies if I offended. I am thousands of years old, and humans are very much as children to me, even if they live to be a hundred." Nessar's eyes widened and he looked at the floor for a moment, suddenly feeling silly. Even at eighty, he was barely a blink in the ancient Weya's existence. "Guardians...I have not seen Guardians for a very long time. What may I do for you?"

Layton looked at his friends and Kiran gestured for him to speak. He had always been more diplomatic than either Kiran or Nessar, and she was more than willing to admit it. Layton carefully moved forward and sat on the edge of the LorMage's bed as he gathered his words.

"One of us may be on the verge of doing something dangerous. We think he is going to an ancient city to find something that may help him. We think we know what it is he is planning, and we want to stop him before he hurts himself or anyone else. We believe he seeks lost Corria."

The smile froze on the ancient Weya's face, then faded. He was silent for a few moments, then spoke in a sad tone. "Indeed, that is a very tragic tale. For a brief time, Corria was a shining jewel of a city. Stunning works of enchanting beauty using gems and precious metals were created there." A frown creased the already deep wrinkles in Eldwynn's face. "But the city is no more. Once they found the Heart, they sealed their doom, for it ignited their greed. That is what destroyed it all."

Kiran moved closer, fascinated. "What is it? The Heart, I mean."

The LorMage turned to face her, his cloudy eyes squinting as he tried to bring her into focus, and then his face brightened. "Ah, I have heard of you, Kiran. I know you by the sapphire in your Jidaan, which even my failing eyes cannot miss. It is an honor." He inclined his head in greeting, then continued. "The Heart is an immense diamond with a gentle pink tint, cut by the Corrian master jewelers into a dazzling gem of incredible beauty. Sunlight

130

breaks into a million rainbows if it hits the Heart, and its brilliance is blinding. It is roughly the size of two fists together, and was considered their crowning achievement. They placed it in a vault, but allowed the Corrian people to view it whenever they wished. They came to believe that it represented the soul of their fair city, though they were wrong."

"What happened at Corria? You said the Heart was their doom, but how?" Nessar's gravelly voice entered the conversation, and Eldwynn turned in his direction.

"Ah, the former thief. Well met, Nessar of Rualtha. I have heard of you, too. Old for a human, but I venture that there is life in you, yet!" He wheezed a laugh that turned into a weak cough. Eldwynn rested his head back on his pillows for a few long moments as he caught his breath, then eased forward once more. "Yes, yes, the Heart. I saw it once. It was truly awe-inspiring. Moreover, it has its own magick, a presence. One must take care not to get lost in its sparkle. You see, the Heart was their doom because they wanted more just like it. Their mines were flush with treasure of all kinds, but it was never enough. They kept digging, deeper and deeper, until one day, they dug so deeply they woke something that should have remained asleep. What they uncovered was spawned from the darkest evil, surely by one of Balroth's servants in the ancient past. It killed everyone, man, woman, and child alike. No one survived that dreadful day."

A cold draft suddenly whisked through the room, ruffling papers and raising gooseflesh on exposed skin. Trian quickly moved to the open doorway where he untied a heavy curtain and let it fall, settling the air in the room once more.

"Well, that wasn't spooky at all," Kiran muttered. She turned her attention back to the Weya. "What was it? Is it still there? Where is the Heart now?"

The LorMage chuckled softly, his laughter dry and rustling as if it were made of paper. "Questions, so full of questions are the young. What came up to devour the people of Corria was never determined. It disappeared back into the mines, taking its food with it. Only scant remains were found; an arm here, a foot there…and blood. Lots of

131

blood. No one stayed to investigate further, for those who did never returned. And the Heart?" The ancient Weya leaned back against his pillows as his energy faded. "No one knows. It may still be there, in its vault. Corria is extremely difficult to reach, and even more difficult to escape, should the evil presence persist. Even the Weya avoid it." Eldwynn sighed and relaxed, seemingly pleased that he could relay the tale to the Guardians. "What use could Gart have for the Heart? Brunar had treasure aplenty in the Hall of Jidaana, gifts from grateful monarchs over the centuries. What is one more diamond, no matter how large?"

Kiran replied, moving closer to the LorMage so that he could hear her better. "Well, we are reasonably certain that he's trying to find the Heart, as well as something called the Blood of Nimshi."

At the mention of the Blood, the LorMage uttered a faint gasp and began to tremble slightly under his covers. When he remained silent, Kiran continued.

"Based on notes we found, we think he is trying to bring back the soul of his long-dead wife so that he can...speak to her, apologize. We're not completely sure on that part."

The ancient Weya recoiled in horror, wheezing and clutching at the front of his robe. His cloudy eyes were wild and terrified. "No!" he whispered, "No, he cannot! He cannot possibly possess the power or the skills to work that spell! If he opens the portal, he might well doom us all! Even the Conclave of LorMages would not dare such a thing!"

Trian quickly moved to one side of the LorMage's bed and placed a reassuring hand on his fragile arm. "LorMage, please, try to remain calm."

The ancient, lined face turned towards the young Weya, the old man's fear plain to see. "You don't understand, Trian, I've already seen it! I had hoped with all of my being that it would not come to pass, that it was nothing but a bad dream. But after all these centuries, it is upon us!" Tears began to make their way down his face.

The Guardians exchanged pained looks, and Kiran tried to keep her voice calm and reassuring. "We're not going to let him do it if we can stop him! Gart is a good man. He saved us all at Alverton Falls. If we can just talk to him, we think we can convince him to let this go."

Nessar added his voice to the conversation. "Barring that, if we can stop him from finding either the Heart or that Blood stuff, then he can't do the summoning. Right?"

The LorMage gazed into the distance for a moment, then slowly nodded his head. "Yes," his voice was a thin whisper. "Yes, the spell requires both the Heart and the Blood. Without either, the portal simply won't open, no matter how strong the will and power of the Mage might be. The energies would not align properly, and a portal could not be created." Then his voice became desperate once more. "Even so, when I tell you that I have already seen it happen, I mean that the vision of what is to be has been with me for thousands of years. You had a vision, a vision that eventually brought you here, yes?"

Layton replied quietly, "Yes, LorMage. In it, we saw Gart, and others. And something vast was approaching, something dangerous. But we did not see what it was." Layton paused a moment as he considered. "I have often wondered since…how did these visions occur to all of us? I have never had one before, and to my knowledge, neither have my friends." He glanced up to see both Kiran and Nessar agreeing with him. Neither had been privy to visions before, especially not at the same moment in time, and with such impact. Layton continued, "What could have caused them?"

The LorMage was still and silent. His breath wheezed slowly in and out, and he remained silent for a time, gathering his thoughts and the strength to continue. When he spoke, his voice carried a faint note of warning. "There are forces of great evil out there, to be sure. So many places in which we should not meddle, for we risk destroying ourselves like children playing with fire." Then he surprised them by smiling widely. "But I must tell you that there are other forces at work, other consciousnesses. For whatever reason, they seem to aid us from time to time. The Goddess Rowann, she has been around far longer than this world upon which we live, you know. She is far more than you or even I understand. I, and others, have spent what seems like an eternity trying to understand magick, its nature, its uses and dangers. Magick connects us to unseen and powerful presences of this tiny world and also to beings that are so far beyond us that we must seem as insignificant insects to them. Our work reaches them much as the music a tiny cricket makes reaches our own ears." He paused to catch his breath. "But even we, Weya or human, might choose to catch a cricket and take it outside our home rather than simply squash it, for no other reason than because it seems right to us to do so."

Suddenly, the LorMage looked at Layton, his milky eyes struggling to focus. He shook his head, frustrated. "Bah! This won't do." He murmured a few words and waved the fingers of his right hand. They glowed briefly, a warm and gentle brightness that reflected in his eyes. When the glow faded, the faint cataracts had disappeared from his corneas, revealing irises that were a beautiful shade of blue.

"LorMage, you must not!" Trian reached over and touched the ancient one's arm, but the LorMage slapped the younger Weya's hand away.

"Yes, yes, I know it tires me! But it is necessary, now leave me be! This is important!" The LorMage turned his newly bright gaze back to Layton and a look of recognition appeared on his face. "Ah," he said, relief in his voice. "Yes, it makes perfect sense, now. Help me sit up, young man." Layton helped him struggle into a sitting position, and the ancient one allowed Trian to help him from the other side. Once he was upright, he struggled to catch his breath, still holding tight to Layton and Trian. His use of magick to clear his eyes had exhausted him down to his bones. As he rested, he gazed upon the faces of the Guardians one by one, carefully examining their features. Finally, one clawed hand rose, one skeletal finger pointing to a shelf carved into the far wall of the chamber. "There...move those things, and press hard on the wall beyond."

Layton walked over and carefully removed the ancient books that the LorMage indicated, then placed his palm on the stone wall as directed. "Here?" he asked.

"Yes, boy, and press with all of your strength!"

Layton pressed his hand into the stone, lightly at first, then harder. A bead of sweat rolled down his face from the effort, then he finally heard a faint click somewhere within the wall. A small section of the stone suddenly slid away, revealing a tiny cube-shaped hollow carved into the wall. Layton peered inside and found a small leather pouch, slightly bigger than his fist. It leaned to one side, as though full of something.

"That's it, boy! Take it. Take it out and bring it here," the ancient LorMage's voice was thick with excitement, overriding his weakness for the moment. Layton complied, reaching in and carefully picking up the pouch. It was simple, made of brown leather, old, but sturdy. It was tightly tied at the top with a slender twine, the string sealed with red wax. It was heavier than it looked. Layton took it and sat on the edge of the LorMage's cot, looking into the Weya's sky-blue eyes.

"I was but a boy when I received this," Eldwynn wheezed, "so many millennia past. Hardly taller than my father's knee, indeed. A human woman gave it to me and told me to keep it safely hidden and secret. At least, I thought she was a human at the time. Over the centuries, I've often pondered that and found myself thinking otherwise. Many times throughout my long life, I thought I saw her watching me from the edge of crowds, from far away, as if checking to see if I had kept my promise. When I would try to catch her, she was always gone." He coughed wetly, then sank back against the pillows as fatigue washed over him. He stayed silent only a moment before continuing, in spite of the effort it cost him. "She came to me while I was playing and made me promise to keep this safe. That one day, it would be necessary to save us all. That pouch should have fallen into dust aeons ago, but it looks the same today as it did then. I've never opened it." He coughed again, his frail body seizing sharply with each exhale, and then he lay back. He stayed silent longer this time before finding the strength to go on. "The woman touched my hand when she gave it to me, and I was given a vision that is still crystal-clear, even though my sight is no longer as such. In my mind's eye, she showed me four faces. One was a man whose face was bitterly scarred on one side, with eyes of ice that pierced me even then. I knew he was a man of immense power."

"Gart." Kiran stated what all the Guardians knew already.

"Yes," the LorMage nodded, the movement paining him. "Yes, he who once saved so many could also damn us all."

Nessar spoke up, his gravelly voice unusually gentle in the quiet of the small room. "And the others?"

The LorMage smiled at the aging human, then cast his gaze back to Layton. One withered hand came up and gently caressed Layton's bearded cheek. Eldwynn's ancient, wrinkled face broke into a wide smile, and his eyes, already beginning to cloud over again, began to stream tears of relief.

"I've waited so long...I'm so tired, so very tired. The faces were yours. All three of you." The LorMage breathed more quickly in his sudden excitement. "I kept it safe until you came. The warrior who travels without moving, who understands the stillness within the motion. The woman with a sharp blade and sharper tongue. And a man old in years but young at heart. You are the hope of the world."

Layton reached up and took the ancient Weya's hand in his own. "What must we do?"

For a few moments, there was no answer. The LorMage simply gazed at Layton as tears continued to fill the deep lines in his skin. Then, as the light began to fade from his eyes, the answer came. "Gart will go to the Shrine...of Malmathas during...the eclipse. Go there. Cast this...over the Gateway. It will seal...the portal...world...will be safe..." The breath finally eased out of the LorMage along with his spirit. He clutched Layton's hand until the end, until finally, it slipped from the warrior's grasp. The LorMage was gone.

Chapter 20

Gart blew the dust from the top of the pedestal in the eastern tower, allowing the runes on its surface to emerge. Under one arm, he held the next artifact, the next piece of the puzzle he knew he must solve. He was not much of an art lover, but he had to admit that the artifacts he had placed in the other towers had been quite beautiful. He had never seen works of such impressive craftsmanship.

The red onyx fire urn in the southern tower had been stunningly wrought, its surface the color of rubies beneath the dust that had covered it. It had not even been moved from its place on the pedestal, though a long-dead tumble of bones nearby indicated that a doomed priest had meant to take it. Gart had double-checked to see that the urn was still in its proper position, then had set a small brazier at the base of the short column. He had lit the oil and watched the flame burn for a moment to be sure it would stay lit, then poured more oil into the ancient urn.

Afterward, he had made his way to the eastern tower, the tower of Air, where he now stood. At first, he was unable to find the artifact, but finally, he located the sprawled form of another robe-clad skeleton several yards from the base of the tower. The priest had actually made it beyond the wall with his prize, but at the last, he had fallen in the same manner as his brethren. His pitiful, huddled form and ancient, decayed cloak had covered the stunning sculpture, and Gart carefully dug it out and cleaned it off.

It was stone, but inlaid with gems and gold and silver threads that brought it to brilliant life. Emerald vines entwined around each other to form a hollow circle. From the topmost arch of the circle hung a score of tiny silver chains and bells, windchimes that sparkled with music at the slightest breeze. Gart had roughly wrapped the piece in cloth to silence it until he was ready, and now he settled the wrapped sculpture onto its base and carefully removed the cover. He aligned the runes along the bottom so that they met properly, then stepped away from the pedestal. He took a moment to admire the way it sparkled beautifully in the sunlight that shone through the holes in the roof. He gazed at it for a few moments, on some level understanding what a treasure it was. Then he sighed. He had no need of it, other than as a tool to get what he needed to fulfill his mission. His face grew stern and he turned his back to the stunning sculpture, heading down the stairs toward the next part of his ritual. Keeping a careful eye out for dangerous creatures, Gart pulled out his notebook and checked his sketches against the nearest buildings he could identify. Making his best guess, he worked his way toward the center of the temple complex.

As Gart walked, he saw what could only have been other priests, barely recognizable as piles of moldering bones and decaying robes. Most appeared to have fallen quickly and without warning. Some were slumped in doorways, others simply sprawled in the street. He noticed that they all seemed to be moving away from the center of the complex, and he wondered for the hundredth time what had actually happened in the Temple of Nimshi. He shrugged at the thought. That was ancient history, and all he needed was the Blood. Once he had it, he could move on to his next target and begin his true quest.

Carefully stepping over another ancient corpse, Gart sighed. *Is it really right, what I'm doing?* he mused, as he so often had over the last few years. At first, he had been at peace with everything. At least, what passed for peace with him. Gradually, though, doubts had crept in. Guilt. Over time, his thoughts had turned darker and angrier. He had begun to pursue ideas that seemed harmless. But the ground upon which he now walked was anything but harmless. *This place is ill. The snake, the dead priests, nothing here is right. It's an evil place that I've come to, of my own choice. Does that make me evil too?*

Unbidden, the image of his wife's face appeared in his mind's eye. The scar tissue on the side of his face pulled tight as an unaccustomed smile found its way there. His heartbeat quickened at the thought of her, and although he was trying to take care with each step, he found himself moving faster towards the center of the temple grounds.

No. I love her. If I do this right, then I can see her again. And I can tell her... Gart's throat closed up with emotion at the thought of seeing her, talking to her, even for a few moments. His vision blurred briefly as tears filled his eyes, and he blinked them away, feeling his customary anger rise at the inconvenience. He had spent so many years angry at the world that the emotion seemed ever present to him. Only Gennie had ever pushed that anger away. Only she had made him truly happy. And soon he would see her again.

Wiping a sleeve across his face, he brought his focus back to the task at hand, picking his way through the misshapen shrubs and gnarled trees that had bullied their way through the pavestones. The map he had carefully drawn in his notebook helped him navigate the temple grounds, once so elegant and beautiful, but now fallen into ruin and decay. Something buzzed loudly and thumped forcefully against Gart's old hat, causing him to flinch away. It hit the ground nearby, and Gart was horrified to see what looked like a centipede with dragonfly wings, an ungainly and malformed thing that skittered into the shadows, clicking its wicked mandibles. Gart repressed a shudder, then resumed his search for the temple center.

He rounded the corner of a stone structure and found what he was looking for: a wide open space surrounded by a circular array of columns and archways. Though much of the stone had fallen, the general pattern of the pillars was clear. Gart moved through the columns and over the fallen debris until he reached the open center of the plaza. Dirt, lichen, and plant growth had obscured the original stone paving, and Gart frowned as he consulted his notes. He needed to see what was beneath it all. Looking back at the ground, he nodded to himself, knowing what he had to do.

He took a deep breath and let it out, then simply stood with his hands at his sides. He knew he could leave his Jidaan in the scabbard on his back for this. Gart flexed his will and instantly, the pommel of his Jidaan flared a brilliant emerald. He smiled faintly to himself as he recalled the very first time he had ignited the power of the Jidaan of Storms. He had called lightning down upon his own head and managed to blow a hole through his left boot. It was a wonder he had not killed himself, but then again, Guardians seemed to be a sturdy lot. His skills had multiplied

139

exponentially since then, and now, he called the power of the Jidaan almost without effort. The weapon glowed brightly, awaiting his command.

It took only an instant for him to form the proper picture in his mind with enough focus and detail that he was certain of the intended effect. Then he released the power of the Jidaan to make it so. The emerald pommel blazed even brighter, and the sickly breeze that had been blowing intermittently all day began to pick up. Gradually, it increased until Gart reached up and held his hat to keep it from blowing away. Debris and leaves began to swirl and churn in a circle in what Gart estimated was the center of the plaza. Faster and faster the wind blew, picking up dirt, rocks, anything that was loose, and a swirling funnel began to take shape.

It was a small vortex, not even a stone's throw across. As it sped faster and faster, it began to scour the centuries of dirt and grime from the stone pavings on the floor of the plaza, carrying it up and into the walls of the tornado. An emerald gleam of power shone from Gart's ordinarily bright blue eyes, and he concentrated on keeping the vortex under tight control. He did not want to destroy any of the surrounding stonework, only clear the thick layer of detritus from the plaza.

When the tornado's walls were heavy with dirt and sickly plant life, he willed the twister upward, sending it high into the sky, safely away from the temple of Nimshi. He sent his awareness with it, so that he might search for a suitable spot, and seeing one, he guided the whirl towards an open field beyond the edges of the forest. When the tornado was directly over the empty land, he let the winds die. The mass of earth and debris continued to spin for a moment, then fell harmlessly to the ground below. Gart released the power of the Jidaan, and the emerald obediently went dark once again. A wave of fatigue hit him, as it always did when he used the Jidaan, but he was ready for it. As he caught his breath, he examined his handiwork.

Where before, the central plaza had been a mess of fallen stone, earth, and malformed plant life, it had now been swept clean and looked almost new. Huge, square pavestones lay exposed beneath Gart's feet. In the center, a waist-high, flat dome had been revealed, nearly twice as wide across as Gart was tall. Surrounding the dome and equidistant from its center, four slender obelisks marked the cardinal directions. Pointed at their tops and thicker around than a man's waist near the bottom, they looked worn and smooth-edged, having been buffeted by the elements for centuries.

That has to be it, Gart thought to himself. He started towards the circular structure, keeping a watchful eye on his surroundings for anything that might try to eat him.

Once he got closer, he could see that the surface of the dome was cut into four equal sections. Gart lifted his gaze and saw the tops of each of the four towers he had visited, each standing taller than anything else on the temple grounds. Each obelisk was aligned perfectly with one of the towers and with one of the triangular panels on the dome. Gart could see that each panel was deeply inscribed with symbols that echoed those on the artifacts and pedestals within each tower. One each for Earth, Fire, Water, and Air. Gart had brought the fifth element with him: the magick of his own spirit.

Yes, this is it, he thought to himself. *When I open this portal, the Blood will be nearly in my grasp. One step closer to Gennie.* He gathered his strength, preparing for the task of opening a passageway that had been sealed centuries ago.

Suddenly, he stopped and turned one ear towards the north. He had heard something, but was unable to define exactly what it had been. A flicker of concern arose in him, since he had left Bessie and Beauty in that direction. Closing his eyes, he reached out with his sensory magick, searching for them, hoping they were unharmed. Moments later, he found Bessie, right where she had been tethered. She was fine, though agitated. Beauty, however, was not where he had left her. Alarmed, Gart expanded his search. He found her several yards away, sitting in the grass, panting good-naturedly.

The coppery tang of blood traveled across the magickal link to Gart's senses, both alarming and puzzling him until he stumbled onto its source: the body of a huge, dead...*thing,* lay not far from where Beauty rested. Gart sighed with relief as he probed the creature, which was missing its head, and therefore harmless. Its body was slightly smaller than Bessie, but larger than Beauty. It was similar to a jungle cat, but no cat had scales and extra limbs. Mutated like everything else in the area, it had a disturbingly alien feel to it. Gart roved over the area with his senses until he discovered the head of the beast nearby, its fanged mouth open and its three eyes staring into the sky. It had not been dead for long, but thanks to Beauty, it was no longer a threat.

Gart reached out and touched Beauty's mind, only to find her generally happy and satisfied, if a little wary. He sent her a wordless inquiry, which she answered in her way. She used images and feelings rather than actual words, but Gart had long since grown adept at understanding her. *Thing was bad. Scared Bessie. Killed it. Tasted awful.*

Gart sent her a feeling of thanks, then removed his awareness from her mind. He allowed himself the ghost of a smile. He knew he could count on Beauty. He had always been able to do that, ever since they found each other decades ago. She had seen far more years than any other dog her age should have, but Gart had found subtle ways to keep her strong with his magick, and he was glad of it. She had been his one constant companion, and he did not know what he would do without her.

Comforted that she was keeping an eye on things, Gart readied himself to take the next step. He pulled out his battered journal and thumbed through it one last time to be sure he had the necessary sequence firmly set in his mind. Then he tucked the little book back into his pack.

He took a deep breath as he cleared his mind for what he was about to do. He had always been able to move things simply by willing them to move, even though he had spent many years trying to suppress that ability and pretend that it did not exist. It was not enough that he had been attacked by a stray mongrel when he was little more than a toddler and given a faceful of terrifying scars; the fact that he had thrown the animal several yards away and viciously broken its neck was what started the rumors. After that, he had been ill-treated by everyone he had ever known. Sideways glances, barely overhead comments and

142

rude laughter, not to mention all the fights he had been goaded into until the young boys of the village finally learned that poking at Gart would only earn them a furious beating. He had been a lonely, angry boy that turned into a brooding, sullen man. Until Gennie.

Gennie had seen through his angry demeanor, and through his scars as well. She saw something in him that he had not known was there, and had fallen in love with him in spite of everything. No matter what anyone else ever said after that, he still had Gennie. He had truly been happy. When Rheann, his daughter, had been born, even the villagers began to warm up to him, as if having such a beautiful baby daughter had affirmed that Gart was not a total monster. Life had been almost good.

When Brunar had found him on the road, he had appeared as a ghostly apparition, holding the spear with the emerald pommel. He said that Gart had been Chosen, that he must come and fight against the evil of Mordak. Gart had refused. It had not been his fight. He had only wanted to be left alone with his family.

Just a few days later, Jor Dayne and a band of vicious creatures attacked Gart's village and killed everyone in sight, including his wife and daughter. All of Gart's happiness had been ripped away in a single night of fire and blood.

Gart had ultimately chosen to accept the Jidaan, seeing it only as a weapon that could bring him revenge. In time, he saw it for what it really was, an instrument for the greater good. But even though he had done his part and saved thousands from Mordak's evil, it had never truly been enough. Nothing had been enough. For a while, Ishabel had helped. The red-haired, feisty clan chieftain had fought alongside him, traveled with him, and even shared his bed for a time. But duty had called her away, and they had parted as friends. Not even Ishabel had been able to help him shed the burden of guilt he carried from Gennie's loss. It had only grown over the years, a weight that pressed harder and harder upon his shoulders each day.

Glancing at each of the towers in turn as he raised his magick, Gart allowed himself a burst of hope. *One step closer,* he repeated to himself. He closed his eyes and then engaged his magick. His body suddenly glowed gold as his power manifested, and four misty arms of energy sprang from him and stretched towards each of the crumbling towers.   He knew he had to focus on all four tasks simultaneously, and his brows knotted with concentration. Strength he had, enough to lift enormous boulders with ease, but this task required precision rather than magickal muscle.   Gradually, awareness of his body fell away as he began to see the pedestals in each of the towers.

Earth, Air, Fire, and Water, he had to engage each of the artifacts at the same time. Carefully, he lifted the bowl of water in the north tower and the jar of dirt he had left in the western tower, guiding them through the air until they were poised just over their respective urns, where he could easily pour their contents into place. The fire urn was a little trickier. Gart lifted the flaming brazier up more slowly, keeping a watchful eye on the flames to see that they did not go out. The Air artifact would be the easiest, and Gart readied himself to use the tiniest bit of power from his Jidaan to engage its chimes.   Heartbeats passed as Gart maintained his focus. He would not be rushed.

Sheathed at his back, the Jidaan's emerald pommel began to glow over Gart's shoulder, and he willed a breeze to blow. Holding the other parts at the ready, he guided the breeze away from himself and through the ruined temple, around the broken buildings and thorny ruins until it approached the tower of Air. He sent the gust of air into the window, and at the precise moment the sparkling, dancing notes of the windchimes rang out, Gart poured earth and water into their urns and set fire to the last artifact.

Gart instantly felt the old magick of the temple awaken, an intense tingling, then a burning that seemed to start deep in his bones. It felt as though his insides were on fire, but he ignored the pain and kept his focus on his goal. *For Gennie.*

He felt the rumble in his feet before he heard it, and the earth began to shake, just as Gart had known it would. Looking at the stone dome ahead of him, he spoke the words with all of his will behind them, "Altak mhi hagath orr!"

144

The rumbling intensified, and the dome split along the creases, the triangular stone panels slowly receding to reveal a darkened tunnel beneath. A set of stone stairs led downwards from the north, disappearing into a stygian darkness.

The panels disappeared completely, leaving a perfectly circular doorway to an underworld Gart knew only little about. Gart leaned over to look inside and saw two more figures covered with decaying fabric. More priests. One of them seemed to have a long piece of wood in his skeletal hands. Puzzled, Gart looked at the wall nearby and saw that the wood lever had been broken off at the base of some sort of mechanism. *The door handle?* Gart thought to himself. The more he looked, the more he decided that it did, indeed, look as though the priest had purposely broken the handle off at its base, rendering the door inoperable from the inside. Moreover, every exposed bone that Gart could see appeared to be broken, some in more than one place.

Well, that can't be good.

Gart looked around and noticed a broken stone bench nearby. Relieved to be using his power in a more familiar way, he picked up the heavy object and moved it easily through the air, the golden glow of his magick radiant in the shadows of the stony ruins. He placed the ragged chunk of granite on the top step, where it would hold the door open if the panels tried to close while he was below ground.

Satisfied that his escape route was assured, Gart pulled a torch from his pack and lit it. Shouldering his pack, he held the torch in his left hand and drew his black-bladed sword with his right. He had other ways of lighting his way, but sometimes, fire more easily kept bad things from getting too close. Remembering his goal, Gart left the world above and stepped into darkness.

145

Chapter 21

Teryn rode behind Reyanna on Bettina, with Ginn riding alongside. They had made good time since leaving the gang of bandits. The road to the north stretched out ahead of them, and they planned to stop for the night within the hour. Having never met a priestess of Rowann, much less one of the spider-riders, Reyanna was most eager to pump Teryn for as much information as she could get.

"So you've been living with a colony of gigantic spiders for the last year?" Reyanna could not keep a note of disbelief out of her voice. Having seen one of those gigantic spiders in the flesh, she was full of questions. "That's amazing!"

Teryn laughed in delight. "Well, thank you! Yes, although I had been told of the possibility when I entered the ranks of the Sisters of Rowann, I never dreamed I would be chosen as one of the emissaries. A new one is chosen every so often, usually each year, give or take. We've learned an awful lot from the Queen, and we like to think that she has learned a lot from us as well. Certainly, they eat far fewer stray travelers now that we help them keep livestock nearby."

Amused, Ginn added, "I'm sure those travelers would be very grateful, if they knew the fate they'd been spared."

"Indeed. The spider colony is isolated enough that they don't see many people, but they much prefer it that way. Humans are not as tasty, they say, and they truly do not wish conflict with our kind. They only want to be left alone to live their lives, as any of us would."

"What kind of things do you learn from her? From the Queen Kulcania, I mean?" Reyanna's eyes were wide as she imagined the queen, big as a house, from Teryn's description, and apparently an adept of a kind of magick that had previously been unknown to the priestesses of Rowann.

Teryn thought for a moment as she decided how to put her answer into words that Reyanna would understand.

The girl was bright and knowledgeable as any Weya Ranger, but thoroughly unschooled in magick, it seemed.

"Well, much of what she teaches us helps us reach deeper within ourselves, if that makes sense. She has a strong connection with the magick of the earth, far stronger than our own, and that's saying something. Through it, we can see things that were hidden from us before; the past, the present, and sometimes even the future, for those of us who are stronger and more experienced. I'm still a young Sister, but I know a thing or two," Teryn smiled slyly as she spoke. "And Kulcania has been most generous with her teaching. She's taught me to memory-walk, and it has been very illuminating."

Ginn spoke up immediately. "Tell me of this 'memory-walk'. What is it?" He cast a glance at Reyanna and raised an eyebrow. With his hands, he signaled her. *Could she help?* She returned his gaze with a slight shrug of her shoulders and signaled back, *I don't know.* Both of them listened intently as Teryn began to speak.

"Well, it's a procedure. A spell, if you will, that allows the priestess to enter a person's mind, and from there, experience a specific memory in a very vibrant and clear way as though she were watching the events unfold around her. It enables her to see things that the person often has forgotten, uncover suppressed memories. For instance, it could be used to discover details that might identify the perpetrator of a crime, or find something that was lost. The process can also be helpful in easing trauma. I'm looking forward to bringing this skill back to the other Sisters and to our community. I think I can help a lot of people with it."

Reyanna's mind churned furiously. She had spent a lot of time thinking about the vision that brought her on this quest, and had been continually frustrated by it. Although certain parts seemed burned into her mind, there was a strong feeling that she had missed much more than she could recall. There were blurry figures that, identified, might at least shed some light on the scene that had struck her with such power.

"What about..." Reyanna paused, wondering if she should continue, but then decided to press on. "What about visions? Let's say that someone experienced a very powerful vision, something that involved other people, as well. Could you help the seer to learn more about it?"

"Hmmmm…" Teryn thought for a moment, then replied with a hint of amusement. "Might this unnamed seer be, shall we say, a 'friend' of yours?"

Reyanna blushed furiously, but Ginn allowed himself to chuckle aloud. "I like you, Sister Teryn. You are quite direct."

"Thank you, kind sir," Teryn bowed as much as she could, seated behind Reyanna. "I've found that it often saves time." To Reyanna, she said, "It's possible, of course. I would need to know more about the situation, but it sounds like something I could work with." She laid a reassuring hand on Reyanna's shoulder. "I'm a priestess of the order of Rowann. I live to serve and help others wherever I may. I would be honored to help you, if I can."

For a time, the only sound was the wind in the trees and the clip-clopping of hooves on the road as Reyanna thought over Teryn's words. She had been taught that the priestesses of Rowann were above reproach. Like the Weya, they believed they should help others wherever possible, and care for the land so that all life would benefit. And apparently, the priestesses were capable warriors, as well. Had she meant any harm to either of them, Teryn would likely have already demonstrated the fact. Finally, Reyanna broke the silence.

"Sister Teryn," she began, "I would very much appreciate your help. I know where we are going, though I am not exactly sure why. I received a powerful vision back in Allinshae, and it frightened me. Our LorMage saw it too. The Elders decided that I should journey to the Keep of the Guardians to find a man named Gart, and since I thought that would be the only way to learn more, I agreed with them. Much has happened since then, and there is so much I don't know. It's hugely frustrating. We've already been attacked by someone who uses evil magick," Reyanna paused as she felt Teryn stiffen in alarm, but pressed on, "and I think it all has to be connected. After what I saw in the vision, I know in my heart that I must do *something*, but I can't be sure that what I'm doing is right. Any light you could shed on my situation would be most welcome, Sister."

Teryn reached around Reyanna's waist and surprised her with a big hug. "It is my great honor to help you, Reyanna! It seems it was no accident that we ran into each other. The goddess Rowann works in odd ways at times. I would not be surprised if this was her doing. When we stop ahead and get settled, I'll see what I can do."

Reyanna's face brightened with a wide smile of relief, and her blue eyes sparkled. "Thank you, Sister. That would mean the world to me. I won't get my hopes up, but anything you could tell me will be more than I know right now."

They rode on, their conversation drifting back to Teryn's time with the Sisters of Rowann, as well as the spider queen, Kulcania. Teryn blushed as Reyanna responded to her stories with bright enthusiasm. Ginn remained quiet, happy to listen to the two women talk. He had lived alone for many years, and had grown used to talking very little, but the sound of feminine voices cheered him mightily, especially Teryn's.

When the sky overhead was turning deep purple, the trio turned off the road and moved into the forest to find a secluded place to camp. Reyanna found a sheltered grove well out of sight of the road, and there they dismounted and began to settle in for the night. The twilight deepened into evening and the stars began to twinkle in the black velvet of the sky, like diamonds sprinkled by the hand of a goddess. Ginn sat near their tiny campfire and heated a small pot of stew for them to share. After they had eaten and tended to their other needs, the two women sat together while Ginn sat away from them. The Weya sat with his back to the fire to preserve his night vision and kept watch.

Teryn took Reyanna's hands in her own and looked into her eyes, surprised at the brightness of them. "Why, Reyanna, your eyes are striking. Almost like those of the Weya."

Reyanna blushed, but she had heard that comment before. "Yes, thank you. I forget about them until I meet someone new. I'm used to them."

Teryn smiled and got back to the task at hand. "All right then, your part of the memory walk is actually very simple; you will close your eyes and think about the vision you had. The rest is up to me. You may not notice anything different while it's happening. You just go through it in your mind, as clearly as possible, and if you reach the end of it, just go back to the beginning again. Keep doing that until I am finished. Do you understand?"

Reyanna nodded, both excited and nervous, but willing to follow Sister Teryn's directions to the letter. Teryn gave Reyanna's hands a reassuring squeeze.

"All right then, take a deep breath and let it out slowly," Reyanna did so, and Teryn repeated the command, and again, Reyanna did as she was bidden. The priestess began to breathe in time with her, gently guiding her to take longer, deeper breaths. In moments, Reyanna was calmer, her heartbeat slower, and her mind more at ease. In a soft, gentle voice, Teryn continued. "Everything is all right. You are calm. Your mind is clear. All is well. Just breathe." Teryn began working the spell silently in her mind as she had been taught, working through the intricate series of visualizations necessary to split her awareness so that she could be in two places at once. She needed to be able to talk to Reyanna, to guide her until she was fully engaged with the memory of her vision, then be ready to send herself into that memory at the same time. It was a challenge, but Sister Teryn had practiced incessantly, and the skill was hers. "Now, take yourself to the beginning. It's all right. Nothing in the vision can touch you, you are just watching. Breathe, relax, everything is all right..." Her voice was its own magick, helping Reyanna drift into a sleep-like state that enabled her to see more clearly. Her chin lowered, and Teryn felt her relax completely. Satisfied that Reyanna was experiencing her memory of the vision, Sister Teryn engaged the spell. She closed her eyes for a moment, and felt the *shift* as her awareness left her body and went somewhere else.

She felt the change before she saw it, a powerful rumbling, an overwhelming vibration that suddenly terrified her. When Sister Teryn opened the eyes of her spirit, she found herself in a nightmare.

150

Chapter 22

"He asked me to lay these out before you arrived." Trian's voice was quiet and firm, though he had to keep wiping at his face with a kerchief to keep the tears from falling onto the books he indicated. "I did not understand why at the time, but now, I see that he must have foreseen your coming." The heartbroken Weya carefully opened the largest book to a place marked with a smaller piece of paper, displaying a detailed map of the continent.

Kiran leaned over the table to get a closer look, and found herself wishing for a kerchief as well. She never thought she would live to see the day when when a Weya just passed away quietly before her eyes; it seemed more fitting that a Weya die under more adventurous circumstances. This just felt wrong. She gathered her wits, sniffed a few times and commented, "This isn't right. Where's Laro? And Rualtha looks so tiny."

Trian pointed one finger to a finely scribed set of runes in one corner of the map. "According to this, it's because this map is from approximately three thousand years ago. Not everything was then as it is now. For instance, Caldea is here, rather than the New Caldea which you may recognize. And here," he indicated another spot on the map, not far from Caldea, "is Corria."

Nessar moved forward, pulling out his journal as he did so. "Perfect. Let me see that." He leaned over the book and squinted at the elegant lines and smooth swirls. The map, although faded with age, was beautiful in the way that only Weya art could be, but Nessar was only concerned with landmarks and distances. He scribbled in his little book until he felt he had every bit of discernable information about Corria's location, then he stood up straight and sighed. "All right, then. We can find this, and with snot-rat here making his Gates, it won't take nearly the time it would otherwise."

Layton raised an eyebrow at the jest, an old nickname Nessar had given him, but he said nothing. He, too, had been saddened at the passing of the LorMage, but moreover, he had been exceedingly shocked at being the focus of a premonition from thousands of years past. He knew he would have to think on that later. For now, they had work to do.

"Ha ha, funny, old man," Kiran retorted, sticking up for Layton. "You're just jealous because he's the good-looking one." Without waiting for a response, she turned her attention to Trian. "What can you tell us about the Blood of Nimshi, or the Shrine of Malmathas?"

Trian had mostly regained his composure, though his bright amber eyes were still red with unshed tears. "Nimshi? Ah..." he stood still for a moment, his mind working furiously. "That does, how do you humans say...ring a bell?" Glad to have something to focus upon, he moved to the other side of the table, where a handful of other books lay neatly stacked. "The LorMage asked that I pull these books out as well, though I recall he went through and discarded several, as though he was not quite certain which ones would be needed. He was frustrated at the last, I gathered. He kept saying he wished he could remember it all. These are the ones he finally settled on, but I don't think they have what you need." Trian moved to the shelves across the room and began to peruse the spines of the orderly rows of books. He stopped once, then again, and finally pulled a slim black volume from a top shelf. "Ah, yes, if it is anywhere, it is in here."

He turned, opened the book, and flipped through the first several pages. Suddenly he stopped, and his breath caught in his throat.

"What is it? What have you found?" Kiran struggled not to be overloud in the small room.

Trian raised his amber gaze from the pages of the book and regarded them all with a worried expression that looked out of place on a Weya. "Your friend is apparently in the habit of finding the most dangerous and tragic places in which to fumble around. Nimshi was a temple of an order that arose to worship an earth power of some kind. That power corrupted the surrounding land, even as they thought it was thriving. It made them all sick, perverting their bodies and minds into something awful, though some resisted its power at the last. It was too late, though. It

152

killed them all. And if Gart is headed there, it may well kill him, too." He closed the book and handed it to Kiran. "Take it. There is one other copy, which we have here. There is a map inside, clear enough that you should read it easily. Corria is much closer, though. I would go there first." Trian pulled the larger map around and scanned it. "Corria is between here and the Shrine of Malmathas, which is in these mountains, here." His finger landed on a jagged little mountain range within the Poravian Mire. Nessar scribbled the location in his journal, quickly sketching the landmarks that surrounded it. "The Shrine is an ancient place of great power, though no one goes there anymore because it's so hard to reach, even for Weya. There are things even we avoid in the Mire." He raised his jeweled eyes to Kiran. "In roughly the middle of the range, there is a deep cleft in the stone of one of the cliffs that faces east. The shrine is inside somewhere. That's all I know."

"Thank you, Trian. We know this must be hard for you." Layton placed a gentle hand on Trian's shoulder.

"Indeed. He was my father. Thank you, Guardian." Trian sighed. "However, the task that awaits you three is far more difficult, I think. I hope the Goddess Rowann guides your steps; you may need the help."

Chapter 23

Ginn glanced over at the two women seated near the campfire, facing each other with both hands entwined. Teryn's voice was low and calming, almost musical, and Ginn could see Reyanna visibly relax. Their eyes were closed; he heard the priestess take a deep breath, then let it out. Suddenly, Ginn felt a hum of power, felt its tingle on his skin. A faint lavender glow surrounded Sister Teryn, shining warmly in the dark. The glow crept down her arms and enveloped her hands, and then Reyanna's as well. It continued up the young woman's arms and quickly covered her entire body, completely enfolding her within the spell that Teryn had wrought.

Ginn nodded to himself. The Priestesses of Rowann had always been strong with their earth magick, and it did not surprise him that even one so young as Teryn was able to raise such an enchantment. Indeed, as one who had spent time with the Spider Queen Kulcania, she was probably one of the more powerful members of her order.

Just then, Ginn felt a subtle change in the atmosphere of the forest around him, and he snapped to alertness. He let his eyes scan the surrounding trees and listened as he had been taught centuries ago, his pointed Weya ears taking in far more sounds than those of the humans. Something thumped out in the dark, and Ginn could tell it was not just an animal. He pulled his bow, held three arrows in the same hand as the bow and nocked a fourth arrow to string with his other hand. He could draw and loose in a single, fluid motion if need be. He turned to glance at the two women, still quiet, still glowing, communing within the structure of Teryn's spell. After reassuring himself that the two were safe where they were, he noiselessly slipped into the forest on the southern side of the clearing, watchful for anything on two legs. In moments, it was as though he had never existed at all, so easily had he disappeared into the trees and brush.

The two women continued to sit in silence, the pale purplish glow of Teryn's magick shimmering gently as the moments crept by. Suddenly, Teryn gasped in horror, and

154

the light of her spell winked out all at once. Her eyes flew open as she scurried away from Reyanna like a crab, only to stumble and land on her back on the grass.

Reyanna's eyes popped open and she, too, gasped as she saw the naked fear on her new friend's face. "Sister Teryn, are you all right? I'm so sorry! What did I do?" She sat forward, reaching out for the fallen priestess, praying fervently that she had not been harmed.

The priestess scrambled to her feet, and once there, managed to catch her breath. Embarrassed, she began to straighten out her clothes and dust them off as she searched for words.

"I..." Teryn began. "I'm so sorry! I should not have reacted that way." She cast her eyes down as they quickly filled with angry tears, and her next words were directed at herself. "I'm a priestess of Rowann, not a scared little girl! I'm better than that!" Then she raised her glittering gaze back to Reyanna's. "Again, I'm deeply sorry. The vision was so strong, I just, well, I wasn't expecting the power of it, that's all. It must have been so frightening for you."

Reyanna instinctively opened her arms and the priestess moved into her comforting embrace. "I'm the one that should be sorry! I should have warned you how intense it was." She held Teryn for a few moments more, allowing the woman to regain her composure. "Can you tell me what you saw? Beyond what I told you, I mean." Sister Teryn sniffed once and then moved away from Reyanna, holding the younger woman at arm's length. Teryn's face brightened.

"Yes! It was scary, but I saw several people quite clearly. I can describe them to you, I think. Some were Weya, others were not. Most importantly, though, I saw..."

Sister Teryn suddenly grunted and fell forward into Reyanna's arms again, stumbling to her knees and nearly taking Reyanna with her to the ground.

"Teryn? Teryn!" As Reyanna helped her down, she saw an arrow jutting from Teryn's back. "What? No!" Furious, she pulled her dagger with one hand and reached for her bow with the other, intending to bring it to herself with her magick. Another arrow slammed into her own chest, high near the shoulder. The impact spun her around and sent her down to one knee in blinding agony, her left arm suddenly useless. A cry of pain and rage erupted from her throat as she knelt in the dirt, helpless and in more pain than ever in her life. "Ginn!" she called, desperately hoping he was nearby.

"Your elf can't help you now, you trollop!" A man's voice, loud and rude, echoed in the clearing. "It cost us some men, but he won't be helping anyone anytime soon!"

Tears of pain and anguish rolled down her face as she stared at the bedraggled, hard-looking man that stepped into view from the trees. She recognized him as one of the bandits they had left tied to the tree with spider silk. Somehow, he had escaped. As she watched, three other men materialized from the far side of the small clearing, also from the same ragged band.

"And I don't see your spider, either! That makes it all so much easier!"

Reyanna tried to move her arm and was rewarded with a blinding bolt of pain. She looked down at Teryn and saw that she was still breathing, but shallowly. Of Ginn, there was no sign. Despair washed over her in an icy flood.

The men began to laugh, and she heard them start arguing over which man would get which girl first. The fact that both were wounded and one possibly near death apparently made no difference to them. They laughed again, and Reyanna felt something snap inside her. Anger flared, a white-hot heat that blossomed deep within her body. She heard herself grunt, not in pain this time, but in wrath. The fire of her magick burned hotly, greater than it ever had before, and she quickly lost herself in it. It scoured away the pain in her shoulder, and she saw the arrow disintegrate as magickal flames burst from her body, enveloping her in a roiling nimbus of fire. She gasped as her clothes burned away, leaving her naked, but unafraid. The slender web of burn scars she had carried since she was a child glowed with white heat. They snaked across her right arm from wrist to shoulder and across her upper back, clearly visible against her pale skin, an incandescent tattoo. She snapped her gaze back to the men and saw that they had abruptly stopped talking and were staring at her. A grin crawled across her face as horror found its place on theirs.

She was an inferno, a bonfire of scorching power. Her eyes, normally a startling shade of blue, were pools of flame. She dropped her dagger to the ground, barely noticing that the leather wrapped around the handle had burned away, and she rose to her full height as she turned to face them. Her smile, dangerous and wild, broadened. She had taken only three steps towards the band before they broke and ran. Or at least, tried to.

Reyanna raised her hands and sent a sheet of molten power blasting from her fingertips. It flew across the little clearing, searing the air as it hungrily sought the fleeing ruffians. It impacted them in their heads and shoulders as they ran, leaving them no time to scream. The power instantly incinerated everything it touched, sending their lifeless bodies hurtling face-first into the earth like discarded ragdolls. They fell in a tumble of lifeless arms and legs at the edge of the clearing, settling into an ignoble mass of bodies.

Reyanna lowered her hands and glared at their corpses, her body still burning, the flames of her magick writhing and roiling around her naked form. She stood there for several heartbeats, a malicious grin still on her face as her power ruled her. Then, her face fell. The flames of her magick dwindled, burning lower and lower as each second passed. Reyanna's fire slowly slithered back inside her body and disappeared, leaving the clearing and its tiny campfire nearly dark by comparison. Reyanna's chin dropped forward, her eyes closed. She swayed unsteadily on her feet, then crumpled into a heap on the grass, unconscious.

A few minutes later, a battered and exhausted Ginn staggered out of the trees near where the outlaws had appeared, his sword bloody and his quiver empty of arrows. His left eye was nearly swollen shut, and he cradled his ribs on that same side as he limped through the dead bodies on the ground. He looked them over in disbelief, taking in the scorched skin and broken necks. He wondered how the priestess had managed to do that, knowing that a Sister's magick was generally used for healing rather than as a weapon. Ginn knew well that the warrior priestesses preferred hand to hand combat due to its honesty, but magick had most certainly been used here.

His eyes fell on Reyanna's naked body on the ground a few yards away, and he gasped at the sight. Grimacing in pain, he began limping quickly towards her, even as he saw the arrow jutting out of Sister Teryn's back where she lay a few feet farther away.

He reached Reyanna first. "Reyanna! Are you hurt?" Ginn grunted in pain as he knelt to check the pulse at her neck. Relieved to find it steady and strong, he quickly moved towards Sister Teryn, who was obviously in far worse shape. He knelt next to her and began to gently probe the arrow wound. "Sister, can you hear me?" He looked down at her face and saw that a lock of her hair was covering her eyes. He used his fingers to move it aside and found her looking up at him, her breaths quick and shallow.

"Ah," she answered, her voice thin and laced with pain, hardly more than a whisper. "Not dead yet. Rowann...still has use for me, I think."

Ginn smiled, ignoring the discomfort it caused his bruised face. "The Goddess has always been wise." He continued to probe the area around the arrow that protruded from her back. The shaft looked well made, and for that, at least, Ginn was thankful. It would likely not splinter in the wound, and he could concentrate on getting the barb out instead. "I can get this out of you, but it's going to hurt. I have to stop the bleeding after that, but I think you'll make it."

A pained grin flickered onto Sister Teryn's face. "Do your worst, sir. I once fell off of the mission's roof into a rosebush. This is nothing." She breathed as deeply as she dared as she gathered her strength. Ginn moved toward the arrow, but suddenly, Teryn stopped him. "Wait. Reyanna...is she all right? I heard some very strange things, but I couldn't see."

Ginn looked over his shoulder at Reyanna before answering. The girl was still curled on her side, sleeping soundly. Her naked skin shone in the light of the silvery moon that had risen, and Ginn saw the tracery of thin burn scars that wound up her right arm and across her upper

158

back. He watched her body rise and fall with the rhythm of her breathing, then turned back to the priestess. "As far as I can tell...yes, she's fine."

As he went to work on the arrow, Ginn wondered if that was completely true.

Chapter 24

Keeping his sword ready and the torch held high, Gart carefully followed the staircase as it plunged deep into the earth. The stairs formed a counterclockwise spiral, moving ever downward, away from the sun and sky and into the dark unknown. Gart tried to reach out with his magick to get an idea of what waited below, but no matter how he tried, he could not sense anything beyond what was a few yards ahead. It was like trying to see underwater in a muddy lake. He grunted in frustration and forced himself to pay extra attention to the input from his eyes and ears. Step by step, he made his way deeper, already missing the open skies above.

He followed the stairs for what seemed like an eternity, looking upwards every so often until the circular hole he had come through was nothing more than a tiny speck of blue in the dark overhead. A shiver rolled down his spine as he realized just how far away from the world above he actually was, but he kept up his pace. Nothing would stop him now that he was this close.

Gradually, the temperature began to rise, and huge beads of sweat began to form on Gart's skin and trickle down his back. Where the air above ground had been muggy, damp, and smelling of rot and decay, the air this far down was dry and smelled of earth. It was a welcome trade, but the heat was starting to take its toll. Gart slid his sword into its scabbard and pulled a waterskin from his pack. He took a long pull on it, then put the skin away. Feeling somewhat refreshed, Gart drew his sword once more and continued his descent.

Finally, Gart saw the spiral stairs end a few flights below. The flickering illumination of his torch revealed that the circular shaft terminated in a flat stone floor, split into four quadrants with the same four elemental symbols deeply engraved in the middle of each one. They were arranged in the same order as the symbols on the upper dome had been, and Gart guessed they also echoed the placement of the towers far above. All was silent but for the shuffling of Gart's boots and the snapping and popping of his torch. Gart reached the bottom and slowly edged out onto the center of the floor, keeping his sword and torch at the ready. He could feel the weight of his Jidaan at his back, and it comforted him.

There was only one exit that Gart could see. A pair of carved pillars stood on either side of an open passageway that led to the south. The same kind of writhing sigils decorated the archway that connected the pillars, and they pulled at Gart's gaze, making his head ache. He shook his head to clear it, and glanced around to confirm that it was the only way out. A wispy, dry breeze came from the tunnel, drying the sweat on Gart's brow. Gart quickly sheathed his sword so he could doff his old hat and wipe the stinging sweat from his eyes. That done, he replaced the hat and brought his sword up as before. Again, he reached out with his magick, but found that his awareness was still somehow limited. Something was dampening it, and that was bothering him more as every moment passed. Nevertheless, he knew that he had to continue. Gart made his way over to the opening, his eyes scouring every inch of the stone that surrounded him. Satisfied that no traps or pitfalls awaited him at the portal, he moved through the archway with purpose.

The tunnel's walls were rough and irregular, and Gart surmised that the archway had been carved around a natural formation. The floor, however, had been smoothed over so that it provided level footing. Gart hurried as much as he dared. Hard-learned lessons had taught him that speed could kill, if it brought him into a bad situation unprepared. He began to control his breathing, slowing it down, and his heartbeat slowed along with it. The thought of untold tons of stone pressing down on him from above still made him uneasy, and he forced himself to stay calm in spite of it. Step by step, he pushed on.

A dim, red glow appeared in the distance, and Gart squinted at it, trying to discern more detail. As he approached, he saw that the tunnel broadened ahead into a much bigger passage that seemed to lead into a large open space. A hot, dry wind made his torch flame dance and his throat ache as he breathed, but he was encouraged. The Blood of Nimshi could not be much farther.

As he approached the opening, the heat grew, suddenly becoming more intense with each step. His lips became parched, his skin began to sting and tears streamed from his eyes as his breathing became more labored. Finally, he was forced to stop to catch his breath. The heat was too much. He leaned his torch against one wall of the tunnel; the cavern ahead appeared to be bright enough that he would not need it anyway.

Gart reached into himself and found his magick awaiting his call. It swirled within him, ready and willing, as always. He cleared his mind, then released the magick to do his bidding. His body glowed a bright gold as his power came to the fore, and he guided the energy until it formed a protective sphere around him. Sending his consciousness into the sphere, he gave it purpose, assigned it function. He willed the sphere to pull heat from its interior and then expel it, thus keeping his body cool. He stood silently for a full minute, adjusting the sphere's process so it would automatically adapt to whatever temperatures he might encounter, leaving him unharmed within its confines. When it functioned as intended, he anchored it to his own center so that it would move as he did.

When he felt all was in order, Gart moved towards the opening again. The strain was considerable, but Gart knew the limits of his magick, and this was well within them. Maintaining the sphere would be a constant drain on his power, so he knew that time would quickly become important. As he stepped through the opening, he felt the stress on his sphere increase tenfold as a wave of intense heat battered it. He forced himself to remain calm as he scanned the new chamber he had just entered.

The stone had become black and porous in the next room, which was easily big enough to hold the entire temple inside its confines. The ruddy glow had come from a wide river of molten magma that wound through the center of the chamber in an undulating, serpentine path. The liquid rock rolled slowly along, its surface changing from red to orange, then yellow, and back to red as it moved through the earth. Its heat was unbearable. The river passed from Gart's left to his right, and he marveled at its terrible beauty. Off to one side, he spotted a bridge of black stone

162

that spanned the flow. It was carved with the same runes as the pillars and archway, and Gart had to avert his eyes.

Then he saw his goal, and his heartbeat quickened. Across the molten river, a path of huge, black flagstones led from the bridge to a great altar that had been carved directly into the far wall of the cavern. Sinister runes had been inlaid into the walls and altar itself, the symbols gleaming with an unknown metal that was apparently impervious to the heat. The center of the altar was dominated by what looked like a fountain, but no water flowed there. Instead, a black, shiny liquid, its surface like that of quicksilver, flowed and bubbled from an ornate aperture that jutted from the stone itself. It cascaded into a circular basin that appeared to drain back into the stone somehow, so that the continuous stream of Blood would not spill over the edges. A sense of dread settled on Gart as he took in the sight. It gave him a chill in spite of the intense heat that surrounded him. Although the fount was his goal, this was not a place where good things happened. Whatever earth power the priests had been worshipping, it had not been the benevolent spirit they might have thought it to be.

A wave of fatigue hit Gart as the intense heat assaulted the outside of his magickal shield. He steadied himself, taking a moment to recover his composure, then he began to hurry toward the bridge. He knew that, although he was stable, he would only be able to hold the shield for a finite amount of time. He did not want to be in the chamber when his strength ran out. He wondered how the former priests of Nimshi had survived the heat and then realized that the lava flow must have been much lower in the trench back then. It had likely risen in the centuries since Nimshi fell.

Moving as fast as he dared, he stepped up to the bridge and began to make his way over it. The heat from below pushed hard at his shield, and he quickened his step so he could escape it as soon as possible. A dozen paces took him to the other side of the bridge, and he was relieved when his boots landed on the black pavestones that marked the path. In spite of the cooler temperature he had created within his magickal bubble, sweat had begun to

163

pour down his face, both from the exertion of holding the bubble in place and from the excitement at locating the Blood of Nimshi. It was right in front of him, mere yards away. He scanned the altar carefully as he approached it, keeping a watchful eye out for traps and other dangers. He saw nothing but carved black stone and the silvery-black liquid that had to be the Blood.

When he reached the base of the altar platform, Gart sheathed his sword and slid his backpack off so that he could retrieve what he needed. He drank more from his waterskin, dismayed to see that it was nearly empty, then tucked it back into place. Then he reached in and grabbed the object he had painstakingly created for just this purpose: a small stone vessel. The vessel was roughly made, a bit larger than an ale mug, but fitted with a stone stopper and lined with lead. Symbols had been chiseled around the lid, looking shaky, but clear and easy to read. Gart would never pass for a skilled craftsman, but it was solid and serviceable. Gart closed the pack and lifted it by one of its straps, carrying it with him as he approached the fountain so that it would remain within his protective shield of magick.

Moving with care, Gart stepped towards the fountain, dropping his pack at his feet so he would have both hands free. He unstoppered the vessel and began to reach for the Blood as it bubbled and flowed out of its spigot and into the basin before him. A sense of pressure, of power, began to make itself known to Gart, and he stopped with his hands raised in front of him, mere inches from the Blood. He shook his head curtly, but the feeling persisted. Then the whispers began, and Gart knew that the Blood was trying to reach him. He knew, too, that his time was running short, as he was growing wearier by the minute.

Frowning with determination, Gart ignored the odd sensations that assaulted him and carefully filled the vessel with the shiny, slippery liquid. When it was nearly full, he moved it away from the flow and used his magick to scrape off the drips that had landed on the jar's outside surface. He had the feeling that touching the stuff with his hands would be a bad idea. He carefully affixed the lid to the jar and twisted it shut, elation filling his heart. Moving more

164

quickly, he wrapped the jar in a cloth and put it into a leather bag, which he tied shut with a leather thong. As sweat poured down his face, stinging his eyes and clouding his vision, he replaced the now-full vessel into his pack and slid his arms through the straps.

As he stood, settling the pack firmly on his back, he noticed something on the opposite side of the altar platform that he had not seen in his rush to get to the Blood: another bundle of bones. This one seemed different somehow, and Gart cocked his head as he tried to understand what was not like the others he had seen.

That's when it moved.

The whispers that had begun when Gart had approached the blood had been sly and sinister, but the voice that suddenly exploded in Gart's mind was overwhelmingly direct. Blinding pain brought Gart to his knees as the voice made its desires known.

BodyIneedabodyI'mfreemineminemine!

The bones that had once been a human being drew together and sat up, the empty eye sockets of its skull burning with a cold blue light that somehow mirrored the mercurial nature of the Blood of Nimshi in the fountain nearby. Moving with unnatural speed, the bones pulled themselves to a standing position. The creature's jaws clicked together as the voice continued to scream in Gart's head.

For a moment, Gart's shield wavered, and scalding heat blasted him from all sides. Gart let out an involuntary yell of pain, but stopped himself before he breathed in again, knowing that he would sear his lungs beyond repair. Momentarily shutting out the voice, the sight of the undead creature that had risen, and the pain, he focused all of his energy on the task of rebuilding his magickal shield. Urgency lent him speed. The shield strengthened, becoming more solid around him again. The instant he felt the overpowering heat dissipate, Gart sucked in a huge lungful of air.

As he caught his balance, Gart saw that the being that had awakened was moving closer to him, its fleshless arms outstretched as it reached for him. It moved with jerky fits and starts, its entire frame trembling on unsteady, bony legs. Gart drew his sword and backed away from the oncoming creature, even as its disembodied voice hammered at his mind.

Bodyyourbodymineminegivemebodywantitnowminem inemine.

"Leave me be," he snarled through clenched teeth, brandishing his ebony blade at the lich. It ignored him, its teeth still chattering. Gart shielded his mind as best he could, but he could still hear a constant, shrill keening in his head as the creature approached. From what Gart could tell, the spirit needed a body, and it apparently thought that his own would do just fine. "I've got no quarrel with you."

The creature shambled forward, its skeletal fingers clawing at the air. It walked up to the edge of Gart's glowing nimbus of magick, where it paused, as if deciding what to do. Then it lunged, passing through the golden sphere of energy as though it did not exist. Gart fell backwards, frantically swiping his blade at the creature as he scrambled away, desperately struggling to maintain the structure of his shield. The blade rang off of the creature's forearm bones as though they were made of solid iron, and two of its bony fingers scratched Gart's face, adding two lines of scarlet to the tracery of scars on his right side.

The instant the lich touched Gart's skin, Gart's mind exploded with images and sounds from a time long past. In between heartbeats he saw the discovery of the cavern that held the Blood, the rise of the temple of Nimshi, and the devotion and reverence of the priests that resided there. He saw them study, saw them work, and then saw them sicken, change, and finally, die. The world had changed around them, perverted by the power of the Blood, and at the end, they finally knew what they had done: unleashed an illness upon the world above. Gart saw a small group of priests agree to destroy it all, to make it so that Nimshi would fade away, unknown and unseen, forever. Four were sent to take the artifacts as far away as possible, thereby removing the means to open the gate to their underworld. And three, including the High Priest of Nimshi, were tasked with destroying the fountain, the source of the Blood, so that no one would be tempted by it again.

In that flash of knowledge, Gart saw the High Priest approach the altar with a great hammer, intent on destroying it utterly. But the man paused. While the other priests looked on, he stopped and simply stared at the fountain, enraptured by it, and then enslaved by it. When he turned, the other two priests recoiled in horror as they saw his eyes, which had become pools of quicksilvery black. One of the priests, a hard man by the look of him, lunged forward and stabbed the High Priest in the chest with a ceremonial dagger. He and his companion turned and ran for the stairs before the High Priest's trembling body had even fallen to the black stones. They had known they were too late to save him, or themselves. The Blood of Nimshi had long ago tainted them beyond redemption, but they could at least keep it from causing pain to others by locking it away, and they hurried to complete their mission. They did not see the High Priest drag himself up to the altar. They did not see him drink the Blood. They did not see what it did to him. They frantically raced up the spiral stairs, fleeing the horror behind them. The managed to close the dome and break off the handle of the mechanism before the High Priest caught up with them at the entrance to the descending shaft. Enraged, the High Priest had vented his frustration on his two former friends. And then, an eternity of silence fell below ground.

Gart grunted in anger at the mental intrusion and shook his head violently to clear it of the High Priest's influence. Only an instant of real time had passed. The unsteady pile of bones was still just outside of arm's reach, two bright spots of Gart's blood on two of its skeletal fingers. As Gart watched, the blood changed color. It crawled over the ancient bones and transformed. It turned into pale skin that covered the ends of the spindly digits.

"Oh, so that's how it is, eh?" Gart gritted his teeth in a grim smile. "You'll take what's mine for yourself?" The bones of the High Priest did not answer, though its skull tilted a bit as if to hear better, its jaws opening and closing spasmodically as it jittered in place.

"I don't think so, Slim."

Gart stepped forward and launched a powerful kick right into the lich's naked sternum, cracking bones under

167

his boot and sending the creature's ribcage and spine hurtling back to crash into pieces against the black altar. Left without support, the creature's skull, arms, and legs fell into a shuddering pile. Gart did not wait to see if the creature put itself back together, but turned and ran for the bridge. The stress of holding the magickal heat shield in place had nearly drained him of strength, and keeping the lich's thoughts out of his head had nearly pushed him to the breaking point. He had to escape, lest he become too tired to keep the intense heat of the magma flow at bay. His boots hit the black stone bridge at a run, and he desperately tried to control his breathing as he crossed the span. In a few steps, he was finally past the scorching fires of the river and safe on the other side. The passage that led to the stairs was only moments away.

MYBODYMYBODYMINEMINEMINE!

The voice exploded in Gart's head, blinding him with agony. His momentum carried him forward, but his mind could no longer control his legs and he crumpled into a heap on the stone, mere yards from the exit. He pressed his palms over his ears in an attempt to shut out the sound, even though he knew it was all in his head. His control over the magickal heat shield finally slipped and it vanished, allowing the heat to flow over him in a scalding tide. Although still intensely hot, he had put enough distance between himself and the magma river that the heat did not kill him outright, though he felt as though he had been cast into a smithy's furnace. Screaming in anger and frustration, Gart focused all of his energy on keeping the voice of the High Priest out of his mind.

Reaching deep within himself, he called up the last reserves of his power and finally sealed off his mind from the relentless demands of the High Priest, leaving Gart in blessed silence at last. Struggling against his fatigue, he sat up and tried to focus. He needed to see where the creature was, for if it reached him, it would clothe itself in Gart's own flesh. A flicker of movement caught his attention near the stone bridge, and Gart saw that the lich had already pulled itself together. The dry skeleton had reformed into a shaky, twitchy semblance of a man and was already lurching its way towards him. Even though he was actively using his magick to keep his mind protected, he could still hear the buzzing of its powerful will like a storm that raged outside a stone cottage. Gart's brows knit in anger. He had reached the end of his patience.

The long-bladed Jidaan that rode in its scabbard across his back was eager to answer his call, and its emerald blazed like green fire at the merest hint of his intent. Gart pulled himself to his feet, keeping his eyes on the shambling, jittering remains of the High Priest that approached. He formed a very clear picture in his mind of what he wanted the Jidaan of Storms to create, and in a flash of emerald, the ancient weapon responded. Gart quickly stepped backwards into the tunnel, for he needed to be out of the chamber before his will was manifested.

In the space between Gart and the oncoming lich, the air began to swirl and rotate, picking up black rock dust as it moved. It formed a whirling, semi-solid column, a swaying pillar nearly as thick as a man. Narrowing his intense blue eyes, Gart focused on the pillar of air, increasing its speed and intensity. It began to pull air from the rest of the room as it grew, and suddenly, a line of fire flew from the nearby river of lava and into the growing whirl, adding touches of scarlet to the small twister. Gart braced himself against the side of the tunnel, thankful that he was finally far enough away that the rocks were not hot enough to burn him. The wind in the huge chamber grew, finally turning into a howling tornado of fire, three times its former size. It stood there, undulating, awaiting Gart's command. Gart saw the undead creature still struggling to move towards him. It had altered its path to skirt the intense vortex, intent on taking Gart's flesh for itself.

Gart smiled. *Not going to happen. Not today, not to me, nor to anyone else. Your day is done.* With a flex of his will, Gart sent the swaying twister straight towards the jittering skeleton. It tried to move away, but was instantly caught in the furious windstorm. Gart watched as its body lost cohesion and disintegrated into a pile of separate bones within the body of the tornado. He saw a leg bone in the swirl, only to watch it disappear a moment later. Elsewhere, the skull surfaced, its empty eyes glaring, but then it, too, disappeared. More glints of dirty white bone flashed briefly into view within the storm, and Gart knew what he had to do to finish this.

With a gesture, he sent the storm up and over the river of lava, guiding it carefully where he wanted it to go. Gart noticed that his outstretched hand was shaking, and he knew he had to hurry. Use of the Jidaan always exacted a powerful toll on his body, and although he had built his strength tenfold over the years, he knew that his stamina was nearing its end. Straining to keep his focus, he slowed the storm until the bones of the High Priest dropped onto the black stone altar that surrounded the fountain of Blood. As soon as all of the pieces were deposited, he moved the storm away from the altar. Gart saw the bones already starting to pull themselves together, heard the inhuman scream of frustration and outrage beating on his mental shields, but he held firm. He still had one task to perform.

Dropping to one knee, Gart took a deep breath and threw everything he had into the storm. He settled it down right over the seething river of lava. The ferocious wind cooled the top of the river into a black, scarlet-cracked crust, but the molten stone underneath was still hellishly hot; Gart scooped up as much of it as his tornado could carry. Even as the disembodied voice of the evil priest screamed silently at him to stop, he carried the enormous load of magma over the altar and positioned it directly over the fountain of bubbling Blood.

With a sigh of relief, he released his control over the magick of the Jidaan. The blazing emerald pommelgem in his weapon suddenly went dark, and the storm simply vanished. Its load of molten rock fell onto the altar, the fountain, and the bones of the High Priest, incinerating them almost instantly and covering the entire altar with rapidly cooling stone. Within moments, the screaming in Gart's head vanished, and where there once had been an ornate altar and fountain, there now sat a massive, squatty hunk of solid igneous rock. The room calmed, the magma in the river began to move along in its customary fashion, and everything finally went quiet.

Gart gave the buried altar a long look, making sure all traces of it were hidden. The bridge remained, but he cared nothing for that. When he was satisfied that the voice

170

was gone and all was well, he turned and staggered away from the fountain chamber, carrying the last of the Blood of Nimshi in his backpack, exhaustion dogging his every step.

When he reached the circular chamber at the bottom of the stairs, Gart finally allowed himself to rest. He pulled out his waterskin and drained it completely, then sat on the bottom step for a few long moments. He looked up into the stairwell, not relishing the climb, but wanting to leave the underground hellhole behind him as quickly as possible. At last, he gathered his feet under him and began to make his way up. He grumbled to himself that the way up was far more exhausting than the way down had been, but that was the way of things. He sighed and continued onward, putting one tired foot in front of the other until his echoing footsteps seemed to blend into a melancholy music, a monotonous drumming that he thought would never end.

I'm almost there, at least, he thought, cheering himself. *I have the Blood, now all I need is the Heart. Then I can see her.* He tried not to get choked up, but failed. The thought of seeing Gennie, even as an apparition, of hearing her voice, moved him as it always did. The last few flights of stairs were blurry through his tears.

Just when he thought he would not be able to take another step, he came upon the ancient skeletons that had sealed themselves in with the devilish High Priest. Gart nodded at them and spoke to the empty air, "Your boss is gone, boys. You can rest easy, wherever you are." He gingerly stepped over their remains and made his way toward the opening. The dome's panels had stayed open after all, but he was still glad he had left the piece of stone there to hold the exit ajar. One could never be too prepared.

Emerging into the sunlight, Gart squinted down at the chunk of granite and stepped over it. In that instant, something crashed into the side of his head. The world flashed white, and then promptly turned upside down. Gart fell face-first to the ground just outside the dome, and the awful taste of the rotten earth gagged him even through the pain that burst in his tortured head. Rough hands grabbed him and he felt his backpack being yanked from his limp body. He tried to struggle, but his arms and legs were not

171

listening. Gart tried to call on his magick, but he was having trouble staying conscious, much less call up his already exhausted power. All he managed was a weak cough that barely got the smelly muck out of his mouth. His backpack was tossed aside, and he felt the familiar weight of the Jidaan suddenly vanishing as it was pulled from its scabbard on his back.

No! He struggled to one knee as he tried to call on its power, hoping that it could bring down lightning to stun his attackers, but a boot slammed into his face before he could even form the thought. He fell, stunned, to his back.

"We've done it, Barovius!" the voice sounded young, and tinged with awe. "We've actually captured a Jidaan! Not only that, the Jidaan of Storms!"

"I know, I know! I was the one to strike him. It's because of me that we have it! Get your paws off it, Arkhan!" a rough-edged voice crowed. "Check his pack! If he brought any of the Blood up from down below, he'd have stowed it there. Go look, damn you!"

Gart's vision swam and his head felt like it was about to split down the middle. He struggled to make his eyes work again. Everything was light, then dark, then light again. Nothing was clear to his sight. He squeezed his eyes shut to keep out the disorienting light and forced himself to heave a deep breath into his lungs, then another. His hands dug into the foul-smelling earth beneath his body as he breathed, vaguely aware that something bad was going on, something very bad. The two voices nearby started arguing, but he tried to shut them out in favor of getting his bearings. Somewhere within him, his magick resided. If he could reach it, he could regain some measure of strength and use it to steady himself. He sighed heavily again and continued his silent struggle while the two men bickered over his weapon.

From somewhere far away, Gart heard something familiar. Running footsteps, but from four feet, not two. An animal was running towards them, panting heavily in its excitement.

Not excitement, Gart absently amended as he drifted in a haze of pain. *That's anger.*

"Watch out!" one of the men yelled, his warning overlapping the other man's howl of fear, which was quickly followed by a loud, ferocious snarling that somehow comforted Gart in his injured stupor. His awareness was fading in and out, but the fierce growls reassured him in a way that no human voice could have. The two unseen men screamed as the animal attacked, and Gart drifted into darkness with a vaguely satisfied smile on his face.

Get 'em, Beauty. I need you this time, he thought. And then everything went dark.

Chapter 25

"This is some rough country. Beautiful, though, I'll grant you." Nessar commented as he admired the land through which they traveled. They were following a tiny trail into the southernmost Blackthorne Mountains, riding upwards as they kept the steep slope on their right. The deep greens and browns of the majestic trees they passed contrasted sharply with the whitish-gray stone of the mountainside, and the effect was breathtaking. "It's been years since I've been this far south. I had forgotten how pretty it is."

Since leaving Elarin Glen, they had made efficient use of Layton's Gates to travel a week's distance in a day, but the thickly forested mountains they rode through hindered such travel for the time being. Thunder rolled through the grey clouds that blanketed the sky above them, and the air was thick with moisture, heralding a storm soon to come.

"Beautiful, maybe, but it's going to be wet before too long. I can keep us dry with my Wards, but I'd just as soon not be sliding the horses down the far side of this mountain on a muddy trail. How much farther do you think we can get before we have to stop?" Kiran said. She knew that even the lightest of her Wards would shield them from the rain, but the road would become a sucking mire as it got wet, especially if the storm had any power to it. The thought suddenly had her scanning the skies, wondering if Gart was out there somewhere, sending a storm to slow them down. *That's silly,* she thought. *He can't even know that we're trying to stop him...I hope.* She had seen his power over the weather firsthand, and was not looking forward to confronting him. She hoped he would listen to reason and abandon his quest. *Riiiiight*, she thought, shaking her head in silence.

They crested a rise, and the land to the west of the peak they skirted spread out before them. Sparkling flashes of blue here and there revealed the presence of streams and lakes. Layton scanned the horizon, looking for landmarks and clearings that he might be able to reach with his Gates to save them time. They were close, by his standards, though ordinary riders would still take days to reach Corria even if they knew where it lay hidden. Layton spotted a dark rock formation jutting through the trees far to the west. Keeping his eyes on it, he spoke to Nessar. "Ness, do you see that peak out there? Is that what we're looking for?"

Ness pulled his journal out of his pocket and thumbed through it. After a moment's perusal, he nodded. "Yep. According to the old maps, Corria is just east of that, so it's between the peak and where we are now." Nessar squinted into the distance. "See that empty spot there at the base? The forest leads all the way up to the base of that peak on all sides, but not there. It seems like a small area from this far away, but that's the city, I'm sure of it." He tucked his journal away again and rubbed his grizzled chin. "What do you think? Can you get us there?"

Layton peered out at the dark rock, estimating the distance. It was going to be a stretch, right up to his limits, in fact. He knew he would need to rest afterwards, and said as much. "I'll have to recover for a time once we get there, but even if I rested for a full day, that's still far better than the time it would take to ride there. I won't need that much time, though." *At least, I hope not,* he thought to himself.

Kiran spoke up. "Hey, a day of watching you snooze is still much better than a week of riding through the forest down there, and that's what it's looking like to me. If you can do it, then let's move. It's starting to rain on us here." Kiran willed a pale blue Ward into being over them all, shielding them from the growing drizzle.

"What, are you worried about your hair?" Ness jibed.

"Don't make me hurt you, old man," Kiran immediately responded with a growl. Nessar scoffed absently, his eyes still on the rock formation ahead, and prepared to toss another barb her way.

Layton interrupted them before they could walk that well-worn path any farther. "If you two are quite finished, I'd appreciate it if you'd pay attention. This is a long way off, and I can only hold the Gates open for a short time." He went silent as he sealed off his awareness from any distractions. Layton brought his formidable powers of

175

concentration to bear and focused on their distant goal, and nothing else. A moment passed, then his face drifted into a gentle half-smile, as it always did when he found his inner stillness, that place within himself in which all was quiet and he was at his strongest. The opal gemstone that was nestled in the pommel of his sheathed Jidaan flared brilliantly to life, and both Nessar and Kiran felt the tingle of its powerful magick on their skin.

In the next instant, a portal appeared on the trail in front of them, a bright circle of sparkling energy that swirled with every color in the rainbow. A tiny flash of light winked into existence on a flat ledge of the distant peak, the twin of the nearer Gate. Layton's gaze was fixed on the far Gate, holding it open with his will. Kiran's eyes widened as she saw how far Layton was going to transport them. During their recent travels, she had noticed that he had improved his ability to use the Jidaan to travel, but this was more than twice the distance she had ever seen him attempt. Already, he was shaking with the effort of holding the portal open at that distance.

Nessar was the first to ride through, followed immediately by Kiran, her Ward vanishing with her as she was transported to the far mountain. Layton followed at the last, just as the rain began to fall in earnest. He and his horse were drenched before they could step through the Gate. Although they were quickly soaked, Layton paid no attention. The instant he joined his friends on the faraway rocky slope, he let the Gates vanish and heaved a sigh of relief. He sagged in his saddle, exhausted to the bone.

"Oh...Goddess..." Layton murmured. "That was...much harder than I thought...it would be." He leaned over his horse's neck, intending to rest for just a moment, but then he kept going, sliding off of his mount to fall in a heap in the gravel below.

"Layton!" Kiran exclaimed as she jumped down from her horse to check on him. She turned him on his back and checked his pulse, only to find it steady and strong. Just then, Layton snored, and Kiran sat back on her heels.

"He's asleep, isn't he?" Nessar chuckled. "Figures. We'll just have to wait until he wakes up to go down there."

Kiran frowned at Layton, unsure whether to be upset that he had exhausted himself or because he had made her think he was injured. "I swear, what a time to take a nap. Ah well, he warned us. And he did save us days of travel. Let's just camp here. I'll build a fire to dry him out some." Kiran moved to her horse to pull down her pack, but stopped. "Wait, what did you say? Go down where?"

Nessar leaned over in the saddle, peering down the side of the small mountain they had reached. He looked at Kiran and then nodded downward again. "Down there. We found it. Take a look."

Kiran walked over to the edge of the slope and gasped as she looked down at what Nessar had seen. "Oh. Oh, my."

The forest canopy was thick and green on all sides, except for a nearly perfect circle directly below them that stretched nearly a mile across. This close, they could see more accurately that the clearing was immense. Their high vantage point gave them an unobstructed view below. They could see the reason for the absence of trees; a cylindrical depression, a huge, circular hole that descended hundreds of feet into the ground. Four massive, tapering spokes of cracked stone criss-crossed the opening, joined at the center by a small obelisk. Far below the crowning structure, they could see the whole of a city, with buildings and towers made of stone. Much of it was overgrown with vines and trees, but still plainly visible to the eye. Parts of the stone spokes had fallen over the centuries, shattering some of the structures beneath. Nessar looked around the forest again before peering back down. "No wonder this place fell off the map. You'd have to know exactly where it sits to find it. Its tallest tower is below the level of the forest floor above, and you can't even see that except from up here."

Kiran whistled in appreciation. "I'm glad we've got him to get us in and out." Kiran cocked a thumb over her shoulder at the dozing Layton. "I'm a fair climber and all, but I don't love the idea of hauling myself out of that by hand."

"I hear that," Nessar agreed. "I know he didn't have much to say about it in his own case, but he's got the right idea. Let's rest up before we head down there. It'll be dark

177

soon, and I'd much rather we all be fresh and ready in the morning. No telling what's down there."

Kiran laughed. "I thought thieves did their best work in the dark?"

Nessar raised one gnarled finger. "*Former* thief, if you please. And although that's true, I have a feeling we'll need the light on our side for this one." Nessar turned his attention back to the ancient city below them while Kiran tended to their sleeping friend. They both knew that he would rouse eventually. Nessar lifted his gaze to peer out across the forest at the mountain they had just vacated. The storm had gained in force and was dropping thick, gray torrents of rain on the slopes below. Even from that distance, he could smell the rain in the air.

Just then, a thick bolt of lightning struck the far peak, followed by another blinding flash. The thunder rumbled its way across the forest until it finally reached Nessar's ears, and the old thief could not help but recall seeing Gart unleash similar bolts of lightning into Mordak's horde of evil creatures, laying waste to an army. *I hope we don't have to fight you, Gart,* Nessar thought. *We've been friends a long time. I hope we can help you see what you're doing is wrong.* Nessar sighed. As if in answer, lightning flashed within the distant storm cloud, a massive web of bright fire that crawled through the darkness before erupting in another bolt that hit the mountaintop below, followed by two more. The thunder that reached Nessar's ears was intense and menacing, and it sent a chill into the old man's bones. Nessar lifted his eyes skyward, directing his thoughts to the Goddess Rowann.

I hope you're not trying to tell me something, lady.

The thunder rolled once more, and Nessar sighed. *Ah, well. What will be, will be.*

Chapter 26

"What happened?" Reyanna sat up, startled. The blanket that had been around her slipped at her sudden movement, baring her naked shoulders to the cool night air. She clutched at it in surprise. "Where are my clothes? And, and..." She suddenly remembered Teryn's injury. "Oh no! Teryn! Ginn! Where...what...?"

"It's all right, Reyanna, we're here." Ginn's quiet, reassuring voice reached her from the opposite side of the campfire, and she relaxed a little. "Teryn is hurt, so I've been tending her." He heard Reyanna's sharp intake of breath, and he added, "She'll be fine, try not to worry. The arrow that wounded her is out, and she's resting now."

Reyanna resettled the blanket on her shoulders, pulling it more tightly around herself as she rose to her feet. She tried to remember what had happened, but met with resistance. She frowned and walked around the campfire to be closer to Ginn and Teryn.

Ginn held a finger to his lips, and Reyanna sat down on a stone, holding her questions for the time being. Ginn tucked the blanket up under Sister Teryn's chin, and she murmured sleepily, though she did not waken. To Reyanna, he explained, "The arrow came out easily enough, but the damage was done. Between her magick and my meager skills, we stopped her bleeding and hurried what healing could be hurried. Even so, it will be long before she can travel easily again." He sighed as he turned toward Reyanna, and she gasped to see his battered face. He laughed sadly. "Yes, I must look a mess. They caught me out there in the woods, in my own world. Laid a trap and like a fool, I walked right into it. The beating I received served me right for not trusting my own judgement."

Reyanna blinked her wide eyes at him, suddenly resembling a blue-eyed owl. "How in the world did they catch you? You're a Weya Ranger!" She was flabbergasted. No ragged outlaw band of humans should ever have been able to sneak up on a Weya, much less a Ranger.

Ginn shook his head, angry at himself. "They were smarter than we thought, and," he drew a small medallion

179

from his belt pouch and tossed it in the grass in front of Reyanna, "they were using magick to hide the sounds of their movements. They made just enough noise to draw me away from camp. The one wearing that simply stepped out from behind a couple of trees as I passed by, and struck me. I never even knew he was there, and my senses are counted good even among Rangers. Others joined in while I was stunned, and it was all I could do to stay alive there for a bit." A rueful smile finally crossed his face. "I did manage to turn the tide there, at the end." Finally, his gaze fell fully on Reyanna's. "I'm glad that you were unharmed. If you don't mind my asking, though, how did you kill those ruffians? And what happened to your clothes? I searched for them, but they're nowhere to be found."

Reyanna looked at Ginn blankly for a few moments and then turned her face away, struggling to find the answers to his questions. "I..." she began, "I don't know, Ginn. I remember sitting with Teryn, thinking about my vision, just as she asked me to." Reyanna frowned as she concentrated. "I remember that my vision scared her. She said so." She pulled the blanket tighter around her shoulders, suddenly cold. "We were talking, and then...wait, she took an arrow in the back! I remember that!" One hand released a corner of the blanket and flew inside to her left shoulder. The skin there was unmarked. "I thought I was hit, too, but..." she sighed in frustration. "I guess I imagined that. I don't remember anything else. I woke up just now, like this. What happened?"

Ginn had been watching her as she spoke, using all of his instincts in an attempt to discern whether she was lying. He stared at her for a moment longer, then sighed himself. She was telling the truth, or at least, what she believed to be truth. Ginn gestured into the woods nearby. "I'm not sure, but something killed those four men, and harshly. That they probably deserved it is not in question. Their necks and skulls were badly broken from what I could tell, and everything from their shoulders up appeared to have been held in a smithy's furnace. It's hard for me to say whether the fire or the pummeling killed them first. Either way, they are just as dead."

180

Reyanna's pretty face went through a series of emotions, from shock and surprise to disgust and then concern. Her eyes flicked towards the sleeping form of Sister Teryn and back to Ginn, who was still watching her intently. "Sister Teryn couldn't have done such a thing," she stated. "Even if she could, she was badly injured. She could barely speak. How…"

Ginn leaned over and put a reassuring hand on her blanketed shoulder. "Reyanna, it had to be you. I'm not sure how, but I do know you are far more powerful than you realize. I think my arm *was* broken by the man-wolf, and you mended it somehow. And those men," he nodded in the direction of the woods, "their demise was likely well-deserved. Somehow, you brought it to them, and with extreme finality. You've got some very powerful magick within you, Reyanna. That's not a bad thing, but I suggest you strive to understand it, and soon."

Reyanna's tears had begun soon after Ginn started to speak, but she remained silent. She gazed into his blue-jeweled eyes and tried to find the words. Finally, she turned from him and looked away into the dark. "I've always had power, Ginn. To move things, or sometimes see things, ever since I was a little girl. But none of the other kids could do the things I could do. I worried they would shun me; I was already different, a human. I thought if I showed them what I could do, they wouldn't like me anymore. And I thought I would get in trouble, maybe taken away from my parents." She turned back to face Ginn, her tears flowing freely now. "That terrified me. I had already lost one set of parents, and I just couldn't lose the ones that had taken me in and loved me. So I shut the power away and tried to forget that I had it. I just wanted to be normal." She laughed a little, then. "Well, as normal as a human living among Weya might be, anyway. I've felt it growing the last few years, but I denied it to myself. I finally felt truly accepted! I had become a Ranger, and everyone seemed to love me. I had everything I wanted! I didn't want anything to change that."

Ginn slowly walked over to her and opened his arms. Reyanna hesitated, but then moved into his gentle embrace. He held her for a few moments without saying

181

anything, just letting her find a sense of security in his arms. He was not as tall as she was, but even so, his presence felt huge to her, and she welcomed it. Finally, he released her and put his hands on her shoulders as he looked into her eyes.

"It's understandable that you were afraid. I will tell you, though, that the Weya are very familiar with magick. We are a people who are very close to the earth. Magick is part of us, even for those of us who do not know many of its uses. Your parents would have been delighted to find that you had gifts, for that is what your power would be considered: a gift. The LorMages would never have cast you out; they would have helped you. I am so sad that you believed otherwise."

Reyanna sniffed and wiped her eyes. She wanted to believe Ginn. He had no reason to lie, and yet, all of her childhood fears struggled to be heard. For once, she decided to ignore them. She sighed, then found her voice again. "I hope it's not too late, then. If I killed those men with magick and don't remember it, then I could hurt other people, too. I don't want that."

Ginn nodded. "I agree. You will have to go and see the LorMages as soon as possible. They will know how best to help you, Reyanna. In the meantime," he nodded to where Sister Teryn lay sleeping, "we can ask her if she has any suggestions when she wakes. In any event, we may have to change our plans."

Reyanna was confused. "What do you mean?"

Ginn sighed as he walked over and picked up a stick to poke at the fire. "Two of those louts escaped with our horses, and although it shames me to say it, I'm injured enough that I won't be able to catch up to them in a reasonable time. Even if I could, or if you went and handled those ruffians yourself to get the horses back, Sister Teryn was badly wounded. She will not be able to travel back to her home right away, not as she is, and most certainly not on the back of Drusilla. I'll have to stay with her here for a few days until she is able to travel." He turned and looked at Reyanna. "I cannot ask you to stay here. Your quest is important enough that you should go on alone. I am sorry that I will not be able to continue on with you."

Reyanna looked at him silently as she pondered that. "You'll have to give me some decent directions, then. I've never been to the Hall of Jidaana, and I don't know how to get there."

"That's not where you need to go," a soft voice said from the other side of the campfire. Sister Teryn had awakened. Reyanna hurried over to her and knelt, taking her hand.

"What's that, Sister?" Reyanna was perplexed. Her mission had been clear, or so the LorMages had said. Go to the Keep of the Guardians and find Gart. "Where else should I be going?"

Sister Teryn smiled weakly and continued. "I walked in your vision, remember? I saw many things, some of which I don't understand at all. I can describe the people I saw but unless you already know them, I'm not sure how that will help. The one thing I did see for sure, though, was where your vision was taking place, and it was not at Guardians Keep."

Ginn and Reyanna looked at each other before looking back at the injured priestess. Reyanna answered first. "If not there, then where?"

Sister Teryn frowned, and she took her time before responding. She was hurting badly, and exhausted to the bone from the pain. "I recognized the mountains behind Gart. It's a small range, and hard to reach, for it sits in the middle of the Poravian Mire. There is an ancient shrine there, and I think that was where he was headed before," she paused, considering, "before that enormous thing showed up. There is a crack in the central cliff face, a wide fissure that leads deep into the stone. The legends say that MageKings battled there in ancient days. The shrine is in the deepest part of the fissure. It is a secluded place of power, although it is seldom visited because one must first brave the Mire. There are also tales of fell things that guard the shrine, left behind from those troubled times. No one has ever seen anything there, but the few Sisters that made the trek in years past spoke of a powerful sense of dread surrounding it." Teryn leaned her head back on the pillow Ginn had made for her, tired from the effort of speaking.

Even so, she felt compelled to continue. "It is very difficult to reach, but that was the place, I'm sure of it."

Reyanna frowned again. "If it is so difficult to reach, how will I get there? Can you tell me the way?"

Suddenly, Sister Teryn smiled widely. "Why yes, I can tell you the way. And moreover, I know exactly how you can get there quickly, and fairly easily." She paused, watching Reyanna's face. "You can ride Drusilla."

"Oh, right. Wait...what?" Reyanna's expression was priceless as she imagined herself riding the giant spider. Although it hurt mightily for Teryn to laugh, she did anyway.

Chapter 27

Lights burned in the windows of the castle in the distance, and a cool wind blew across the murky lake, causing the small campfire to flicker. Shadows danced on the surrounding rocks, ancient sentinels seemingly keeping watch on the lake and its stony shore. Melidia rarely came out this far from her fortress, but certain conditions existed in the earth and the dark, cracked monoliths at the lake's edge that she had long since learned to use for her sorcerous endeavors. It stank of old magick, a rank, fetid smell of rituals most foul. Aside from the sighs of the wind and the crackling flames, all was silent in the hollow.

Beyond the fire, a large circle had been carefully chiseled into the hard-packed, rocky earth, and within that circle, a slightly smaller circle resided. Between the two were inscribed runes of ill aspect. Those figures irritated the eye, and inspired feelings of dread in those who dwelt too long upon them. Many of the symbols were still sticky with crimson stains, the cost of dark magick paid in blood. To one side, Melidia sat on a padded wooden chair brought from her castle for this purpose. Her eyes were open, but saw nothing of the lake, fire, or starry sky above. She was dreaming bloody dreams of power, engaging in a ferocious meditation as she waited for news.

Above the center of the inscribed circles, the air suddenly darkened, as though the shadows had gathered there. The darkness roiled and writhed, becoming larger with every passing moment, until it was as tall as a man. The circles beneath began to glow with a scarlet brightness that lent no warmth, only a bloody illumination that was echoed in the vulgar symbols between them. The air crackled with malevolent energy as the power within the circles grew.

The shadows thickened and then solidified, taking the shape of two men close together, one supporting the other. There was a blinding crimson flash, and where shadows had been, Barovius and Arkhan now stood. They fell forward, landing hard on the pebbled soil, obliterating the lines of the mystic circle that had brought them back from Nimshi. They lay there, gasping in agony from the strain of the journey, and from their wounds.

Both men were covered in deep scratches, and Arkhan's left arm was badly broken and bleeding. He had been shaken like a rag doll and thrown headfirst into a stone, leaving him nearly senseless. Barovius would have lost a leg, had his leather boots not been so sturdy. As it was, his left calf had been crushed by Beauty's mighty jaws. He would have a limp for the remainder of his days, but at least he still had the foot. He knew that Arkhan might not be so lucky with his arm.

The noise and light of the portal brought Melidia out of her meditations. She instantly rose to her feet, a dagger in her hand in case more than her lackeys had arrived. When she saw the two men on the ground, curled around their pain, she frowned in disgust and sheathed her dagger. "Just look at you!" she spat. "Idiots! I told you exactly what to do and he *still* got the better of you!"

Barovious slowly rose to a knee. Blood had spattered across his face in a crimson spray, staining his teeth as he grinned triumphantly at the sorceress. "That was his damned dog; it was big as a pony! We didn't see the beast in time before it attacked us. I took care of it, though. Stabbed it until it finally released Arkhan." He paused for a moment, then grinned wider. "And we have this," Barovius shoved Arkhan out of the way and pulled something from underneath his bleeding body. Its blade gleamed dully in the firelight, and he relished Melidia's gasp of surprise.

For all her authority and power, the sight of the ancient weapon awed her. Her voice was a whisper. "The Jidaan of Storms! I never believed you could wrest that from him!"

Barovius jammed the Jidaan's darkened pommel into the earth at his feet, roughly using it as a crutch so that he could stand. Leaving Arkhan to fend for himself, he stumbled over to a nearby stone and eased himself into a seated position upon it, keeping his injured leg held out straight and sighing with relief. He laid the Jidaan across his lap, marveling at its beauty and heft. The emerald in its pommel stayed dark, almost black, in his hands, and the weapon felt far heavier than it looked. He traced a finger over the elegant runes that adorned the blade only to yank his hand back with a yelp as he cut himself somehow on the inscription. He stuck his finger in his mouth, then cast his gaze back to Melidia, who was staring at the Jidaan with unsettling intensity. She took a step towards him.

"Oh, no," he growled, "you'll not get your hands on this. Not until I say so. I nearly died for this, and its mine!" Barovius tightened his hold on the Jidaan's wooden shaft. It felt oddly slippery in his grasp, but he gripped it as firmly as he could.

Melidia narrowed her eyes as she shifted her gaze to glare at Barovius, but said nothing. She knew far more about the weapon than the bald sorcerer, and she understood that it was completely useless to the likes of him. Only a Chosen could ignite its power, and Barovius was certainly not one of those exalted few. Besides, she had time. She would take the weapon from him and delve into its secrets eventually.

Let him think he's won this round, she thought. *He can toy with the Jidaan all he wants, it won't work for him. More importantly, Gart doesn't have it - its power is lost to him.* A grim smile played across her ruby lips. *That will make things much easier.*

Dismissing Barovius from her attention, she turned toward Arkhan. The younger man had struggled into a kneeling position, cradling his ruined arm. In a cold voice, she asked, "Did you get the Blood, at least?"

Quietly, his voice remarkably steady, he replied, "No." His face remained expressionless as he watched Melidia clench her fists in frustration. "The dog came out of nowhere just as I was about to check Gart's backpack. If he brought any of the Blood out of the chamber, then he still has it." He paused, considering. "I must tend to my wounds. If you want the Blood, you will have to get it yourself."

Melidia glared at Arkhan, but knew there was nothing to be done. She could see his injuries quite clearly as he cradled his wounded arm, and knew that he would likely lose it. The dog had not only shredded the skin and muscle, but badly broken the bones beneath as well. The sorceress raised an eyebrow as she surveyed the youthful wizard. Although his face was pale and he was trembling

187

slightly, he showed no other signs of the agony he was in. *Impressive,* she thought, though her words were dismissive. "Fine. Go and see to your injuries, then make your way back to the castle. I'll explain the next stage of the plan tomorrow."

Arkhan said nothing, but slowly got to his feet and walked toward the path that led back to the castle, his eyes focused straight ahead. When he had gone, Barovius grumbled, "You'll want to keep an eye on that one. Something's not right with him."

Melidia stared after the young shapemelder. She had always sensed that Arkhan was something other than he presented, but had never been able to see beyond his outer shell. His magick was strong, and that was why she had recruited him. Even so, Barovius had a point. Not that she could trust him either. She turned her gaze on him and engaged a bit of her lustmagick so she could enjoy watching him squirm.

Barovius' breath caught in his throat as he suddenly realized just how alluring Melidia was. He swallowed a few times and stammered before she cut him off.

"Yes, you're right, Barovius, my lovely," Melidia smiled as she angled herself to better display her body. She enjoyed watching his cheeks flush at the sight of her. He may have been old and wrinkled, but he was still young enough to be strongly affected by her charms, especially when they were enhanced with magick. "I have some scrying to do. I need to see where that little girl ended up. Something about her has been nagging at the back of my mind, and I think she's more important than we at first thought. Once I see where she is, we may need to eliminate her. Then we still have to deal with Gart. Keep the Jidaan safe," she saw the bald wizard jealously clutch the spear to himself and felt her tenuous hold on him waver. *Gently,* she reminded herself. If Barovius thought for one second that she was trying to enspell him, he would fight her tooth and nail. As it was, he still thought their endeavor was at least half his own idea. *The moron.* "We will explore its uses when this is done. For now, it is enough that it is in our hands."

"*MY* hands," Barovius corrected, irritated. He already had plans for the fabled weapon, plans that did not include Arkhan and Melidia. However, it served his purposes to stay with them a little longer. The gold Melidia had promised would set him up for a life of luxury, and now he had a score to settle with Gart. *Sic your dog on me, will you? I'll kill you with your own weapon and laugh while I do it!* The thought of plunging the razor-tipped Jidaan into Gart's chest made Barovius smile.

Suddenly, the Jidaan slipped from his grasp and thumped to the ground at his feet. He reached down and snatched it back up again, glaring at Melidia as he did so.

She managed not to roll her eyes at him, but just barely. Turning her back on Barovius, Melidia began the short journey back to her castle, where she could cast her scrying spells more effectively. The more she thought about it, the more certain she was the dark-haired young woman would be playing a bigger part in their little drama…a much bigger part. And Melidia wanted to know what it was.

189

Chapter 28

The heartbeat was loud in Gart's mind. LUBDUB. LUBDUB. It was a comforting sound that cheered him. For a while, he did nothing but listen to it. He floated, drifting in the warm darkness, quietly existing with no memory of the past or thoughts of the future.

The beat began to slow. Imperceptibly at first, but the time between pulses gradually lengthened. The beats became quieter and less insistent. Gart continued to drift, but concern touched him. Something about that slowing beat just was not right. He began to think again, to wonder. What was that sound? It seemed familiar. Gart suddenly decided that he really needed to know what it was and why it was slowing. Somehow, he knew it would be a bad thing if the sound stopped. He became aware of a dull, throbbing pain that seemed to come from everywhere at once, but that only served to spur him on. The beat slowed further, and the pain got worse. Gart struggled harder.

And suddenly, he was awake. Gart found himself face-down in a patch of vile-smelling earth, and slowly began to push himself away from it. He spat the foulness from his mouth and managed to get up on his elbows. Something warm and big was pressed up against his right side. Even though the movement caused bright spots of agony to dance before him, he turned to see that Beauty was lying next to him. He also saw that she was covered with blood.

Alarmed, he struggled to a kneeling position and reached for her. "Beauty? What happened, girl? Are you...?" His voice trailed off as he touched her and found her body warm, but limp. "No. Oh, no. Beauty!" Gart staggered around her enormous form so that he could examine her. He was horrified to see several ghastly stab wounds in her huge chest and rib cage. "Beauty? What did they do to you? Oh no..." Her chest rose and fell, and Gart's spirits rose for a moment. Then he saw the bloody foam that came from her nostrils and her mouth with each painful breath. Tears came unbidden as he scratched her ears the way he knew she liked. Frantically, he tried to figure out what to do.

As he touched her, his magick connected with her mind as it had in the past, and his heart nearly broke. She was dying, the dagger having pierced her lungs and nicked her heart. Her only emotion, even through all the pain, was joy at hearing Gart call her name and touch her. The purity of her love for him burned into his soul, and Gart hung his head and cried silently, ignoring the pain of his injured skull.

In her mind, he saw disjointed visions of what had happened. She had heard the men too late, and came running when she sensed Gart among them, heard the sound of him being attacked. Nothing had mattered to her but defending him. It could have been an army, and she would have flung herself headlong into it without a second thought. In the end, it was only two men, and Gart saw their faces clearly in Beauty's memory. He marked those faces well, vowing that they would pay for what they had done. He saw the younger one as Beauty mangled his left forearm, felt her remembered pain as the older, bald one stabbed her. She had turned on her new attacker and bit him ferociously in the lower leg, but she was not as quick as she once was, and her wounds slowed her further. The sneering bald man had been more nimble. He escaped from her massive jaws, and the dagger had seemed to be everywhere at once, slashing, stabbing, hurting. When she couldn't catch him again and the agony had become too great, she retreated to stand over Gart, intent on protecting him to her last breath. Fortunately, the bald man chose to escape rather than press his attack. He gathered up his wounded comrade and they stumbled out of sight, taking Gart's Jidaan with them. The vision faded, and Gart found himself back in the here and now. He looked down into Beauty's bloody face, and she moaned quietly, trying to lick his hand. She was dying, but her thoughts were only of Gart, of protecting him, reassuring him.

Guilt slammed into him like a hammer. His quest had caused this, his selfish need to see Gennie again. Furious, he shook his head and shoved those thoughts aside. He already knew he would continue the quest, even if he hated himself for it. For now, though, his only focus was Beauty.

"No," Gart said angrily. "No, I can fix this." He tried to clear his mind, but the pain in his skull made concentration difficult. He cursed, and tried again, searching for the powerful magick he knew he possessed. It answered. Delving into his power, he sent it into his injured companion, searching for ways to aid in healing her. He found the deepest wounds the dagger had made and did his best to repair the damage, but it was extensive. He carefully mended sliced tissues, stopped bleeding where he found it, but it seemed amazingly complicated. He wished he had spent more time in the library in the Hall of Jidaana looking at the healing scrolls, rather than the ones he had been poring over for the last few years. Determined, he pressed on. He found her heart, still beating, but weakly, leaking blood from one side where the dagger had clipped it. Straining to use his magick so delicately, he eased the edges of the wound together and sealed them shut. When he had repaired everything he felt he could, he withdrew his magick from her and sighed with relief.

"There," he said softly near the dog's ear. "That should do it. If you rest, you should be all right, girl."

Beauty looked up at him, her brown eyes filled with love. She licked his hand again, her huge tongue leaving bloody streaks on his skin, and then she died. Her breath left her body in a long, slow wheeze, and she fell still.

"No! No! I fixed everything!" Gart exclaimed, horrified. Again, he reached into her body with his magick and found her heart. It was whole, but still. He cradled it with his magick, squeezed it so that it pumped. He tried to mimic the strength and pattern that he had felt from her over the years. Again and again, he squeezed her heart, praying fervently to the Goddess Rowann that Beauty would live.

At last, Beauty shuddered and heaved a huge sigh, followed by another. Gart laughed and cried at the same time as he stroked her head again. "I've got you. I've got you, girl, you'll be all right." He continued to pump her heart until he felt the pattern was right, then withdrew his magick once more.

Instantly, her heart stopped. It refused to beat on its own.

"NO!" Gart yelled, diving in yet again with his power. He reached her heart instantly this time and pumped it, being careful not to squeeze it too hard, but keeping the strong, steady rhythm she needed. Beauty whined and snorted. Her tail wagged slowly as she looked up at Gart.

Cautiously, Gart began to withdraw his magick again, but the heart simply would not continue moving without his power animating it. Beauty was alive and fairly healthy, but only as long as Gart could keep her heart beating. They sat together for a few minutes as Gart got a feel for the process. He gently stroked her neck, tracing the thick network of scars she had gained from years of fierce dogfighting. Through the connection of Gart's magick, Beauty spoke.

Men bad. But tasted good. Bit them, they bit back. Protect Gart. Love Gart. Her chest ached deeply and she was thoroughly exhausted, but as long as Gart was there, everything was all right. She was his and he was hers, and they were together. She had not a care in the world, although she felt that a nap would not be a bad idea.

Gart wiped his face with his sleeve. He would have to use a constant flow of magick to keep Beauty alive. It would be exhausting, but he had no choice. He would have to figure out a way to do it, even while he was sleeping. He sighed and scratched Beauty's ears again. "This is going to be tough. But you're worth it, girl."

Beauty huffed softly at him and laid her massive head across Gart's knee. Through the magick that connected them, she could now understand him better than ever. And she agreed wholeheartedly: she was most definitely worth it. Happily enjoying her master's touch as he continued to stroke her, Beauty drifted into a contented doze, completely oblivious to Gart's silent tears, even the ones that fell on her head.

Chapter 29

"You can get us down there easily, right Layton? No climbing?" Kiran's eyebrow was raised so high it was in danger of disappearing into her hairline.

"Of course!" he answered brightly, then gave her a quizzical look. "You've ridden through mountains before. And we used to do training runs all the time with Brunar when we were newly Chosen as Guardians, remember? Why so skittish all of a sudden?" He finished loading a small backpack with things he thought might be useful in the ruins below and shouldered the pack. His opal-pommeled Jidaan leaned against the rock upon which he sat. He picked it up, enjoying the feel of the ancient weapon as he always did.

Kiran leaned carefully over the edge of the wide pit, her breathing shallow and rapid as she surveyed the city of Corria, far below. She straightened up and turned slowly away from it before she visibly relaxed. "I'm not gonna lie, it's been a long while since we were young and stupid, running Brunar's conditioning courses. In case you hadn't noticed, I'm not the willowy little thing I was back then. And I haven't spent a lot of time running around mountain peaks, either. Running my mercenary service has kept me busy at the inn, and I've kept my feet on the ground." Layton just stared at her for a moment, and she scowled, adding, "Hey, I'm still tough enough to handle myself, and you know it!"

Layton chuckled. "Kiran, I've never once thought any differently. I'd rather have you fighting at my back than anyone I know, all of my best students included. And most of them hate heights, too."

Kiran nodded sharply. "Exactly! I'd still be the match of most of those overgrown children at your school...and don't forget it!"

Nessar interjected at last. "If you two are finished babbling at each other, let's get down there and get this over with. I'm not getting any younger."

Layton laughed and stood up. "That's for sure, Ness. Let's leave the horses here. Everything seems too

194

congested down there for the horses to do any real good; we'll move better on foot."

"Agreed," Nessar grunted in reply. "Let's go."

Layton stepped over to the ledge and looked down into the deep, cylindrical hole that sheltered the city of Corria. It looked for all the world as if the city had formed above ground, then suddenly drilled its way hundreds of feet down into the earth. The walls of the pit were sheer and covered with lush vegetation. Shrubs, plants, and even small trees had taken hold in the earth and rock below. Birds could be seen flying to and from nests among the foliage. A misty haze hovered in the center of the shaft, and Layton could see that, if the low cloud were thicker, it would easily shelter the city from sight. Fortunately, the mist was thin enough for him to spot a viable entry point in the city below, and he cleared his mind so that he could use his Gift.

The pommel of his Jidaan flared brilliantly to life as he called to it, and a circular Gate appeared before him. Slightly wider than an ordinary door, its surface was a constant swirl of white energy mixed with every color imaginable. Keeping his focus on the Gate, Layton gestured to Kiran. "All set. We'll come out in the open space next to that fallen archway down there in the southeastern part of the city. Step through whenever you're ready."

Kiran glanced over the edge one last time and spotted the glowing twin to the Gate that stood before her. "All right, then. Hopefully, this will be quick and easy." She left her Jidaan strapped to her back, but pulled her short sword and held it at the ready as she stepped into the portal and disappeared.

Nessar stepped through without a word, choosing to save his breath in case he needed it to run later. His ebony-pommeled Jidaan bounced a little as he moved and he absently tightened its straps without looking, again instinctively preparing in case speed became necessary. Between one step and the next, he found himself suddenly standing in the ruins of Corria. Layton stepped through a moment later and the opalescent Gate vanished, leaving the area in shadow.

Nessar looked up to see the bright circle of sky far overhead. The sunlight struck the wall of the pit at a slant,

195

but he knew that it would creep downwards as the sun rose. "We'll have full light within the hour, but not for long," he observed, whispering. "I brought an oil lantern in case we need it. If we're here after dark, it'll be pitch black down here."

"I'm hoping we'll be out of here long before then," Kiran replied quietly. Her jade green eyes scanned the ancient city for any signs of threat, but there was no movement. Although birdsong and the sound of the wind rustling the leaves could be heard from far above, it was distant and quiet. The air in the crater was still, leaving them all with the sensation of being in a graveyard. The stone buildings and statues were green with life, as vines and plants had crawled over much of the exposed stone. The outlines of the structures that had once been impressive and beautiful were blurred and misshapen. Even so, beautiful flowers bloomed here and there, lending bright spots of color to the green of leaf and gray of stone.

"Look there," Nessar pointed to the southern wall of the steep pit, indicating a huge and ornate archway carved into the rock. The entrance to the passage was easily wide enough to drive two wagons through at once. Its interior was dark, but a huge pile of rubble was still visible, completely filling the tunnel. "I wondered how they got in and out of here. There had to be a way, but that one is blocked." Nessar craned his neck to look around and added, "There are similar exits to the north and east, and those are blocked as well."

"Well, that figures," Kiran whispered back, her tone dripping with irony. "Can't have an easy way out of here, nooooo. And why are we whispering?"

Layton's eyes were focused to the east, looking for anything that could be a problem. "Because we don't know what killed everyone down here. For all we know, it could still be lurking nearby. This is not an easy place to escape, unless whatever they awoke could fly. The LorMage said that it came from deep in their mines, so it likely went back there." He turned and looked at Kiran. "If it's all right with you, I'd just as soon let it sleep, whatever it is." He waggled his eyebrows at her, and his attempt at humor made her

196

want to either chuckle or punch him, but she did neither. Ultimately, his thinking was sound.

Nessar whispered at them both. "Let's move in, but stay in sight of each other. If we need to speak, let's use the Mindspeech. The Heart is supposed to be in a museum of some kind, if it's still here. Let's fan out and see what we can find." He pointed to the north, where the bulk of the city lay before them.

Kiran and Layton nodded. Layton drew his Jidaan and held it in a relaxed guard position as he moved forward, his boots making almost no sound. Kiran quietly drew her sword, choosing to leave her Jidaan resting comfortably in the scabbard on her back. She was amazed at how quickly she had become reaccustomed to it; it had begun to feel like a part of her body almost immediately. Nessar left his Jidaan scabbarded also, preferring to leave both hands free. Even without using his Jidaan's power of Stealth, he was completely silent, and Kiran had to keep an eye on him to be sure where he was.

Walking carefully, they spread out and slowly made their way through the abandoned city, moving through the ancient, ivy-covered buildings. Doorways stood yawning open, leading into clusters of shadows that gave little clue as to what else might be inside. At one point, Kiran startled a flight of birds that, in turn, startled her when they burst through an open window of the structure she was searching. Otherwise, the three Guardians found little to tell them more than they already knew.

As they moved closer to the center of the city, Kiran's voice echoed in Layton's and Nessar's minds. *Hey, does anyone else see that huge, ominous cave in the cliff to the west?*

The two men swiveled their heads in that direction and they both quickly saw what Kiran was talking about.

You mean the one that looks like it could hide a dragon and still have room left over? Layton responded.

The beat of silence that followed was heavy with irritation, and Layton grinned; he could imagine her rolling her eyes at him.

That would be the one, Laytie honey, Kiran retorted, dripping with sweetness before reverting to her usual

197

sarcasm. *Five gold pieces says that the museum is in there somewhere. Where it's dark. And where the monsters probably live.*

Nessar calmly interjected. *Well, that fits what the LorMage told us. They dug too deep and awoke something that lived within the earth. So yes, whatever killed everyone is likely down there somewhere. We have yet to see anything up here that remotely resembles the Heart, so we'll have to check it out. Let's go.*

Sighing, Kiran shifted direction towards the enormous cavern entrance, keeping a close eye on her surroundings. They had passed vine covered statues, archways, and buildings that had been beautiful once, but nothing that looked like a massive diamond. She kept her sword ready and reached out with her senses as Brunar had once taught her, searching out the terrain a few yards farther than she could easily see.

Soon, the trio stood at the line of shadow that separated the rest of the city from the darkness of the cavern. Layton pulled a torch from his backpack and was about to light it when Kiran waved a hand to stop him. She beckoned him and Nessar closer, then pointed into the gloom, squinting into the shadows.

There's light in there. Look.

The two men stared where she was pointing, striving to see what she saw. Kiran stepped into the darkness and disappeared from their sight for a moment, but immediately her voice sounded inside their heads again. *Ok, wow. Get in here and let your eyes adjust. You'll see.*

They edged inside the dimness to stand next to Kiran and waited for their eyes to adjust. Gradually, they became aware of a faint green light that seemed to come up from down below. As their pupils dilated and they were able to focus, their jaws slowly dropped open as the interior of the cavern became visible to them.

It was enormous.

The city that sat outside the cavern was only a small part of Corria, dwarfed by the ornate and extensive structures inside vast open space within the mountain. While the city outside had been overgrown with plant life as the forest gradually worked to reclaim it, the structures

198

inside the cavern were exposed and bare, and their unusual beauty was plain to see. The Guardians turned their heads slowly from one side to the other, taking it all in.

The ceiling was barely visible in the shadows far overhead, and covered with wicked stalactites. The Guardians stood at the beginning of an elegant stone bridge. The slender structure curved gently to the left, then the right, before reaching the far side. Its sinuous design appeared to serve no apparent purpose other than to make the bridge pleasing to the eye. The bridge spanned a bottomless ravine that shimmered and glowed with a pale emerald light that almost seemed alive.

Across the chasm, the bridge reached the opposing ledge and opened out into a wide, circular courtyard. The space was surrounded by benches and statues of muscled men and women in various poses, all arranged around a central fountain, its stream of water long since dried up. Along the walls in either direction were square and rectangular structures whose original purpose was long-forgotten. Bold designs were chiseled into the stone, running along the outward faces of the structures, connecting them all with a sweeping, graceful curlicue. On their rooftops stood railings and balconies where the people of Corria must have enjoyed the spectacular view of the cavern. Spots of the same glowing green illuminated the city in several places, somehow housed in globes of translucent glass that reminded the Guardians of Brunar's globelights. Where those of the Mage burned steadily, the cold green fires shimmered and moved, gently swaying within their clear prisons and casting their viridian light all around. Meandering staircases had been carved into the stone to lead to other dwellings higher up, and from those structures, more stairs led higher still. The interior of the cavern was covered in sculpted chambers. Once a thriving metropolis, now the windows and open doors looked like the empty eye sockets on a skull, lifeless and silent.

Off to their left, one structure stretched high up along the wall, easily four or five stories tall. Facing the wide walkway that ran along the front of all of the chambers was a huge and ornate double door, one side of which was open a crack. Nessar marked it as the first place he would search for the Heart, then edged over toward the side of the bridge.

Nessar leaned over the railing and stared down into the shifting light for a time, the green brightness playing over his face and neck, before he turned back to his friends. *The bottom is too far below; I can't see it. I would guess there's glowing lichen down there making the light, but honestly, I can't tell from here.*

Kiran bent down and picked up a small rock, then dropped it over the side. It fell into the emerald abyss below, disappearing into the pale green light. They listened for several heartbeats, but heard nothing. As far as they knew, it never hit bottom.

Well, whatever it is, it's pretty far down there. Let's get moving, I don't like being hemmed in here. Kiran's fear was shared by the others, and they nodded in agreement. Moving quietly and scanning the wondrous city before them, they headed across the stone bridge, treading carefully with each step.

As they approached the halfway point, they heard and felt a sharp cracking sound that froze them in their tracks. A thin crack appeared in the stone beneath their feet, crawling insistently from right to left across their intended path. Quickly, they stepped backwards a few paces until they were well clear of the widening crack. Other rumblings caused the bridge beneath their feet to vibrate more. With a great ripping, shearing sound of stone grinding on stone, the most slender part of the graceful bridge detached itself from the rest of the causeway and plummeted into the wavering river of emerald light below. A few smaller chunks of debris from the jagged edges of the remaining bridge followed, but as before, there was no sound of the rubble impacting anything as it fell. The Guardians stared at the wide gap that now separated them from the other side. The brief echoes faded away almost at once, leaving the trio in silence once more.

Well, that's just wonderful, Kiran silently commented. *At least it was relatively quiet. Whatever emptied out this town can just stay asleep a little while longer, if I have anything to say about it.*

In answer, Layton engaged the power of his Jidaan and created a pair of Gates, one right in front of them and the other in the courtyard across the broken bridge. Without hesitation, he stepped into it and appeared in the courtyard, closely followed by Nessar and Kiran. He turned and gave her a wink as he let the Gates vanish, and she rolled her eyes at his smugness.

All right, then, Nessar's voice broke the silence in their minds. *I want to have a look inside that fancy building.* He pointed to the tall edifice that had captured his attention. *If the Heart is anywhere, it'll most likely be in there. The LorMage mentioned a museum, and that definitely fits the bill.* He cast a glance at the pair and grinned slyly. *This kind of thing is right up my alley. If it's a museum as they said, there may be safeguards in place around the thing. I'll handle any issues of that sort, and then bring it out.*

Kiran and Layton nodded their agreement, and Layton responded, *All right, old friend, we'll keep watch out here. If anything goes amiss, we'll let you know right away.*

Kiran's mental voice had a hint of amusement in it. *It is occasionally good to have a thief of impressive skill on your side. Get to work, old man; make yourself useful.* Though her words were joking, she reached out and squeezed his arm gently, giving him a look that told him to be careful or else she'd put her boot in his arse. He patted her hand and smiled at her in reassurance. Then he turned to head towards the museum, and engaged the power of his Jidaan. The midnight onyx stone in the spear's pommel came to life, its inner darkness roiling briefly as Nessar called to it, and then the old man simply ceased to exist. It was not just that he was invisible; he made no sound whatsoever, and left no tracks on the ground. Within moments, they saw the already open door to the tallest building push farther inwards just enough to admit someone of Nessar's slim build, and then it moved no more. He was inside.

Hels bells, it always gives me the willies when he does that. It's been over twenty years, and I'm still not used to seeing him just...vanish, Kiran commented, eliciting a quiet chuckle from Layton.

Me too, Kiran. I mean, he's just...gone.

Exactly! Kiran gestured, glad that she was not the only one who was unnerved by the completeness of Nessar's disappearance. *Ah, well, maybe I'll get used to it one day. Let's go check things out around the fancy building that he's going to search. I'd like to know what's nearby in case something goes wrong.*

Layton nodded and moved silently forward to examine the chambers nearest the museum on the left, and Kiran quietly worked her way over to the right, both keeping eyes and ears wide open in case something did not take kindly to their intrusion.

*   *   *   *   *   *

Inside the museum, ancient, unlit torches were placed in sconces around the walls. Nessar was pleased to discover that the green, glowing lights were also mounted in every room. Although the light they emitted wavered and moved, he could see quite well without having to use a torch. He smiled absently as he thought about how the Jidaan would hide him even if he were holding a blazing torch aloft in a completely darkened room. He would be able to see better, but anyone outside of the ancient spear's influence would be blind.

The Jidaan's magick hummed through his body, and he welcomed it, although it taxed him, and was exhausting if he used it for too long. However, he had practiced over the years until he could maintain the use of his Gift of Stealth for hours if need be. It was a far cry from when he was first Chosen to wield the Jidaan of Stealth, back when he nearly passed out from using its power for only a few minutes. The old man nodded to himself, pleased at his own progress.

The first room he entered held a central table of marble, shaped like a crescent moon. Along the walls, he saw paintings of several types. Most were still firmly anchored, though some had slipped and fallen to the floor over the centuries. Nessar looked at them, wondering at the skill and talent that must have been employed by the ancient artists. While most were obviously impressionistic paintings, their images hinting at figures rather than clearly depicting them, a few were astonishingly life-like. Some were enormous works of art, while others were barely the size of two spread hands.

Although he knew his mission was urgent, the paintings caused Nessar to spend a few extra moments in contemplation, wondering how anyone could render such realistic pictures using nothing but canvas, paints, knives, and brushes. On one small canvas, a female warrior sat astride a rearing horse, shield in one hand, a sword in the other, her dark hair blowing in the wind. She wore long greaves that protected her shins and knees, and a brief breastplate that had been chiseled to resemble an eagle in flight. Her hair was kept away from her face with a narrow circlet that glimmered gold even in the room's green light, and her expression was fierce, indomitable. Nessar stared at the painting for a long while, captivated. There were no placards he could see, no mention of artist or subject, but the woman enchanted him. He left her only reluctantly, silently promising himself that he could see her again if he hurried.

The first floor of the museum had several large rooms, and he carefully inspected them all. Some held various types of pottery, while others had sculptures of all sizes. Nessar spent a moment looking over one particularly voluptuous depiction of the Goddess Rowann before he chided himself again to find the Heart. *I may be old,* he thought to himself, *but I'm far from dead.* Impressed with the work of the ancient Corrians, he moved on to the adjoining room, eager to see the next display.

Arms and armor were next, and although Nessar could appreciate a good weapon as much as the next thief, he moved through the room quickly. If all went well, he might send Layton back in to have a look, knowing that the younger man would likely burst with joy to see so many bladed and pointy things in one place.

Other rooms awaited, and Nessar moved through them without encountering any problems or traps. Apparently, the Corrians had been a very trusting people, and chose to leave their treasures on display without any

203

magickal theft deterrents. They must have simply stationed guards throughout the museum to keep everyone honest.

At that thought, Nessar stopped in his tracks. *Yes, there would have been guards. So where are they? We've not seen the remains of even a single body since we entered the city. Even a skeleton turned to dust would leave its armor behind. Unless...*Nessar turned quickly to look over his shoulder, reassuring himself that he was still alone in the ancient museum. Finally he pulled a slender dagger from its sheath at his belt and held it at the ready. *Unless whatever killed them all also took their bodies away. For lunch or whatever. Yeah, that's not good.*

Resolving to be more careful, Nessar eased towards the rearmost chamber in the building. Where all of the rooms had open doorways, this one had a large double-door, its heavy wooden beams banded with iron.

There you go. That's the only room on this floor I haven't tried. He moved toward the door and soon felt the tingle of magick as he approached. *Yep. Thought so.* He edged closer, being careful not to trip any of the light wards he felt around the door.

When he was younger, he had always had a knack for sniffing out traps and avoiding them. Sometimes, he had simply followed his stronger instincts and unknowingly dismantled magickal wards without truly knowing what it was that he was doing. He had spent years honing his skills as a thief and gained a reputation as the best in the business, able to succeed at nearly impossible missions where many had previously failed. He had been a shadow, a ghost, a legend. In time, he had risen in the ranks of the Thieves Guild of Rualtha by the strength of his skills alone.

Once he became Guildmaster, however, everything had changed. No longer was he searching for ways to challenge his skills of stealth, lockpicking, climbing, and other such talents. No, he abruptly found himself to be an administrator, overseeing a bunch of quarrelsome and egotistical morons who all had very strong opinions as to exactly what he should have been doing. He had tried to be fair, and that had gained him enemies. He had tried to be kind, and that had lost him respect. By the time he had been Chosen to wield a Jidaan as a Guardian, he was more than ready to leave the whole thing behind. But even now, decades later, he still relished the opportunity to use his hard-won skills. It had never been about the money; it had been the thrill, the challenge.

During the ceremony when his Jidaan had Chosen him as its one and only wielder, the ancient weapon had awakened his slumbering magick, made him intensely aware of the power that had always been within his own body, and then amplified it. His normal senses had become highly acute, and when he focused his magick, he could clearly interpret sensations that had only been vague instincts before. After years of practicing with his magick, mystical traps might as well have had a written sign on them, so visible to his perceptions were they.

Now, as he approached the doors, he explored the wards he felt there and found them to be simple alarms, likely meant to alert someone nearby in the event of an attempted theft. Although there was no one left to answer the alarms, he reached out with his magick and gently disabled them, not wanting any sudden gongs to sound or bells to ring unexpectedly during his visit. When the alarms were nullified, he knelt to inspect the physical locks on the doors. They were an old design, but far more intricate than he had expected.

Ah, yes, he thought as he pulled an old set of high quality lockpicks from a pouch on his belt. *Time to put these old things to good use.* The picks had been a gift from his mentor, a crafty old buzzard known as One-handed Willie for obvious reasons. They had never been far from Nessar since, and he was an expert in their use. It was only a matter of seconds before he heard a sharp click from within the doors, and he grinned in triumph. He stowed the lockpicks away again, oiled the hinges as best he could with oil he carried just for that purpose, and then tried the door. It opened with a soft rattle and swung easily at Nessar's touch.

The inside of the room was a thief's dream come true. Nessar's mouth dropped open as he eased inside, shocked at the wealth that was displayed in the large chamber. Diamonds, emeralds, rubies, gems of all types and sizes were displayed everywhere in all manner of jewelry. Jewel encrusted ornaments of gold and silver adorned life-sized statues all around the room, and alcoves carved in the walls held piles of precious coins and gemstones. Elegant weapons stood in beautiful displays, their hilts glittering with gold and jewels. Had Nessar not seen the extensive and wealthy treasury back at Guardians Keep, he would have been completely thunderstruck at the sight. Even so, he was mightily impressed at what the Corrians had managed to fashion out of the prizes they had dug from beneath the mountain.

Nessar let his gaze travel over the abundant riches in the room and searched for the Heart. He reasoned that it might be in the back, so he carefully made his way deeper into the chamber, still cloaked by the power of his Jidaan.

As he approached the rear of the treasure room, Nessar caught sight of the Heart of Corria at last. It stood alone on a pedestal, illuminated by a single shaft of golden light that fell from an unseen source in the high ceiling. It glittered and sparkled in a dazzling array of colors, though the stone itself had a pink cast to it. It was as the LorMage had said, a faceted diamond the size of two fists placed together, but its stunning beauty made it seem much larger. Nessar stood still for a time, gazing into the depths of the gemstone. *Magnificent,* he thought. Truly, it was the most beautiful thing he had ever laid eyes on. He stood there, staring into it, lost in it, drifting on its endless array of colors. Time slowed.

A distant noise disturbed Nessar's enjoyment of the Heart, and he ignored it. The noise came again, more insistently, and Nessar finally broke free of the spell of the Heart. He shook his head and stepped back, away from the dazzling gem, averting his eyes as he fought to clear his mind.

No wonder the Corrians got greedy, Nessar thought. *That thing has its own power...it must have done something to them. I don't know what else it can do, but we'll have to be careful with it. Can't have it mucking around in our minds, turning us into a bunch of drooling slackjaws.*

Not wanting to take any chances, he quickly dropped his backpack and pulled out a thick leather sack, which he turned inside out, then pulled over his right hand like a sock

206

puppet. Carefully keeping his eyes off of the Heart, he reached out with his magick and checked for any traps or alarms, but found none. He took a deep breath, then moved with the speed of a much younger man. Nessar stepped up to the pedestal that held the Heart, grabbed it with his right hand, then quickly pulled the leather sack back down over it, instantly covering the massive diamond. He tied the thong at the neck of the bag tightly, then double-knotted the thin leather string just to be sure. Breathing a sigh of relief, Nessar strode over to his backpack and stuffed the sack down among his other things, nestling it safely in the bottom. He then slipped his arms back into the straps and allowed himself to relax. He'd done it. He'd taken the Heart of Corria. Gart could never use it for his infernal summoning ritual now.

Just then, he heard an echo of the noise that had roused him from his magickal stupor earlier. He had forgotten about it, but in his mind, he heard a muffled, distant sound that sounded like a familiar voice. His eyes widened as he realized who it was.

Kiran! I'm coming! He ran back towards the huge doors to the chamber, still cloaked under the power of his Jidaan, and was grateful to discover they still stood slightly open, just as he had left them. He slipped out of the treasure room, and as soon as he stepped away from the doors, he felt as though a thick, unseen blanket had been removed from his head as Kiran's voice exploded in his mind.

Gods dammit, you old fool, get your wrinkly arse out here and help us! They're everywhere!

Nessar sprinted down the central hallway, angling around the benches and exhibits that were scattered there, and neared the front doors. One door was still closed, the other pushed inwards as it had been when he had entered the museum. As he raced towards it, he caught sight of the bright blue glow of Kiran's power. Remembering that he was still unseen, he released his Gift and became visible once more. He gasped with relief as the stress of maintaining the cloak of Stealth fell away from him and his Jidaan slept again. Nessar pulled both his daggers and slipped through the gap between the doors, ready to fight.

He found himself standing with Kiran behind a glowing wall of dazzling blue light, a Ward, created by the power of the Jidaan she carried. Kiran stood with her arms sternly folded, just outside the massive doors. Her pale green eyes narrowed as they surveyed her surroundings. The pommel of her Jidaan was on fire where it rested just above her right shoulder, blazing as if the entire blue sky above had been collected in its tiny gemstone. Outside the shimmering shield of energy, an army of hideous creatures were flinging themselves at the barrier, heedless of the injuries they sustained as they slammed into its unyielding surface.

They were human-sized, and humanoid in shape, but there the resemblance ended. Their skin was pale, almost white, and rough with bumps that looked much like those of a toad. The creatures appeared to be blind, since they had no visible eyes, but huge, vertical nostrils dominated the center of their vaguely canine faces. Their jaws grinned widely, displaying rows of wicked fangs. Wiry arms ended in hands that had slender, grasping digits, and their legs were bent backwards like those of birds. Housed in fingers and toes were deadly talons, each as long as Kiran's fingers.

Blowing a stray lock of her hair out of her face, Kiran turned to glance at her old friend, who stood at her side, his mouth open in shock at the sight of the sea of creatures that opposed them.

"I think we can stop worrying about being quiet now. They're awake. Whatever they are."

Nessar stared at the roiling mob of beings that pressed up against Kiran's Ward, his words having deserted him completely. He suddenly realized that Layton was not standing with them, and asked, "Where's Layton? Wasn't he with you?"

Kiran sighed and pointed off to their left. Nessar looked and saw Layton. The warrior was seated on the ground, unconscious, resting with his back to the museum door and his Jidaan lying in his lap. Three of the creatures lay dead at his feet, one neatly cloven from collarbone to groin, leaving a ghastly smear of greenish ichor. His chin was resting on his chest, and he was silent.

"Um...what happened?"

Kiran turned her angry gaze back towards the creatures, not wanting to see Layton's still form or Nessar's judgmental look as she spoke. "They swarmed us from everywhere at once. They were so quiet, we didn't hear them, and didn't sense them coming either. The dead ones there were the first to attack. Layton killed them just as you'd expect he would, then promptly tripped and hit his head on the wall. Knocked himself out colder than a codfish."

There was a long beat of silence before Nessar finally said, "Seriously?"

Kiran fumed silently before answering, her tone dripping with irony. "Yep. The Weaponsmaster, a man whom I've seen dancing atop the walls of Laro, slaying Gholans, Morcats, undead soldiers by the hundreds, nimbler than any acrobat I've ever seen, tripped on a rock and knocked himself unconscious. I tell you what, would you mind dragging him inside so that we can shut the door and I can drop this Ward? I'd have pulled him in there myself, but I didn't want to chance losing my concentration and letting any of these…things," she gestured at the silent beings, "in there with us. Each time they strike the Ward, it drains me a little, and they're pretty persistent; I can't hold this forever."

Nessar wasted no time. He sheathed his daggers and grabbed Layton under his arms while Kiran stepped carefully around the dead creatures and picked up the opal-pommeled Jidaan. Nessar grunted with effort, surprised at how solid the once-wiry fighter had become, then slid him through the space between the doors. Kiran moved in behind the pair, allowing her Ward to shrink to follow them.

Once they were inside the museum, Nessar laid Layton against the wall while Kiran pulled the weighty door closed. She made sure she heard the latch click solidly in place, then she picked up the reinforcing bar that stood off to one side. The ironwood beam had obviously been meant for two people to lift, but she engaged her magick to enhance her strength and hefted it by herself, moving it carefully into place with a loud thump. Once she was satisfied that the windowless building appeared secure, she relaxed and let the Ward outside fall with visible relief. An instant later, the door began to shake as the silent creatures outside began their assault, intent on breaking through to reach their prey.

She turned to Nessar, who was examining Layton's head. "How is he?"

Nessar grimaced and continued looking the younger man over. "Well, it's a nasty knock, that's for sure. He'll feel that one for a long while, and he'll have a goose egg back there that'll sting like Hel. Once he comes to, we'll know more."

Kiran shook her head. "I hope he's all right. If he dies, I'll never be able to give him Hel about this. As inconvenient as it is, I can hardly wait to rib him about it later." A thoughtful look crossed her face then. "I guess even Weaponsmasters can lose a step as they get older."

Nessar turned and regarded her with a raised eyebrow. "Speak for yourself, missy! I feel like a young man of sixty, I'll have you know!"

Kiran scoffed. "Pfft! You're an exception, you old codger." Suddenly, her eyes widened. "Wait, did you find it? The Heart?"

Nessar grinned and doffed his backpack. Kneeling on the floor next to Layton, he reached in and pulled out the leather sack that held their prize.

"Yep! Watch out, though, it has a way about it. Easy to get lost in the thing, so keep your wits sharp." He tossed it to Kiran, who deftly caught it and untied the bag. She was surprised at the weight of it, and whistled softly as she reached inside for the gem.

"Oh..." she said, holding the stunning diamond up to the light, where it glinted and sparkled like nothing she had ever seen. "Oh, yes, that's...the..." her voice trailed off as she lost herself in the Heart. The colors danced and twirled, rainbows of beauty that swirled in her mind. She swirled with them.

Nessar snatched the Heart from her and stuffed it back in the sack, breaking the spell. Kiran instantly snapped out of her trance and sputtered, "What in the Hel? That thing is dangerous! Goddess, what was that?"

Nessar placed the sack back at the bottom of his backpack and shrugged it onto his shoulders once more. "I told you, Kir, it has a way about it. I think the room upstairs had a magickal dampening property to it, the effect wasn't so strong there. No wonder the folks here got crazy with their digging! It's got its own power, though I don't know what good could come of something like that."

Kiran shook her head to clear it. "I hear that, old man. Yes, if Gart is already obsessed, we definitely had better keep that thing out of his hands. There's no telling what it might do to him."

Just then, Layton coughed weakly and his eyelids fluttered open. He groaned and leaned forward, reaching one hand up to probe the swelling on the back of his skull. Kiran rushed over and knelt close by, relief flooding her at the sight of Layton struggling awake. He brought his hand down from his head, and found no blood there. Kiran instantly took it in hers. "Well, there you are, you clumsy arseling! How do you feel?"

Layton squeezed his eyes shut and reopened them a few times as he tried to get them to focus. He gazed at Kiran for a moment, then at Nessar, then he focused on Kiran again and stared intently at her face. For a long time, he said nothing.

"Layton?" Nessar gently urged. "How are you, man?"

"Yes, tell us that you're OK so you can Gate us out of here," Kiran half-joked. "There's a whole mess of nasty creatures outside, and we need your magick to get us across that broken bridge."

Layton kept staring at Kiran, still silent. His brows furrowed as he looked away, deep in thought, then he looked into her eyes again, his confusion plain on his face.

"What magick? I'm sorry, but I don't know what you're talking about. Who are you? And who is Layton?"

Chapter 30

Reyanna held tightly to the slender reins in her hands, though they seemed to do her little good. Her legs ached from clinging to the saddle between her thighs, and she was grateful for the buckled straps that held her legs firmly in place. Although she had been riding Drusilla a couple of hours already, she felt she would never be used to the abrupt changes in height and orientation that the enormous spider was capable of as she made her way rapidly through the forest. Her long, spindly legs skittered along on either side of Reyanna, constantly moving, mesmerizing in their rhythmic motion. Sometimes Drusilla walked along the top branches of the larger trees as easily as Reyanna might walk along a paved pathway, but then she would suddenly dive into the forest below, climbing straight down the trunk of a huge oak, righting herself on the forest floor to continue her eastward trek.

"I must say, Drusilla, you are a wonder," Reyanna said, meaning every word. An odd and alien sense of pleasure skated along the edge of Reyanna's consciousness, a sensation she had come to recognize as Drusilla's way of communicating with her. There were no words, only feelings, but Reyanna was slowly beginning to understand more of the spider's way of speaking. "You are welcome!" she said, and was instantly rewarded by another of the odd tinglings. Reyanna smiled to herself and took another deep breath. She would have to rest soon. Reyanna had no idea how long Drusilla could keep moving, but she, herself, would need a break. She was well-accustomed to riding a horse, but a giant spider? Her body was protesting in a thousand ways. "Hopefully, I'll get used to it at some point," she said absently, keeping her eyes on the forest ahead.

The hours passed quickly, and Reyanna finally discovered how to ride in the saddle more smoothly despite Drusilla's sharp changes in direction. As the afternoon eased towards evening, she began thinking of finding a place to camp for the night. Just then, Drusilla decided to leave the forest floor. She scampered up into the trees and popped out on top of the canopy of thick branches, affording

Reyanna a clear view of the forest for leagues in all directions. It spread out before her, a seemingly endless and gently undulating ocean of green leaves. Far to the west, she could see just a hint of a dark ridge of mountains that looked like an island in an emerald sea. She knew that somewhere beyond it, she would find the ruddy mountains that contained her destination. Much closer, and of distinctly more interest, a few slender columns of smoke rose out of the forest to the north, most likely a settlement of some sort. She had never been this far west, so Reyanna had no idea whether it was a town, a farm, or a single dwelling. Whatever it might be, she thought that a bed might be nice for the evening if she could get it. She had a decent amount of money, and the timing was perfect.

With a bit of pressure from her thighs and a mental command to Drusilla, the young woman found herself traveling directly towards the columns of smoke in the distance, angling slightly away from the mountains. *It won't take too much time off my journey,* she thought. *We can be gone again before morning. I need rest, or I'll be good for nothing when I get where I'm going.*

A tingling burst of feeling from Drusilla surprised Reyanna, laden with what felt like humor. As strong as she was, the spider apparently agreed that some rest was in order. Reyanna's eyes widened, as did her smile. "Drusilla!" she admonished in mock reproach. "Are you telling me that I should lose some weight so that I'll be easier to carry?"

The silent reply was somewhere in the affirmative, but Reyanna could swear that the huge arachnid was teasing her. "Really, Drusilla. How rude!" Tired as she was, she laughed aloud, and if Drusilla had been capable, she would have laughed as well.

As they neared the source of the smoke, the odor of cooking meat finally found Reyanna's nostrils, and her mouth immediately began to water. Suddenly, the thought occurred to her that whoever she was likely to meet was probably not used to seeing gigantic spiders, much less a woman riding on one.

"Drusilla, let me find a place to dismount where they won't see you. You can go hunting and rest tonight, then meet me again before dawn, and we'll be on our way

213

again." Reyanna held on tighter as the spider dug down into the canopy of leaves and headed straight for the forest floor.

As the sunlight disappeared, hidden by the thick branches overhead, Reyanna blinked until her eyes adjusted enough to see the grass and shrubs beneath them. Drusilla's long, almost dainty legs found the earth and she leveled out again, gently settling down so that Reyanna could dismount. The Ranger unbuckled herself from the saddle and stepped down, pulling her pack down with her. She gave the spider an affectionate pat on her abdomen, pleased with the tingle of thanks and affection she received from Drusilla in return. Although initially anxious around the enormous spider, Reyanna had come to know Drusilla during their journey, and she smiled as she realized that she had become fond of her.

"All right, then, be safe out there. I'll see you here in the morning."

Drusilla turned her entire body to face Reyanna and stared at her with all eight of her eyes, the two largest only a foot or two away from the girl. Reyanna felt...concern? "I'll be fine, Drusilla. Really." Reyanna could tell that Drusilla had doubts about that, but the great beast turned without clarifying them and scuttled off into the forest. She looked at the spot where Drusilla had disappeared for a few moments, then shouldered her bag and turned towards the settlement. Although she was tired to the bone, it felt good to be walking under her own power again, and she relished the feel of using her legs as they had been intended.

She strolled through the forest for only a few minutes before the smell of cooking meat intensified. Along with it came the sounds of voices and hammering. She quickened her step when she saw the trees thin out ahead of her, and she emerged from the forest into a wide clearing. A well-worn dirt road ran out of the trees on her left. It crossed the middle of the clearing and passed in front of a wooden building that sat a little way from the worn path, which continued off into the woods to the northeast. The structure was a wide, squat building with a porch that ran all the way across the front. A wagon pulled by a pair of tired looking horses obscured one side of the porch, and a trio of burly men were carrying bundles from inside the building and loading them into the wagon for transport. Two of the workers were younger men, one brown haired and the other coal black, both following orders from a bear of a man with a bushy, graying beard and a bald head.

The older man saw her first as she came out of the forest, and he told the other two to continue loading the wagon. He pulled a square of cloth from the pocket of his trousers and wiped his face and head with it. As he put it back into its accustomed pocket, he tilted his head to one side as he approached and addressed Reyanna.

"Say there, missy," he said, a hint of wariness in his voice. "We don't get many folks just poppin' outta the woods like that. Nothin' that way but forest for days. You lost?" He raised one bushy eyebrow at her as he patiently awaited her response.

Suddenly, Reyanna's mind was awhirl as she thought about what she should say. Her first instinct was always to simply tell the truth, but there were other factors to consider. She was a target; someone was sending deadly magickal creatures to attack her, and she had no idea whether she could protect anyone she met if more beasts were to arrive. Even if they were completely innocent, knowing who she was might put them in danger. *Better safe than sorry, for both me and the people here,* she thought.

Reyanna mustered a dazzling smile for the man, and was relieved when she saw him relax. "Yes! I left the road to avoid a group of rough-looking men and managed to lose my way."

The man frowned and deep lines creased his wide forehead in concern. "I'm sorry that happened, but I'm glad you're still in one piece. They might have been harmless, but these days, you can never tell. A young lass like yourself alone on the road would have been an easy target for a bunch of thugs." Then his demeanor brightened. "You need a place to stay? There's a room still available, and the evening meal should be ready soon. Won't cost you too much, either."

Reyanna's smile flashed again. "That sounds perfect. Please show me the way."

The man turned and looked at the young men who were supposed to be loading the wagon. Both had stopped to gawk at Reyanna's raven hair and blue eyes, not to mention her graceful curves. "Close your mouths, lads, gawking ain't polite. And get back to work!" The youths snapped out of their momentary trance and bashfully went back to their tasks, suddenly looking everywhere but at the young woman. "My apologies for my sons' lack of manners, miss. I didn't raise them in a barn. Well, not completely, anyways. They should know better."

Reyanna was not sure who was more embarrassed, the young men for being caught staring, or herself. "No offense taken, sir. At least they didn't whistle at me."

The man laughed, a loud and hearty chuckle. "Oh, they know I'd have boxed their ears for that, for sure! Pardon my saying, but you are quite pleasing to look upon, milady, but that's no excuse. I'll not have that kind of disrespect visited on a lady by my boys."

He glared balefully at them and they muttered a quiet, "Yes, Pa!" and moved a little faster.

More quietly, he added as he looked back at Reyanna, "They're good boys, though. I love them dearly, lunkheads though they often are." He offered a sly wink that made Reyanna giggle. "I'm Geoff. Those two are Arlen and Baylen. We've a few regulars who come in for the evening meal, but they won't bother you."

"I'm sure we'll all get along just fine, Geoff. I'm...Reyna." Although she hated to be dishonest, she strongly felt that she should not use her real name, hoping that an alias might throw her pursuers off the trail. "And I'm very pleased to make your acquaintance, Geoff." She tilted her head and curtseyed briefly.

Geoff smiled, showing big, blocky teeth through his beard as he bowed low with exaggerated majesty in return. When he had finished, he said, "Well met, Lady Reyna! Come on, I'll introduce you to my wife, Vania, and then get you settled." He led her up the steps and held the door open for her.

216

The inn was simple, but well-made and clean, and it was obvious that Geoff took great pride in it. A spacious common room had a few sturdy tables and chairs scattered throughout, and a huge fireplace dominated one corner. Vania was a bustling little woman, filled with energy, and she delighted in meeting Reyanna before rushing back to the kitchen to make a special dessert in her honor. Smiling, Geoff watched her go and remarked, "Oh, I do love that little woman. Especially when she gets all excited like that. She just loves when new people stop by. Which is probably why we run an inn instead of a farm or something like that. New folks all the time."

Geoff led her up the stairs and turned down a hallway, walking to the last door on his right. He opened it and gestured for her to step inside. "Here you are, Reyna. I hope you're comfortable here. Dinner will likely start in a quarter hour, so I hope we see you down there soon."

The room was like the rest of the inn, simple, but clean and well-kept. Reyanna only had eyes for the soft-looking bed. She set her traveling pack and weapons on the floor and promptly walked over to it. She sat down with a sigh, luxuriating in the feel of it after so many days sleeping on the ground. "It's lovely, Geoff! Thank you so much!"

"My pleasure, milady." He gently closed the door, leaving Reyanna alone in the quiet. She flopped down on her back, intending to relax for only a moment.

It was fully dark when her eyes opened again and she was dismayed to find that she had curled up on the bed and fallen deeply asleep. A blanket had been placed over her during the night. She also noticed that her boots were off and standing together at the foot of the bed, though she did not remember removing them. The smell of cooked beef caught her attention and she saw a covered platter and a large earthenware mug sitting on a desk in the corner. In front of it was a folded sheet of paper with her name carefully written in blocky script.

She stretched, enjoying the sensation to the full, and then walked over to the desk. She picked up the note and read:

Reyna,

When you did not come down for dinner, I worried for you, so I came in and saw you sleeping like you really needed it. I took off your boots so you'd be more comfortable and left some food for you. I hope you like the tarts!

Vania

She lifted the cover from the platter and found a bowl of thick beef stew, a chunk of buttered bread, and three small pastries. Her eyes misted at Vania's kindness. After the things she had faced lately, the sense of relief and safety she felt at the inn was almost overwhelming. She knew she still had a long and dangerous way to go, but rest and a good meal would help her face it. She pulled up a stool and tucked into the food, intent on enjoying every morsel.

She finished it all and took a long pull on the mug of ale before wiping her lips with the napkin Vania had left. Reyanna belched in a very unladylike fashion, then pushed the platter aside. She walked to the window and looked outside, gauging by the moon's position in the clear sky that it was not quite midnight. *Good!* she thought. *I can still sleep for a few hours before I leave to find Drusilla.* She took a few minutes to tend to other bodily needs, then went back to the remains of her meal on the desk. She dug in her money pouch and left a silver piece beside the tray, then added another out of gratitude. She slid back under the covers, feeling better than she had felt since the vision had struck her. She turned on her side, closed her eyes, and was back asleep in moments, lulled by the gentle sound of the wind outside her window.

The dream started not long after. It was a gradual thing, as Reyanna had immediately drifted into a deep sleep, but she found herself aware of her surroundings again. She was not entirely sure whether she was dreaming or awake. The bed felt the same, soft and comfortable, just as before, but everything felt different. There was a strange reddish light in the room that had not been there before. She had rolled over onto her back, and now it felt like the

218

blanket weighed a thousand pounds. Reyanna tried to roll over again, but found that she could not. She was still heavily drowsy. She tried to just relax and wait it out.

"Who are you?" the voice said, feminine and curious, and laced with menace. A bolt of fear surged through Reyanna as she tried to turn her head only to find that she could not. She was held fast, a statue, unable to do anything but breathe and move her eyes. She strained to find the source of the voice. Her heart began to thunder beneath her ribs, but she said nothing. "Who are you? Each time I scry, I see your face. I've sent creatures to dispatch you, just in case you might somehow seek to hinder my plans, but you keep escaping somehow. How is that, my little pet? There must be something special about you, yes?"

Reyanna struggled to turn her head and finally saw a shape, a woman, standing a few feet away. The strange, wavering light was actually coming from her. Her curvaceous body was shimmering, shifting, as if it were a reflection on a pool of water. Reyanna realized with a start that she could see through the woman as if she were a ghost. Her skin was pale as the moon, her hair radiantly scarlet and her lips the same bloody shade. She was stunningly beautiful, yet she exuded malice and cruelty as well.

Reyanna's mind was racing. She could not move, she could not cry out, and she had no idea who the woman was. Even so, she took care to examine her face, struggling to memorize every detail of the crimson-haired apparition. She felt her magick begin to awaken, deep in the center of her body. It began to roil and writhe, squirming in its eagerness to be used. She felt her body begin to respond, slowly breaking the unseen shackles that held her immobile.

The stranger's gasp almost startled Reyanna. "Such strength!" Suddenly, the bonds fell back onto Reyanna, mercilessly pinning her to the bed, crushing her under an immoveable weight. "Well, I never suspected you had that much power in you! You certainly don't seem to be a mage, nor a priestess...hmmm. No matter. If you can do that much, then you're definitely a danger to me, even if you don't know what you're doing. Such a pity."

The ghostly woman walked over to where Reyanna had left her pack and looked down at it. Moving leisurely, she bent to rummage around in it, then stood tall again. Reyanna's dagger shone bloody in the spectral light, its undeniable solidity a stark contrast to the insubstantial fist that held it. "Such a pity," the woman said again as she walked to Reyanna's bedside.

Reyanna's eyes widened in fear. She knew the strange woman was going to kill her as she lay helpless, and for a moment, terror gripped her heart in its icy talons. Then, when Reyanna thought she could take no more, the fear was replaced by something stronger, something that began to burn white-hot in her breast.

Rage.

Reyanna had bent her will towards the task of being a Weya Ranger for well over a decade, forcing herself to endure far more than her Weya classmates. They recovered faster, ran farther and with much less strain than she. They melted into the forest as if born to do so, while Reyanna had struggled along clumsily at first, bumbling through the foliage like a wounded bull. She had endured their quiet, jewel-eyed stares, their silent pity, and set herself to work twice as hard. The Weya children never said a word about how slow she was compared to them. They never had to. Reyanna could read it all in their faces. She swore that she would be the best of them someday, a child's promise with the unbending solidity only a furious child could harbor.

She had loosed arrows at targets in all kinds of weather, from standing, kneeling, hiding in trees, even while running in the dark. She had practiced with her bow until her fingers bled, but she had never once given up. She learned every track of every animal that lived in the forests, and recognized every call, hoot, and howl.

She constantly pushed herself to the limits of her body and mind, always striving to be something more than she had started out to be. The aches, the scrapes, the bruises, all were suffered without complaint, though she often cried in the night where no one would see her. Each time, she had dried her tears and woke the next day even more determined to do better. She had even pushed her magick away, hidden it deep inside herself in an attempt to achieve everything honestly from her own work.

In the end, she had done it. Finally, she had been accepted into the Rangers, and all of her classmates had rejoiced with her. In her mind, she had finally earned their respect. She was a Ranger, the only human Ranger in Weya history. Her adoptive parents had been so proud they had cried unabashedly at her induction ceremony.

And now, here she was, held immobile in a bed by a woman she did not even know, mixed up in something she still did not understand. She was going to die without even the chance to prove herself as a Ranger.

No. She thought as her rage grew upon itself. She focused on the word, that simple expression of defiance. Her anger continued to build. It consumed her, pushing everything else away. *No.* Her magick seethed inside her, straining to escape the confines of her imprisoned body. *NO.*

Reyanna sucked in a deep breath and released her pent up anger with a yell that burst from her lips, startling the spectral woman. "NOOO!" Reyanna's magick exploded from within her in a searing, burning rush, and her world went completely white. The power instantly incinerated her clothing and the thick blanket, vaporizing them into nothingness, dispelling Melidia's most powerful binding ward as though it had never existed.

Melidia's shade gasped in shock at the explosion. Reyanna's dagger, held up only by the strength of Melidia's concentration and will, dropped to the floor with a clatter. Although she was in no physical danger, the sorceress instinctively threw her arms over her face and vanished, her astral self escaping back into her body nearly a continent away. The crimson glow, already eclipsed by the burning white fire of Reyanna's magick, vanished entirely as Melidia disappeared. On the remains of the bed, Reyanna sat up, her eyes burning with fiery power and a sly grin upon her lips. All traces of fear had vanished, replaced by an inhuman arrogance that shone from her as brightly as a bonfire. Reyanna, the young human woman, was gone; in her place was something far greater.

The door slammed open, kicked in from the other side. Drawn by the commotion and Reyanna's scream, Arlen stood framed in the doorway. His dark hair was tousled from sleep, and he was naked to the waist. In his hands, he held a stout club with some authority. His face was set in a determined scowl until he saw the naked Reyanna on the bed, magickal flames flowing from her, burning everything they touched. The walls and ceiling were ablaze, though Arlen did not quite register the fact, for his attention was riveted to the naked woman amid the flames. He had never seen anything so beautiful, yet so deadly. He stood frozen, his eyes wide, his mouth open in shock.

Reyanna got to her feet in one graceful, swaying movement. The smile never left her face, though her eyes were still filled with fire. She took a single, sensual step toward the door, then another.

"Arlen! What's going...on?" Baylen had rushed to aid his brother. His face appeared over Arlen's shoulder, only to assume the same expression of surprise. They both froze, and it almost meant their deaths.

Still smiling, Reyanna lifted both hands and unleashed a torrent of magickal flame at the two men, a ferocious blast that seared the air as it passed. Arlen and Baylen dove in separate directions, tumbling to the wooden floor. The molten energy burst through the doorway to incinerate the wall beyond it into fiery rubble, sending chunks of wooden planks, roofing shingles, and other debris flying out into the road and leaving a gaping hole in the side of the inn. A rainstorm had sprung up during the night, and droplets rained into the hallway through the hole, but evaporated instantly upon encountering Reyanna's power. Both men crawled desperately away from the blistering heat. The other doors down the hall had been flung open and owl-eyed guests peered in horror at the devastation.

"Get downstairs!" Arlen yelled as he struggled to his feet. "Now! Get out as fast as you can!" The other patrons needed no urging. Soon the few other residents of the inn were stampeding down the stairs to safety. Arlen watched them go and then turned back to the blaze. Reyanna's room had been the last one at the end of the hall, and Baylen had crawled as far away from the conflagration as he could.

222

Arlen peered through the flames and smoke to see his brother curled in a ball on the floor, trying desperately to shrink away from the searing heat. He did not appear injured, but the fire was eating its way through the surrounding walls and ceiling at an alarming rate.

Just then, Reyanna walked out of her room to stand between the two brothers. Arlen stared at her and realized that she was not actually touching the floor. Her toes floated nearly a foot from the burning floorboards in the hallway, her body held aloft by the fiery blaze of her magick. Slowly, she turned towards Arlen, her sweet smile belying the fierce power that burned in her eyes.

"No! P-please!" Arlen held his hands up in front of him, desperately trying to dissuade her. "Please stop! Why are you doing this? Please!"

Reyanna slowly cocked her head to one side as she looked at him, as though he was an interesting but unimportant specimen to be examined. One arm rose in an elegant gesture and Arlen knew his life was measured in moments.

"Who…what are you?" Arlen fell to his knees and covered his head with his arms, not noticing the tears that fell from his cheeks.

"Reyna, STOP!"

Reyanna tilted her chin up and focused her blank, fiery eyes on the source of the voice. The burly innkeeper, Geoff, had finally made it up the stairs and interposed himself between Reyanna and his son, who still cowered on the floor. The older man's eyes were wild with fear, but he stood his ground with his hands out in front of him.

"Milady, no! Whatever is wrong, this is not the way! Leave my boys alone!" Geoff pleaded with the flaming apparition that had already destroyed a large chunk of his home and business and still threatened to kill his sons. "We don't want any trouble, just let us go!" Vania suddenly appeared and grabbed her husband around his waist, crying in terror but unwilling to let him face this unknown daemon alone. Geoff tried to dislodge her and shove her behind him, but she held fast. Arlen clambered to his feet and stood alongside his parents, wrapping his arms around his mother and trying to shield her as best he could.

223

Reyanna watched the frightened family as they clutched each other. Her dark hair billowed around her face, moved by the heat and flames without being consumed by them. The thin tracery of scars that crawled from her arm to her back, neck, and jaw, shone brightly as slender rivers of molten gold. She was strikingly beautiful, but no less terrifying for it. Her blank, fiery gaze flicked to the older man that had stepped between her and the insignificant boy who had accosted her. For a moment, her sly smile remained as cold and heartless as ever. Then, her brow wrinkled slightly as though something had occurred to her. Her head tilted to one side and her smile slowly turned into a frown of puzzlement. Her outstretched arm, poised to unleash a torrent of flame so intense it would vaporize anything it touched, lowered to her side instead. Her head tilted again as her frown deepened. She floated there, unmoving, for a few moments as Geoff and his family prayed to the Goddess Rowann to save them.

As if in answer, Reyanna's eyelids closed and the blaze of power that held her aloft suddenly vanished. The heat, unbearably intense before, instantly diminished. Without warning, she fell hard to the floor in a seemingly boneless tangle of limbs, her forehead striking the planks below with a loud *thunk*. No longer held at bay by her power, the rain began to pour in through the hole in the wall she had created, and smoke began to billow through the hallway as what flames remained lost their hold on the quickly-sodden wood.

Immediately, Geoff turned to Arlen. "Get buckets of water! Now! The rain will help, but we've got to save what we can!" He leaned over to look into Reyanna's room and was astonished to see that it was still mostly intact. The flames were centered around the doorway and ceiling, although the bed was a burnt mess. "If we hurry, we can stop this before it gets any worse!"

"Yes, Pa!" Arlen turned to head down the stairs and nearly ran into one of the other guests with a bucket of water. He grabbed it and then edged into Reyanna's room, followed closely by other men carrying more buckets.

Geoff leaped forward, skirting the unconscious form of the girl on the smoldering floor and rushing to Baylen, who was already getting to his feet on the other side of the hallway. The young man was shaking and blistered from Reyanna's fire, but otherwise unharmed. The lad had his eyes riveted on Reyanna's still form.

"She," Baylen stammered, "she tried to kill us, Pa,"

Geoff looked over at the girl, who now looked much smaller, tiny even, now that her power had been extinguished. He was desperately trying to reconcile the sweet young woman he had allowed into his home with the deadly fire-daemon she had somehow become. "Aye," he said in a low voice. "But in the end, she didn't, now did she? She stopped. That counts for something, I think. I don't think she knows what she's doing, son."

Once he was assured that Baylen was basically uninjured, he turned his attention to the girl. She lay where she had fallen, still unconscious. Rain had soaked her completely, plastering her hair to the floor, but she did not wake. Vania came forward with a blanket she had grabbed from one of the other rooms and covered her damp, naked body. Geoff scooped her up as though she were only a drowsy kitten and carried her down the stairs and into the kitchen. He laid her down softly in one corner and then turned to his wife.

"Watch her. If she wakes, keep her calm and don't let her leave."

Vania was terrified, but nevertheless responded with her usual sass, "I'm thinking she could certainly walk out of here if she has a mind to, but I'll keep watch over her well enough."

Geoff did not respond, but closed the door sharply. He reopened it a moment later and tossed a charred, damp knapsack to Vania, who caught it and immediately dropped it in disgust. A bow and quiver of arrows followed, and a dagger as well.

"They're hers! From the room!" Then Geoff was gone again, and Vania was left alone with the sleeping girl. Reyna, as Vania knew her, slept peacefully, a dark bruise on her forehead the only sign of what had happened. Vania stared at her for a time, then began pacing back and forth in her agitation.

225

This girl, she thought, *she almost killed us all! She can't be human!* Vania turned to look at her and saw how young she looked, how vulnerable. Vania resumed her pacing, listening to the muffled yells of the men outside as they fought the flames down the hall. Vania glanced at the girl every so often, but she remained silent. Her chest gently rose and fell as she breathed, but otherwise, she remained asleep. Seeing her that way, Vania found herself conflicted.

A part of her had wanted to scream at her husband when the girl had fallen, telling him to plunge his dagger into her heart so that she could not rise and hurl flames at them again. *My boys!* Vania thought. *She nearly killed both my boys!* Certainly, she had nearly demolished their home and their livelihood with her magick. She *had* to be evil. Vania remembered meeting her the previous evening; the girl had seemed so sweet, and a little lost. Vania had sensed nothing evil in her then, but reasoned that people could hide almost anything. She turned to stare at the young woman, trying to read her face for any signs of her intent. Vania saw nothing but the lovely face of an exhausted, bruised young woman. Her hair was still damp from the rain that had fallen through the giant hole she had made in the side of the inn. There was no sign of the fearsome, fiery creature she had become. She was little more than a girl.

Vania steeled herself and walked over to check the pulse at Reyna's throat. She found it to be steady and strong. Looking down at her, Vania tried to maintain her righteous anger, but found that she could not. She traced her fingers gently along the network of thin scars that marred the girl's otherwise smooth skin. They were thinnest along her jawline, almost invisible unless you knew where to look. From there, they flowed down her neck and back, and down her right arm. Thinking of the pain those burns must have caused the girl, Vania sighed and sank down to the edge of the bed next to her, smoothing a lock of raven-black hair away from the girl's face. *You're lucky.* Vania thought. *The Goddess Rowann must have a plan for you, else we might have killed you the moment you fell.* Even as she thought it, she knew that Geoff would have done no such thing. He liked to get to the bottom of things before he acted. Geoff liked answers, and often had more questions than a man had a right to. He was a caring and thoughtful man, and if he had decided to keep the girl safe, then Vania trusted him enough to do the same. Besides, with her boys unharmed, the thought of plunging a knife into Reyna's heart while she slept made Vania more than a little sick inside.

Finally, a smile curled one side of Vania's mouth. *Indeed, it must have been Rowann's will that brought you to us; you'd have been killed or run out of town by anyone else after all that.*

Just then, Baylen opened the kitchen door and poked his head inside. Sweat and rainwater dripped from his hair, making smears in the black soot that covered his face. His teeth shone white in a grin as a spoke. "We stopped it! The fire is out! Pa says we've got a lot of work to do to patch the big hole in the wall in the hallway and repair the damage in her room as well. Part of the ceiling and roof burned away in there, too, but it's nowhere near as bad as we thought it would be, especially after how hot it was." His forehead furrowed as he frowned. "It's funny, but it's like the fire just died along with her. I mean, when she passed out. It disappeared when she hit the floor, is what I'm saying." His eyes fell on the girl and widened. Lowering his voice, he continued. "She's not going to do anything like that again...is she?"

Relieved at the news, Vania sighed heavily before answering. "Well, of that, I can't be sure, Baylen. She's quiet now, at least. I suppose we'll just have to ask her when she wakes and hope for the best."

Baylen nodded solemnly, then heard Geoff bellowing for him to go and grab a canvas from the barn. "Back to it, then. Be careful, Ma."

Vania watched her son shut the door and felt tears of relief well up and roll down her face as he left. He was safe, they all were, and she was grateful. She wiped her tears and then looked down at the sleeping girl again, wondering what in the world to do with her. She hoped that keeping her alive wasn't a mistake.

227

Chapter 31

The ancient doors rattled as hundreds of deadly creatures tried to get through them. Aside from the noise at the doors, the outside was eerily silent. Inside the museum, the green, wavering lights cast shifting shadows on the three Guardians. Kiran and Nessar stared at Layton, who was still seated on the floor with a confused look on his face, though it could be argued that Kiran and Nessar were more confused than he was.

Nessar found his voice first. "What? That's you, lad! Don't tell me that knock on the head..." Nessar's voice trailed off as he vaguely recalled a tale he had heard back in Rualtha; a wealthy landowner had taken a spill down his own spiral staircase, banging his head in the process. When he had regained consciousness, he had no recollection whatsoever of whom or where he was. It had caused quite a stir of gossip throughout town until a priestess of Rowann had been called in to heal him. Nessar groaned and rubbed his face roughly with one callused hand.

Kiran's approach was different. She leaned over, firmly grabbed Layton by both shoulders, and looked deeply into his eyes. "Layton, quit kidding around, man! Look, I'm Kiran, that's Nessar, and there is a swarm of ugly creatures out there that seem intent on having us for lunch. We need you to snap out of it and Gate us out of this place so we can escape this hole!" She had managed to keep her tone somewhat level, but her frustration was rising.

Layton scowled and rubbed his head again as he tried to process what he had heard. His head was aching fiercely and his guts were roiling with nausea. He glanced from Kiran to Nessar and back again before gently shaking his head. "I'm so sorry, but I don't know either of you. And I don't recognize Layton, either, even though you say that's who I am. Not that I could tell you my real name, though. That seems to have escaped me at the moment." When Kiran sat back on her heels and sternly folded her arms, he added, "I'm really sorry!"

Kiran glared at Nessar. "Well, this is just wonderful. Layton's Gates are our one way out of here, and his mind is apparently out to lunch. What are we going to do, Ness?"

The old man thought for a moment before responding. "Well, I could try to sneak us out of here with my Jidaan. You know it renders me invisible to eyes and ears."

"What about to smell?" Kiran retorted. "Those things don't have any eyes! I have no doubt they could smell fly droppings at fifty paces; they'd most certainly smell the likes of us."

"I would think that's covered, too," Nessar mused. "Though I haven't tested it specifically. The only problem I'm seeing with the whole idea is there are so many creatures that there's no room to move around them. Unseen and unheard doesn't mean they can't touch us, magick of the Jidaan or no. One of them bumps into us, and that would be it. They'd rip us to pieces, whether they smelled us or not."

Kiran harrumphed in frustration. "Cripes. I could Ward us in that case, but it would still be a problem. We'll just have to figure out something else. Is there another way out of here?"

Nessar shook his head. "Not that I saw." He paused then, frowning. "Wait, there was a stairwell that I didn't stop to investigate. If it leads to the roof, we might be able to see another way out."

Kiran thought about that. "It might also let in a flood of those uglies, if they're already on the roof waiting for us." She sighed. "Even so, it's worth a look." She stood up and offered a hand to the confused Layton. "Can you stand up?"

Layton took her hand and slowly got to his feet, wincing as he did so. He rubbed the back of his head with one hand, then nodded. "Yes, I'm well enough, I think. What was your name again?"

Kiran sighed. "Kiran. This is Nessar. We've all known each other for nearly twenty-five years. We're Guardians, Chosen by the Jidaan to be protectors of the Realm. Or something like that, I'm not much for fancy talk. Here," she bent to retrieve his Jidaan and handed it to him. "This is yours. Do you remember how to use it at all?"

229

He hefted it in his hands, feeling the weight of it. "It's lighter than I expected!" To Kiran's dismay, he began to clumsily move the blade through the air. He looked like someone who had never held a weapon. "I guess...the sharp end goes into the bad guy?" Although Layton's memory had departed, and he still felt sick to his stomach, the tiniest bit of his boyish excitement and usual good humor still forced their way out.

Nessar groaned and Kiran sighed again. "Right. In this case, they're pale, creepy monsters with sharp claws, lots of teeth, and no eyes. Just keep that thing pointed in a safe direction and follow us." To Nessar, she continued, "Where's the door, Ness? We may as well get on with it."

"Follow me, then," Nessar replied, and he walked down the hallway of the ancient museum, Kiran and Layton following closely behind. As he passed the painting of the warrior woman he had seen before, he snatched it off the wall and put it in his pack without slowing.

Kiran saw him do it, and in spite of her frustration at their situation, she almost laughed. "A little souvenir, Ness?"

"What can I say? It speaks to me. I like it. It's doing no one any good here, and it'll look great in my living room."

Kiran's mood brightened in spite of herself. They had been through a lot worse than this together, and if Nessar was planning on hanging that painting in his little cottage in Tamaransett, then he was confident they would find a way to safety somehow. As usual.

"Fine, let's pick up the pace a bit. I'd like to see us get out of here sooner rather than never. One wrong move and those things will be sucking the marrow out of our bones."

"That's my girl. Always such a ray of sunshine."

Nessar reached the door and motioned his two companions to silence. He carefully placed a hand on the ancient wood, then laid his ear on its dusty surface. When he heard and felt nothing, he nodded at them and carefully opened the door, his dagger appearing in his other hand as if by magick.

The door swung open with a creak, just as it had when he checked it earlier. It revealed a stairway that curled in on itself as it rose into the upper levels of the museum. The stairs were lit from above by the same shimmering greenish light, so at least they were in no danger of stumbling in the dark.

So far, so good. Give me a minute and I'll take a quick look. Nessar's voice echoed in Kiran's and Layton's minds. Layton looked thoroughly startled at the sound of a voice in his head. He was about to ask about it when Kiran glared so hard at him that he closed his mouth with a snap. She nodded grimly at him and then turned her attention back to Nessar. The old man ignited the power of his Jidaan and simply vanished. Layton's astonishment was evident, but Kiran again shushed him, this time with a raised finger. She gritted her teeth in frustration and tried to use one of Brunar's breathing exercises to calm herself.

Moments passed, and suddenly Nessar snapped into view on the stairs, his face alight and smiling. "I have good news and not so good news."

Kiran rolled her eyes. "I may punch you in the neck, Nessar. What's the good news?"

Amused as always by Kiran's attitude, he explained. "This stairwell goes all the way to the roof. There are no creepies up there, and as far as I can tell, we'll be safe while we take a look around and get our bearings."

Layton quietly entered the conversation. "What's the not so good news?"

Nessar suppressed a chuckle. "Well, the reason they can't reach us is that there's no rooftop close enough for them to make the jump. Which means it's going to be difficult for us," his eyes twinkled with mischief, "but maybe not impossible. Come on, I'll show you." He turned and headed up the stairs, far spryer than any eighty-year-old that Kiran had ever seen.

"He's enjoying this, I just know it," she mumbled as she mounted the stairs. Layton trailed after her, staying silent for the moment, but following closely. He still had no idea what was going on, who he was, or why they were in this predicament. And his head still felt as though it was being used as a drum.

The pair followed Nessar up the winding staircase, passing doors at each floor similar to the one they had used to enter the stairwell. When they had passed five such doors, the stairs ran out, and they found themselves on a landing with a single, ornate door in one wall. Nessar stood there, waiting for them with a sly grin on his face.

Kiran was irritated. "You seem to be having fun, old man."

Nessar chuckled briefly and ran one hand through his sparse white hair. "You know, I guess I am. Tending the farm and writing my books has its charms, but it's too comfortable." He smiled, showing teeth that were still strong despite his age. "This here is a bit more exciting, wouldn't you say?"

Kiran sighed loudly and shook her head, but in her heart, she was thinking exactly the same thing. At first, she had taken up the inn and mercenary contractor business so that she could settle down and get away from the dangers that the Guardians had faced, both during the war with Mordak and afterward. She had been truly happy there with Oswald, and relieved to be out of harm's way for a change. She had felt safe, and as Nessar had said, comfortable.

Then months had stretched into years, and she had begun to feel itchy inside, anxious. The recent fight with the louts at the inn had been most welcome, in fact. She had felt almost alive again. Now, there was a horde of dangerous monsters outside who would kill them all without hesitation, Layton had his brains addled, and they were all trying desperately to find a way to escape so they could stop Gart from destroying the world. It was a decidedly uncomfortable situation. And she loved every minute of it.

"I hate to admit it, but...yes. Now show us what's up here so we can get on with it." Kiran refused to allow herself to smile at the old man, but his grin widened as she knew it would. He pushed open the door and gestured for her and Layton to step through.

Once through the door, they found themselves on the roof of the museum, not quite a hundred feet above the stone floor of the cavern. The roof had a waist-high parapet, which they leaned on as they looked down at the sea of constantly-moving creatures, an ocean of pale, deadly

232

beings that covered every inch of open space below. They had stopped their attack on the door and now skittered quietly as they searched around the perimeter of the museum, hunting for a way in. They found that the doors and windows were few and solidly barred, so they continued probing the walls. At times, they crawled over each other without noticing, finding their way with their heightened senses of smell and hearing. They often emitted a sharp popping sound from deep in their throats, then turned their heads side to side as they interpreted the signals they received in return, naturally echolocating to make up for their lack of vision. Here and there, a hideous, eyeless face would turn up to gaze in their direction for a few moments before looking away again. Kiran shuddered at the sight.

"Brrr," she said as the chill rolled down her spine. "They're giving me the creepy crawlies. Do you see any way out of here?" Even as she said it, she was scanning the nearest rooftops for an escape route.

Nessar had spent many hours traversing rooftops during his time as a thief in Rualtha, and his practiced eye wandered over the surrounding structures, assessing the possibilities. Unfortunately, the neighboring rooftops were too far to easily reach, even with their enhanced jumping ability. He frowned as he turned the problem over in his mind. "Well, even if we could make it to the other rooftops, we still have the same problem we have here: we have to get back to ground level, make our way through the swarm down there, and get across the chasm somehow. I'm not yet seeing how to do that."

"Wow, there certainly are a lot of them down there. What are they, again?" Still queasy, Layton clutched tightly to the top of the stone parapet as he stared at the pale beings that stood between them and the ravine.

His eyes still roving slowly around the cavern as he searched for a way out, Nessar replied absently, "Some kind of underground creature I've never heard of. They don't appear to be friendly, judging from the fact that they killed everyone in this city centuries ago and tried to kill you and Kiran earlier today."

Layton scowled. "Right. Not friendly. Got it." He rubbed the back of his head, wishing he could make more

233

sense out of the situation. He did not like being confused. He ran his hands over his torso as if getting accustomed to it, and when his hands found his sword hilt, he took a step back and drew it from its scabbard. He waved it around clumsily for a few moments, then slid it back into its scabbard, nearly cutting himself in the process. He cursed absently, exasperated. The blade had felt alien and peculiar to him. However, at the edge of his consciousness was the feeling that something vast awaited if he could only grasp it, like a thought on the tip of his tongue.

Kiran watched him and rolled her eyes, though she said nothing. Instead, she scanned the roiling crowd below and tried to figure out how they could get through it, and then find a way across a chasm that appeared to have no bottom. Every inch of open space between the buildings and the near side of the ravine seemed to be covered with the creatures, with almost no space whatsoever in which to move, even if Nessar's Jidaan could render them all invisible. She thought about simply throwing a Ward around them all and working their way through the mob, but even if they reached the edge, how would they get across? The wide channel was much too far to jump, even with their abilities. A glance upward told her that the ceiling of the cavern would be nearly impossible to climb as they would be hanging upside down the entire time, even if they had the gear to do it. Kiran had to admit she was stumped, and that infuriated her. She tried to think back to her time with Brunar, back when she was young and newly-Chosen. He had said something that was nagging at the back of her mind.

Before she could grasp it, Nessar spoke again, his voice quiet. "I swear, it's like we stuck a toe in an anthill or something, the way they've swarmed all over everything down there."

Kiran grunted in agreement. "Right. And I'd hate to see the queen of that anthill."

Nessar grimaced and turned to look at her in disgust. "Did you really just say that? Are you *trying* to bring more trouble down on us right now? 'Cause that's how you bring more trouble."

234

Just then, they heard a muffled grunt from Layton and the grinding sound of stone against stone. They quickly turned to see what had happened and saw Layton leaning over the parapet, looking at them in alarm as rock dust floated around him. A portion of the wall was suddenly missing.

"Whoops," he said with a grimace. "A piece of the wall broke away while I was leaning on it. It fell…"

They heard the rubble landing in the crowd below with the meaty sound of stone impacting on pale, leathery flesh. Only one of them had been killed outright by the largest chunk of debris that had fallen, while a few others clutched their injuries, moaning piteously in agony, their odd-sounding cries echoing in the cavern. The other cave dwellers instantly stopped moving, ignoring the few injured. As one, their eyeless faces turned upwards, towards the trio of humans atop the museum. There was a moment of stillness, and then the entire horde burst into motion, swarming the face of the building. They crawled on top of each other as they used their powerful claws to dig into the stone, pulling themselves upwards. Where they could not reach the stone, they grabbed the bodies of their fellows. The roiling mass of creatures began to make its way up the wall.

"Yeah, that's not good. Sorry." Layton apologized as Kiran swore.

"Hurry! Back into the museum!" Nessar took one look at the frantically climbing mob and was suddenly worried that they might not make it back to the doors in time. He grabbed Layton's arm and pulled him away from the wall only to see him stumble and fall to his knees, his features contorted in agony. The sudden movement had aggravated his head injury. "Kiran, help me with him!" Nessar called, and Kiran quickly came around and grabbed him by his free arm. Together, they hefted him to his feet, and Layton struggled to keep his balance.

"I'm sorry," he apologized as he tried to hurry, but he stumbled again. Kiran and Nessar started dragging him towards the door to the stairwell.

Just then, the first of the monsters made it to the roof. The beast caught wind of them immediately and

235

yowled, a bloodthirsty cry instantly echoed by the others close behind. They swarmed over the edge and onto the roof in a ferocious wave, each eager to sink its talons into human flesh. The lead creature opened its jaws wide to reveal rows of sharp fangs. It sprang towards the retreating Guardians with its claws extended, already relishing the meal to come.

Layton might have forgotten how to use the Gift of his Jidaan, but Kiran had not. The leaping creature slammed face-first into a Ward of shimmering blue energy, breaking its neck on impact. Its body slid down the impenetrable barrier of magick as Kiran and Nessar helped Layton to his feet and into the stairwell. The pommel of her Jidaan glowed a bright, cerulean blue as she created the wall that protected them from the onslaught of the sightless beasts. They clawed ineffectually at the Ward as the Guardians pulled the door shut and latched it. Only then did Kiran allow the Ward to disappear. Instantly, the creatures attacked the walls and door of the stairwell, searching for a way in. Although the walls were made of stone, the door was not, and as a roof access, had not been made nearly as sturdily as the entrances at ground level. Their frantic clawing began to tear chunks out of the wood.

The sounds of the cracking, ripping wood above gave Nessar and Kiran additional motivation to hurry down the stairs. Layton had finally regained some of his composure and was moving under his own power, though it was obvious he was still hurting and groggy. In moments, they reached the ground floor, where they immediately set about barring the door to the stairwell with a heavy stone bench and a few other things that seemed heavy enough to hold the door closed a while longer.

Looking at the makeshift barricade, Nessar commented, "That's not going to hold for too long. We're going to have to make a run for it."

"Through those things? I can Ward us for a while, Ness, but even if I get us to the edge, how are we going to cross the ravine? I don't have a magick carpet in my backpack. Do you? We can't jump it, it's too far."

Layton's voice was quiet. He had sat down and was carefully probing the goose egg on the back of his skull with

236

his fingers. "That blue wall you made was pretty impressive."

Kiran glared at him but said, "Thanks."

Layton continued, "It's a wall, right? Solid?"

Kiran raised an eyebrow at him. "More or less, yes. I can shape it into different things, and it can be solid or not, depending on what I want it to do. What are you getting at?"

Layton grimaced as a fresh throb of pain hit his head. "Ow. Um, a bridge is just a horizontal wall. Could you make a bridge across the ravine?"

Kiran blinked at him for a moment, stunned. She vacillated between wanting to kick him and hug him, and maybe kick herself for not thinking of it in the first place. Now, they had a chance. "Layton, that's the best idea you've had in a long time. I can do that, I think. It'll be far, so I'll have to make the Ward pretty narrow; the bigger the Ward, the harder it is for me to maintain. Even so, we just need it to be wide enough to run across." She turned to Nessar. "Ness? Any ideas on getting to the edge of the ravine without becoming lunch for these things?"

Nessar had been pacing, thinking on that very topic. Finally, he stopped and snapped his fingers. "I think so!" He turned an apologetic smile to Kiran. "But it's going to require more work from you. I can hide us to a certain extent, but once we start moving, they'll know where we are anyway. Speed will be our best bet, but I think it'll work if you can do it."

Kiran sighed. "Do what, Ness? I can rest after we get out of here. What is it?"

Nessar explained his plan and both Layton and Kiran just looked at him. Finally, Layton issued a pained chuckle, and the other two turned to regard him. "I have to say, if this is the kind of thing we do all the time, it's much more interesting than standing guard at a dull old castle."

Kiran brightened. "Your memory is coming back?"

Layton's smile faded. "Not really. Although I must have done that at some point, because I do remember that it was incredibly, painfully boring." Then his smile returned. "This is definitely not boring." He rose to his feet. "OK, I'm with you. I'm sorry I'm not more help, but I'm getting my feet under me. I can keep up with you, at least."

Nessar nodded. "All right then. Bring it in close, and we'll see if we can get the door open without attracting too much attention. Right now, they're focused on the roof, so we should be all right for a few more..." Nessar trailed off as they all heard the door crash in at the top of the stairwell. Vibrations reached them through the stone at their feet as the frantic creatures swarmed down into the stairwell in a pale-skinned flood, eager to attack. Nessar amended his assessment. "Welp, time to go. Cross your fingers, hope this works. Kiran, if you would unbar the door, we'll get moving."

Kiran quickly hefted the huge beam out of the door's locking brackets and laid it off to one side before joining them again. The trio stood as close as possible to each other while still allowing for room to move. Nessar engaged the power of his Jidaan, and Layton saw the pommel of the sheathed weapon swirl with inky blackness as it awoke to the old man's call. He felt an odd tingling sensation flow in a wave from the top of his aching head down to his toes. When he looked down, he was astonished to find that his feet, along with the rest of him, had completely vanished. Of Kiran and Nessar, there was no sign; they had vanished too, cloaked by the power of the Jidaan of Stealth.

A firm, callused hand suddenly closed on Layton's wrist and Nessar's voice echoed in his mind. *Here, grab hold of my belt in the back, and grab Kiran's too.* Layton did as he was told and quickly found the appropriate handhold on Nessar's belt. Kiran found his other hand and guided it as well.

Watch the hands, old buddy. I'm a married woman, you know. Kiran said, a thread of humor lacing her words. She knew Layton would blush at that, though the Jidaan of Stealth hid his reddening cheeks. Nevertheless, he grabbed her belt firmly.

Unseen, Nessar opened the museum's main door a crack. Fortunately, the crowd that had been attacking the door had thinned, focused as they were on the far side of the wall. None were paying attention to the door, and the

238

Jidaan kept it silent. Nessar opened it a touch wider, and still, none of the creatures noticed.

On three, we sprint for the edge of the ravine just opposite the remains of the bridge. From there, Kiran will have to make a way across. Are you ready with the Ward, Kiran?

Oh yeah! Kiran's mental voice carried a note of eagerness and excitement. She was ready to roll. *Just say the word, old man, and we'll plow these things out of the way like water before a ship's prow.*

Right then. One. Two. THREE!

Layton felt his companions burst into action and he sprinted after them, directly into the horde of creatures outside the museum. He felt a surge of energy as well as a sense of pure exhilaration from Kiran, and he watched as Kiran's unseen Ward, shaped into a huge plow-shaped wedge that surrounded them, knifed through the crowd of cave-dwellers, shunting them aside before they even knew what had hit them. As each creature struck the Ward and flew away, Kiran accepted the strain and grunted with the effort, but she held steady and strong. The unseen trio plowed their way through the bewildered throng, finally bursting through their lines and leaving the bulk of them behind as they found open space close to the ravine.

Nessar released the power of his Jidaan with a relieved sigh. Its cloak of invisibility dissipated, leaving them in full view of the mob, but fortunately, the cave-beings were still confused by their soundless crossing. Kiran's wedge-shaped Ward vanished as well, and she immediately set herself to the task of creating a bridge across the wide, bottomless ravine that separated them from freedom. She tried to ignore the shimmering, ever-shifting green luminescence that shone up from below, a pale, milky emerald energy that spoke of a power she did not understand and did not want to.

Narrowing her eyes in concentration, Kiran gauged the distance from their location to the remains of the stone bridge. It was far enough to be a challenge if she had been fresh, but she was already tired. Nevertheless, she dug deep and ignited her power again. At her command, the sapphire pommelgem in her Jidaan flared brilliantly, eager

239

to do its work. She raised both hands and gestured out at the empty space above the ravine, focusing her will. The Jidaan responded, and a narrow bridge burst into being across the divide. As it reached the far side and anchored itself to the broken walkway, Kiran's voice echoed in their minds. *Get moving; I can't hold this for long! Move your arses! Hustle, hustle!*

Nessar started across, keeping his eyes focused on the far side. Layton looked at Kiran, intending to let her go before him, but she reached out and promptly kicked him in the buttocks to urge him on. *Go! I come last so I can make sure this works!* Sweat had already begun to roll down her face. She suddenly wished she had kept up her training better over the years. *GO, you stupid fart!* Layton finally clenched his teeth against the pain in his head and sprinted away on the narrow bridge of magick, trusting her to follow.

As Kiran took the first step onto the bridge, a sound made her turn. The motion was too quick, and her left foot slipped out from under her. It saved her life.

The cave-dwellers had spotted them, whether by sound or smell, she would never know, and a crowd of them was almost upon her. The first of them leaped at her, but her fall let her evade its frantic attack, and the hapless creature fell pinwheeling into the silent deep of the ravine.

"Dammit!" Kiran muttered as she sat up, both frustrated at her own clumsiness and relieved that it had worked in her favor. She stood, pulling a throwing dagger with each hand and letting them fly in the same motion. They caught the next two creatures in the throat. They died before their bodies hit the floor, impeding the others in their struggle to reach her. Without hesitation, Kiran turned and sprinted across the Ward-bridge, pumping her arms and legs for all she was worth. The monsters followed, swarming the bridge she had created, lusting for her blood.

Layton and Nessar were already on the remains of the stone bridge, yelling encouragement, their hands outstretched. She doubled her effort, finally leaping the last few feet into their waiting arms.

"Gotcha!" Nessar exclaimed. He wrapped his arms around her as they tumbled in a heap. She gasped in relief.

240

"Kiran, the bridge!" Layton drew his sword and held it in unschooled hands as the cave-dwellers approached, bravely interposing himself between them and his friends, though he barely knew which end of the sword to use.

"What? Oh!" With a wave of her hand, the blazing blue pommelgem of the weapon strapped to her back went dark and the Ward-bridge vanished, sending dozens of the snarling, clicking creatures falling to their deaths far below. "Right, I forgot there for a second. Whew!" Nessar helped her to her feet, and she cast a menacing glance at the horde massed at the far edge of the ravine. "Yeah, take that, you creepies! What've you got? Huh? Nothing, that's what!"

Nessar chuckled as he made sure she was OK to stand on her own. "All right, all right, if you've finished talking trash to the cave beasts, let's find a way out of here." He looked at Layton, who had resheathed his sword, though with great effort. "How are you feeling, lad? Anything coming back to you yet?"

Layton frowned and rubbed his head. The constant, throbbing pain and nausea made it difficult for him to think clearly, but what thoughts he could put in order still did not tell him much. He had a sense that it was all there, just around some corner in his mind, but he had no idea which corner. He carefully shook his head, mindful of the pain that caused. "I'm sorry, not much yet. I'm just trying to put one foot in front of the other for now."

Nessar nodded. "All right then, we'll just have to figure out something else. Let's get back to the exposed part of the city and see if we can find another way back to the top." He cast a glance back at the milling army of cave-dwellers that had massed on the far edge of the ravine. The shimmering green light from down below illuminated them, making them even more ghoulish. He turned to make his way back out into the light, the others all too happy to follow him.

As they stepped off the broken remnant of the stone bridge, the stone beneath them rumbled. They all staggered, struggling to stay on their feet as the earth shook. Just as suddenly as it had begun, the rumbling stopped, leaving the trio stumbling to stay upright.

"That can't be good," Kiran muttered.

The ground rumbled again, more strongly this time, and all three Guardians were thrown from their feet. A roar shook the world, the battle cry of some enormous, unseen beast announcing its presence. Across the ravine, the cave dwellers suddenly turned and ran, climbing over each other as they hastened back to the dark tunnels and chambers from which they had come. In moments, not a single one of the pale creatures could be seen. Watching them go, Nessar said, "Yeah. And that doesn't bode well either. Run!"

Chapter 32

Beauty sniffed the ground as she walked, following the two day old trail left by the men that had attacked Gart and hurt her. Their scent clung to the grass and plants, and their blood was a strong, coppery taste that stood out as easily to her senses as if it were a trail of fire. She could feel Gart's approval more strongly than ever, and she happily moved faster in pursuit of the men.

Gart trailed along behind her on Bessie, his black-bladed sword in his fist and angry cobalt eyes scanning the forest ahead for signs of their attackers. *Barovius and Arkhan,* Gart reminded himself. He had heard them address each other after knocking him nearly senseless as they bickered over his Jidaan. Through Beauty's memories, he had a picture of them in his mind as well, and connected their voices to their faces. He had never seen them before, but they had made a grave mistake when they had hurt Beauty. He could have ignored an attack upon himself, but whatever happened now, he would eventually hunt them down and make them pay. With any luck, Beauty would help him find them sooner rather than later, which would suit him just fine.

Bessie stumbled on the rocky, uneven path, then quickly righted herself. Gart cursed in frustration. Beauty sensed his momentary distress through the constant flow of magick he maintained to keep her heart beating, and she stopped in her tracks. She raised her huge head and turned to look at him, her sudden worry flowing back along the link to him.

"I'm fine, girl. Keep at it." Gart's voice was tired, but the reassurance calmed her. With a satisfied *whuff*, she lowered her snout to the ground to catch the scent again, then loped forward as she found it.

Gart was exhausted and his head felt like it was two sizes larger than normal. Nevertheless, his anger lent him strength. They had his Jidaan. The thought of it being in their hands offended him deeply. As far as he knew, it was useless to them. Even if they were users of magick, the Jidaan had Chosen *him*, and he alone could wield its Gift.

Even so, the loss of it left a void that surprised him with its enormity. It had been a part of him for over twenty years, and its comforting weight had always been within arm's reach or on his back. Moreover, the Jidaan had been joined to him through the magick they shared, and the lack of that slumbering power was staggering. He could still sense the weather patterns in the surrounding atmosphere, but it was like playing dice with mittens on. Everything was muted and difficult to feel.

Gart knew he could continue without the Jidaan, but if he could catch the injured pair quickly, there was a chance he could get it back and have justice for Beauty as well. That chance was worth the effort, at least for a while longer. If they did not find them soon, he would have to call off the search and turn aside. He still had the Blood, and all he needed was the Heart of Corria, but time was drawing short. He scowled as he peered into the thinning trees ahead, hoping he could catch sight of them.

Beauty crested a small rise and disappeared beyond it. Gart felt a swell of emotion from Beauty before she barked twice, signifying that she had reached the end of her search, but was not necessarily happy about it. Gart urged Bessie to the top of the hill and found Beauty in the hollow beyond. She was sniffing at a circular patch of earth that had been scraped bare. The exposed ground looked burnt and dark, and Gart immediately sensed that something ill had occurred there. Flies buzzed in the air, an irritating sound that grated on his already raw nerves. Through his link with Beauty, he experienced an awful odor that combined rotting flesh and sulfur, and he was suddenly glad that his nose was not nearly as good as hers. As he eased Bessie down into the hollow, he felt the sense of wrongness from the spot intensifying. *This is a place of foul magick,* he thought. He had visited more than a few places like this in the last several years, as well as many that vibrated with a brighter, more wholesome power. Some were more ancient than others. This one felt new, like a recent, still-bleeding scrape, but at least it seemed small and confined to the naked earth ahead. Bessie felt the wrongness too and whinnied disapprovingly. Gart angled her away from the angry patch of dirt and dismounted several yards away

244

where she felt less affected. He tethered her to a rock, then came over to join Beauty, whose ragged ears were laid back. She was not pleased to be here, but at least felt no imminent danger. Gart reassured her with a scratch on her furry head and examined her find, letting Beauty wander as she would.

Two concentric circles had been roughly inscribed in the ground, the space between them filled with ugly symbols. Gart knelt to examine the marks and made a face as he smelled the old blood that had been poured into the sigils. He glanced off to one side to see Beauty snuffling at something. It was the corpse of a deer, the source of the blood that had energized the arrangement. He worried that she might eat it, but was relieved to see her quickly step away from the carcass. It had been befouled by the ritual. He turned his attention back to the rings.

"Blast," Gart mumbled to himself as he assessed the design. From his research, he knew a portal ring when he saw one, and this one had surely been used by the two men to escape. Although it was certainly possible that it could transport Gart to his assailants, he had no knowledge of how to properly engage such a construct of dark magick, and he knew the wounded pair had already had ample time to arrange a suitable welcome even if he could figure out how to do so. A flicker of hot rage and frustration rolled through him, but he contained that fire. He took a deep breath and held it for a moment. Long practice had taught him to keep that rage from pushing him over the edge. As he released the air from his lungs, he sent the rage flowing out along with it, lest it cloud his judgement any further than it already had.

Beauty felt his momentary anger and whined softly, wordlessly asking after her master. Gart called her to him and could not help but smile when he felt her joy as she heard his voice calling her name. In spite of his weariness, pain, and anger, his smile remained as he watched her approach. Others might have been terrified by her deeply scarred face with its permanent snarl and huge, jagged fangs that could easily crush muscle and bone. Instead, he saw the light of happiness in her eyes, and her huge tongue lolling as she panted at him. He knelt to wrap his arms around her muscled neck and shoulders and hugged her hard. Doing so pushed some of his anger away.

"Well, it looks like we'll have to find them another day, Beauty," he said, as he released her. He stood once more, and idly scratched behind her bedraggled ears with one hand. "They're long gone and I can't follow them through the door they made. We've got other pressing matters that need our attention; mine, anyhow." Beauty looked up at him and moaned deep in her throat, happy as could be. Gart's heart broke a little as he felt her love for him. It shone pure and bright in spite of everything that had just happened. She had nearly died because he insisted on pursuing his own goals, and she cared not a bit. Guilt turned his stomach into a knot as he thought about how much she loved him. He began to wonder if his quest was worth it.

He loved Gennie with every fiber of his being. It had been over two decades since he had lost her, but lately, the pain of that loss had steadily grown until he felt it almost every second. More and more, he felt compelled to seek her, to bring her back so that he could talk to her just once more. Some tiny, dim part of him knew that he was being unreasonable, but he always pressed on and ignored those thoughts.

Years ago, Gennie's murder had both devastated and enraged him. His rage had fueled a different quest back then, one that had almost gotten him killed. Gart's brows knitted into a well-used scowl as the memories drifted back to him.

Led by the half-daemon Jor Dayne, the marauding squad of Gholans and undead Riders had destroyed his village. The hideous creatures had killed everyone, including his daughter, Rheann. Jor Dayne had slain his dear Gennie right in front of him before he had been knocked senseless by a falling blade that should have killed him.

When Gart woke, his world had been ripped asunder. After sending his wife's body into the flames of a burning barn so that she could rest with their daughter, Gart had set out for revenge. He plunged after the evil horde with little thought as to how he would survive the encounter. In truth, he realized over the years that he had never intended to survive that meeting. But then his life had been spared by a lone Weya who saved him when the Gholans and Riders turned to fight, and his body and soul had been further aided by the spirit of RaeLynn, the Lady of the Lake of Whispered Sorrows. She had tended his wounds and shown him that others fought as he did, others felt the same pain he felt. He had shifted his goal then, and took the first steps on a path that led first to the Jidaan of Storms, and ultimately to a confrontation with Mordak. In the end, justice had been served, and those responsible for Gart's loss had paid with their lives.

By then, he had no longer been fighting only for Gennie and Rheann. He had found something within himself during the war against Mordak, something unexpected. He had fought for something far greater than himself and his own desires, and it had meant something to him. Others had showered him with praise, regardless of the thick scars on his face, and he had felt accepted and loved. For years afterwards, he had traveled with Beauty and Ishabel, had spent time with Agatha learning how to use the powers at his command. Eventually, he had felt something that closely resembled peace. More time passed, and Gart thought he had moved on. All seemed right with the world, or as right as Gart might ever see, anyway.

Gart had trouble pinpointing the change. He found himself thinking of Gennie again. First, thoughts of her came only occasionally, but then more often. Soon, he found himself lapsing into long, sullen silences as his heart ached for her. In time, his preoccupation had pushed Ishabel away. He remembered her saying that she was a living, breathing woman, and that she deserved more than the distracted shadow of himself that he had become. Even now, he could hear and feel the wooden doors slam shut behind her as she left the small home they had rented together, the sound reverberating in his bones. He had just stared after her, silent and stern, his heart aching twice as much, but he had let her go.

Fortunately, Beauty had no problems sharing him with a ghost from the past. He was glad of that, for he had come to need the dog's companionship just as much as she seemed to need his. Her huge, warm presence soothed him and helped him feel less alone, even as he continued to despair over Gennie's loss.

He began to daydream of Gennie constantly, and as he lay awake one night after Ishabel had left, an idea crept in: his magick was strong; could he find a way to see her again? In light of what he had learned about magick, he began to think it might be possible. He had seen and experienced such wonders, things that had seemed impossible until he had watched Agatha do them. He recalled the lessons she had taught, and more importantly, the lessons she had not. Some subjects, she had purposely shied away from. "You're too green, yet, lad. You're strong as a bull, but the skill for some things takes time to refine. And you're just a baby to the likes of me." She had cackled as he had scowled, but he had known that she was right.

Gart knew that Guardians' Keep had archives that were second to none. Agatha had said so. If there was a way to reach Gennie, it would likely be found there. Suddenly filled with purpose, Gart had roused Beauty and left at the break of dawn, bound for the Keep and its archives, determined to find a method of contacting Gennie.

It had taken years of arduous research, but Gart had, indeed, found a way. It had cost him much, and he had been places and seen things that he almost wished he had not, but if that was the price he paid to see Gennie, then he deemed it all worthwhile. He was tireless in his pursuit of his goal, implacable, unstoppable. In the end, he finally had pieced together a ritual that could work. It had to work! It was dangerous, yes, but Gart reassured himself that he could do it. He could keep the spell under control; he knew he could. Even as doubts arose in his mind, half-formed and uncomfortable, the image of Gennie's face always washed them all away. He decided to pursue it, no matter the cost.

Gart heard Beauty whine, and was suddenly brought back from his musings by her enormous tongue as it slapped and licked his face. He was surprised and startled, but rather than being upset, he allowed himself to laugh as he fended off her playful advances and finally wrapped his arms around her thick neck. "All right, all right, enough of that. Let's get moving. We've got our own portal to find, and it's in the other direction. Come on, girl."

He stood and headed towards Bessie, wiping his face on his sleeve, not realizing that most of the wetness there was from his tears.

THE END

Afterword

By now, I hope you're dying to hear what happens next. Never fear, the next part of the story is just around the corner. Be patient. The nice guy part of me wants to assure you that it's already completed, so you won't have long to wait. The author part of me hopes that you flung this book across the room because you were upset that this part is over. Unless it's on your e-reader. Don't fling that.

Thanks for tolerating my nonsense, reader. And I hope you're enjoying the tale.

For updates about new releases,
exclusive promotions,
and a complimentary short story,
visit the author's website
and sign up for the VIP mailing list
at

http://www.whitmcclendon.com

Also By Whit McClendon

Mage's Burden, Gart's Road, and A Mage Awakens, all in one action-packed volume!

Look for it on Amazon, iBooks, and BarnesandNoble.com!

About The Author

Whit McClendon was born on October 31, 1969 in Freeport, Tx. He grew up in Angleton Texas and was active in martial arts, track and field, and playing the clarinet in band. One year at Texas A & M proved that lacrosse was far more fun than electrical engineering, and he eventually graduated with a degree in Engineering Design Graphics from Brazosport College. After working in the petrochemical field as a CAD drafter for many years, Whit finally realized his life's dream of becoming a full-time martial arts instructor. He now lives with his family in Katy, Texas, plays lacrosse as often as possible, and runs Jade Mountain Martial Arts. He laughs a lot more now than he did when he worked at the engineering firm.

whitmcc@jidaan.com
www.jidaan.com
www.jmma.org

www.ingramcontent.com/pod-product-compliance
Lightning Source LLC
Chambersburg PA
CBHW070340260626
47160CB00003B/1103